So You Call Yourself a Man

So You Call Yourself a Man

Carl Weber

KENSINGTON PUBLISHING CORP.

DAFINA BOOKS are published by

Kensington Publishing Corp.
850 Third Avenue
New York, NY 10022

Dafina Books and the Dafina logo Reg. U.S. Pat. & TM Off.

ISBN 0-7582-0718-2

Printed in the United States of America

This book is dedicated to my grandmother,
Sarah Weber,
who at ninety-two years old is still
driving a car and showing me
how to live life to the fullest.

Love you Nana.

Acknowledgments

First off, I have to thank my fans for their support of *The Preacher's Son*. Without them, making the *New York Times* bestseller list would not have been possible. I guess they love drama even more than I thought, because I can't begin to tell you how humbled I was to walk into stores around the country and have hundreds of people waiting to listen to me read excerpts or to get their books autographed. It is you the fans that keep me writing, and I will continue to do my best and not disappoint you. So keep the letters and e-mails coming.

Next, I'd like to thank my staff and partners at Urban Entertainment for putting up with me during the long hard road to finishing *So You Call Yourself a Man*: Roy Glenn, Arvita Glenn, Harold Gilliam, Smiley Guirand, Dwight Keys, Maria Delongoria, Richard Holland, Robilyn Heath, Alisha Yvonne, Kevin Dwyer and Dwayne Dumpson. Guys, I hope you can see where I'm going with this thing of ours because the sky is the limit.☺

Many thanks to Valerie Skinner, Linda Williams, Alisha Yvonne, Anita from Sag Harbor (my old babysitter), and Britney from Sag Harbor (my kids' babysitter); your input on *So You Call Yourself a Man* was instrumental in helping me put out the best book I could.

How could I forget my two good friends Karen Thomas, my editor and Marie Brown, my agent? You two have been around since my infancy in this industry and have taught me more about publishing than any twenty people combined. I will always be in your debt and hope that you will always be there to smack me back down to size if my head gets too big. Thanks for all that you've done and will do.

Last but not least, I'd like to thank my wife, Martha. Without her help I would never have finished *So You Call Yourself a Man* on time. She edited, retyped, criticized, and even wrote some of this book when I couldn't keep my eyes open any longer. Through good times and bad you've always been there for me. Thanks so much.

E-mail me at: www.urbanbooks@hotmail.com
Visit my web site at: Carlweber.net

1

James

Call me kinky, but there is nothing in the world that turns me on more than hearing a woman scream pleasurable obscenities as I make love to her. And that's exactly what my lovely wife, Cathy, was doing as I held onto her hips and plunged into her from behind. Our two boys, James Jr. and Michael, were with my mother for the weekend, and Cathy and I were taking advantage of their absence by spending some quality time together. We'd gone out to dinner with my buddy Brent and his fiancée, Alison, taken in a movie, then came home and finished off a bottle of wine before making love on the living room sofa. We were now on our second round in our bedroom, going at it like two lusty college students in heat.

"I love you, James," my wife moaned affectionately, clutching the sheets as one climax took over for another.

"I love you too," I growled back as my body stiffened and my own pleasure erupted.

Totally spent, Cathy lay flat on her stomach while I gently collapsed onto her back, gasping for air. After a brief recovery, I slid my sweat-soaked body off hers. She snuggled up next to me and I wrapped my arm around her, pulling her in close, her back to my front. I was so exhausted, I wanted to just close my eyes and let the sedative of sex take me to dreamland. But I couldn't do that because it was against the rules—rules we'd created almost two years ago to keep our marriage together. Rules that had made this the happiest two years of my life. Somehow, I was going to have to force myself to stay awake at least ten more minutes and talk to her before allowing myself the enjoyment of sleep.

I kissed her neck, whispering in her ear, "You okay? Do you want me to go down on you or anything?"

"No, baby. I'm fine just like this. All I want you to do is hold me." I did as I was told and she snuggled her backside against me. A few seconds later, I could hear her snoring lightly.

I loved Cathy more than anything in the world. Sure, we had our problems over the years like most couples. Hell, I even thought we were gonna divorce a few years ago, but we worked it out and things had never been better as far as I was concerned. I couldn't see myself with any other woman. I'd loved her since the day we met in our junior year at Virginia State University. She was my soul mate, and I'd do anything and everything to keep her and my boys safe and out of harm's way. I kissed her neck again, then dozed off to sleep.

I couldn't have been asleep more than five or ten minutes before my cell phone rang. Instinctively, I reached over and picked it up from my night table, glancing at the caller ID before hitting the talk button. The screen read UNAVAILABLE, and my eyes wandered to the clock radio on my night table. *One twenty-one a.m. Who the hell is calling me at this time of night?* Then it hit me. There was only one person who would call me at this time from an unavailable number—my best friend, Sonny Harrison. Sonny always used calling cards, so his home number never showed up on my caller ID. His wife and I didn't get along too tough, so he probably waited until she was asleep before picking up the phone to call. He was flying in from Seattle sometime tomorrow to look for a job, and hopefully he was going to stay long enough to attend Brent's wedding. Brent, the third friend in our tight circle, was getting married in two weeks, and he and I were supposed to pick Sonny up at the airport. Sonny was probably calling to let me know what time his flight would arrive.

"Hello?"

"James?" It wasn't Sonny. It was a woman, a familiar voice, but in my tired state, I just couldn't make out the voice. "James?" the woman asked again.

"Yeah, who is this?"

"Michelle."

The hair on the back of my neck stood up, and every muscle in my body tightened. I hadn't heard Michelle's voice in years. Why the hell was she calling me, especially at this time of night?

I could feel Cathy start to stir next to me, and fear ran through my body. I immediately cupped the phone and rolled over on my right side, away from my wife.

I'd met Michelle a few years back, during the time Cathy and I were having our marital problems and contemplating divorce. Michelle was living with her mother. Their house was a daily stop on my old UPS route. Her mother was addicted to the Home Shopping Network, and was constantly ordering nonsense she didn't need. Looking back at things, I wished I had never met her, but in all honesty, she filled a void in my life at a very unhappy time. She was exactly what I needed to realize that what I had at home was worth fighting for.

Funny thing is, in the beginning, I never even thought about messing with Michelle. She was just the woman who answered the door when I dropped off her mother's packages. I mean, she was nice enough and had a decent body, but she wasn't gonna win any beauty contests with those rollers and that sweatsuit she wore when she answered the door every morning. As time went on, however, her appearance started to change. At first it was subtle; the scarf and rollers she usually wore to the door had disappeared, and her hair was now combed in various styles. Then one morning she surprised me by answering the door wearing makeup. And if that wasn't enough, I knew something was definitely up when she stopped wearing the beat-up old gray sweatsuit and started to answer the door wearing a negligee with a sheer robe. Being a flirtatious guy, I gave her a few compliments on her improved appearance. Yeah, I know I was a married man headed down the road to disaster, but boys will be boys, and I was just seeking some much-needed attention that I wasn't getting at home.

I really didn't think anything would start between me and Michelle. That changed, though, when she was more than a little receptive to my flirtation and started giving it back even more aggressively. We played this little back-and-forth game over the next couple of weeks. I don't have to tell you what happened after that. Let's just say it happened every day for six months, even when I didn't have any packages to deliver to her house. Now that I think back on it, I don't think I'd ever been so happy to go to work in my entire life.

"Michelle, why are you calling me at this time of night?" I was whispering but my voice was cold and serious.

"Well, if you had answered when I called you earlier, we wouldn't be going through this now. I been blowing up your phone since five o'clock this afternoon, and it just keeps sending me to your voice mail. By the way, your box is full. Haven't you checked your messages?"

"No, I haven't. I've been busy, spending time with *my wife.*" I glanced at Cathy to see if I was talking too loud. She seemed to still be asleep.

"You don't have to get nasty with me, James. I know you're married, remember? You act like she's right next to you or something."

"*Ahhh, yeah*, where else would she be at this time of night?" I couldn't resist the sarcasm. "Now look, it's late. And I don't do booty calls anymore. So please don't call me again, okay?"

"Don't you hang up this phone, James Robinson!" she demanded. "We need to talk now. And I really don't care if your wife is there or not. This is important."

I didn't like her attitude. I was thinking about hanging up. The only thing that stopped me was the fact that Michelle was stubborn and would probably call back. One call at 1:30 in the morning Cathy might ignore or sleep through, but a second call would have her radar up like she was NASA waiting for the space shuttle to land. "Look, I don't have time for this."

"Well, make time, dammit. Unless you want me to show up at your doorstep with your son."

If she didn't have my attention before, she sure as hell had it now. I swear I could feel my heart stop. "Hold on a sec." I cupped my hand over the phone then swung my feet off the bed to sit up. Cathy turned toward me.

"Baby, who's that on the phone?" She was still half-asleep.

I turned toward her and forced a smile. "Ah, it's just Sonny. I've gotta write down his flight information. I'll be right back."

"Aw'ight. Tell 'im I said hi." She rolled back over, pulling the covers around her neck. I left the room, heading downstairs as quickly as possible. When I reached the family room, I turned on the television for background noise and brought the phone to my ear.

"What the hell is this about, Michelle? You told me the baby wasn't mine." Now that I was not within earshot of Cathy, I had a real attitude.

There was a hesitation on the line.

"I know that, James, but I was wrong." There was a strange tone to her voice, not the attitude I expected. It was more like exhaustion. If I didn't know better, I might have thought she didn't want to be having this conversation with me. But I did know better, and I was sure Michelle was up to something.

"What do you mean you was wrong? Why you trying to play me, Michelle? You know that baby ain't mine. You told me yourself, he looks just like your boyfriend. He don't look nothin' like me."

"Ain't nobody trying to play you, James. And his looks ain't got nothin' to do with who his daddy is. But trust me, he does look like you, just like you." The attitude had crept back into her voice. "I just want you to take care of your responsibility. I can't do this by myself anymore."

"Responsibility! What responsibility? That baby ain't mine. I rode past you and his daddy pushing a stroller down the street a few months ago. You looked like one big, happy family. Why you trying to put this on me now? I work for UPS. I don't own it. I ain't got no money. Damn."

"You think I want this? I don't want this. But I wouldn't even be talking to you if Trent hadn't failed a paternity test. The baby's not his, James. DNA tests don't lie."

There was silence on my end. I wasn't sure what to say. I wanted to ask, "Well, whose baby is it?" but common sense told me that wasn't a good idea, especially since she had my cell number, my home number, and my address. If she wanted to, she could make my life a living hell.

As if she was reading my mind she said, "You're the only other one I was sleeping with, James, so don't come out your face with any stupidness."

God, I wish I had never met her.

"What do you want from me, Michelle?"

"We need to talk face-to-face. All I want you to do is take care of your son. I don't want anything else. But I can't do this by myself."

"Aw'ight, but I can't do it tomorrow. It'll have to be Monday."

"Okay, I can wait 'til Monday. But don't let me come looking for you, James, 'cause I ain't calling your cell phone looking for you anymore. I'm calling your house." Why I called that girl from my home number when we were sleeping together I'll never know. I felt like kicking myself for being so damn stupid.

"Don't worry. I'll call you." I clicked off the phone then walked up the stairs as if I was in a trance. How the hell was I gonna tell Cathy if I did really have another son?

2

Sonny

I stepped off the escalator and changed the time on my watch before heading toward the United Airlines baggage claim carousel. It was 9:00 a.m. back in Seattle, where my wife Jessica was probably just finishing up breakfast for the kids. I was about to pull out my cell and give her a call, but before I could get it out of my jacket, I was knocked to the ground by two middle-aged white guys in suits. They didn't even look back to see if I was all right. All I heard from one of them was, "Sorry," as he raced past me. Well, there was no question I wasn't in Seattle anymore, that was for sure. I was back in my hometown of New York City, where rudeness rules, everything is more expensive, and life just seems to move at a quicker pace. God, do I love this city.

I brushed myself off and continued toward the baggage claim. I thought about calling Jessica again but decided against it when I saw that she'd left three text messages on my phone. I'd only been in New York a few minutes, and it was probably better if I let her and the kids have a chance to miss me for a while. Besides, she'd call back. That I was sure of. Jessica couldn't go more than a few hours without talking to me.

A half-hour later, I was standing on the sidewalk outside the baggage claim area, smoking a cigarette. As I predicted, Jessica had called back not once but twice, and now that we'd hung up, I was doing some window-shopping. New York might be fast, but it had some of the best window-shopping in the world. "Window-shopping" was a term I came up with after Jessica and I got married and she would catch me looking at another woman's ass. Let's get something straight, though. I never cheated on my wife. Hell, I was too damn busy trying to keep her happy so she wouldn't cheat on me. You see, I'm an ass man. I can't help looking when a nice booty walks by me, but I don't touch. When Jessica caught me checking out someone's rear, I told her, "Don't worry, baby. I'm just window-shopping. A brother's got no intentions to buy generic when he's got brand-name at home." Then I'd slap her playfully on what quite honestly might be the most beautiful butt I'd ever seen. She never gave me any argument about that, probably because she knew how much I loved her and how committed I was to her and our family. I was about as devoted a family man as you can get. That was the main reason I was back in New York looking for a job. I needed to take care of my family properly.

"Sonnyyyyyyyyyy!"

I looked up and saw the resident pretty boy, one of my best friends, Brent Williams, headed my way through the crowd. After all these years, he was still probably the most handsome brother I'd ever met, and it had been that way since we were in grade school. When Brent was around, it was the women who did the window-shopping, and that's what most of them standing outside the baggage claim area were doing as he walked by. I couldn't help but laugh as I watched all the turned heads and not-so-subtle double takes. That Brent drove women crazy.

A good six feet three inches tall, Brent had chiseled bronze features with a low military cut and a body that women lusted after. Even under his suit jacket, it was obvious to anyone within eyesight that he was ripped. The thing I liked about Brent was that unlike most pretty boys, he didn't let his good looks go to his head. Oh, he'd had his share of women over the years—lots of women—but he never made a big deal about his looks or the attention women gave him. To be honest, he seemed to resent it at times. I guess that's why he had so much trouble keeping a steady relationship. He wanted someone who was attracted to the man inside, someone who shared his interests and wasn't just looking for an arm ornament she could show off to her girlfriends. I know it almost sounds like what a woman looks for in a man, but you'd be surprised how hard a good woman is to find, and Brent had been searching for his Mrs. Right for quite a while. That's why James and I were so happy when he met Alison. She's a little big for my taste, but she's the perfect woman for Brent, especially with her being a Sunday school teacher and him recently being saved and wanting to go into the clergy.

"Sonny! Man, it's good to see you." Brent wrapped his arms around me and gave me a brotherly hug. "I missed you, man. Dag-gone, I wish you'd move back to New York."

I smiled as I hugged him back. "I missed you too, bro. And believe it or not, I might be moving back to New York sooner than you think if James can get me a job as a driver working at UPS."

Brent straightened his back, cynicism written across his face. I was too embarrassed to tell him I'd been out of work the past three months and that James was my only hope for employment. "And Jessica is cool with that? She's actually going to let you be a driver?"

I let out an aggravated sigh. Brent and James didn't like my wife because they thought she was too high-maintenance and controlling. They were under the impression that Jessica had me henpecked. They believed she moved me to Seattle three years ago so that I would be away from their influence.

I looked him straight in the eyes. "It was her idea. She knows how much I miss you guys and New York. Contrary to popular belief, she wants me to be happy, Brent."

"I hear you, man. God does say, let those without sin cast the first stone." Brent released me and picked up one of my bags. "Maybe I misjudged her, Sonny."

"There ain't no maybe to it, bro. You and James been misjudging my wife since day one. She's a good woman, Brent, the best, and I don't know what I'd do without her. I've only been away from her half a day and I already feel lost. I just wish you guys could understand that."

"I hear you, man, and I'm glad you're happy." His voice was less enthusiastic than his words.

"Excuse me." I glanced toward the voice to see this fine, brown-skinned flight attendant staring directly into Brent's face like he was a rock star or something, but it wasn't just her face I was looking at, 'cause the girl had an ass like Jennifer Lopez. Brent turned his head to acknowledge her presence, but his eyes never acknowledged her beauty or her phenomenal ass.

"Can I help you?" he asked.

She smiled seductively, her eyes locked on his. "Maybe we can help each other. My name's Yvonne. I'm from Atlanta, but my crew is on an eighteen-hour layover. I'm staying over at the airport Ramada and wanted to know if you'd like to join me for a drink." She removed a small business card from her bag, and without even waiting for Brent's answer, she offered it to him. He accepted it with his free hand. "Here's my card. My cell phone number is on the back. You can call me anytime." She winked, this time waiting for his answer.

The way she was looking at him screamed, *I'm gonna rock your world*, and made me wanna say, "Damn, can he bring a friend? All I wanna do is watch."

Brent glanced at the card then at me. "Yvonne, is it?"

"Yes." She nodded, her smile growing wide, like a fisherman who'd just caught the big one. Only this fish was the one that got away, because Brent pushed the card back in her hand.

"What are you doing?" Her smile had disappeared.

"I'm flattered. Believe me, I'm flattered." He answered. "But I'm engaged, and I'm sure my fiancée wouldn't be too happy with me taking you out for a drink or calling you, no mater what time it is." He wasn't being rude, but there was a definite seriousness to his voice.

Yvonne obviously didn't want to accept defeat. "Well, what she doesn't know won't hurt her, will it?" She took a step closer and tried to push the card back into his hand. "And I sure as hell ain't gonna tell her, so you ain't got nothin' to worry about."

"I didn't have anything to worry about in the first place because I'm not meeting you," Brent told her with finality. He turned to me. "You ready to go, Sonny?"

"Yeah, sure."

"Good, 'cause James is waiting in the car, and for some reason he's got a stick up his butt." He reached down and picked up my other bag. "Oh, and Ms. Yvonne, you have a blessed day, and remember, keep Jesus first."

I looked at the woman, who looked like she was picking her ego up off the ground. "Don't feel bad. He does that to all the pretty girls."

As we walked away, I glanced at Brent. He seemed unfazed by what had just transpired. Damn, now that's what I call devoted. And they call me whipped. I didn't know what Alison had between her legs, but that shit must have been the bomb.

B

Brent

After eating twenty-four-ounce steaks, drinking German beer, and smoking twenty-dollar imported cigars with Sonny and James as we reminisced about the good old days, I finally arrived back home about 8:00 that evening. First thing I did when I hit the door was grab my Bible from the coffee table and get down on my knees to pray. My mind had been consumed with lustful thoughts ever since we left the airport. It didn't help when, after his third beer, James finally lightened up from the funk he was in and started talking about the bachelor party he was planning on throwing me. Even down on my knees about to pray, I still couldn't shake the thought of all that beautiful brown flesh they were going to parade in front of me. I loved those guys, but they had a way of bringing out the devil in me.

"Dear Lord," I said, lowering my head in prayer. "Please forgive me my lustful, heathenous thoughts that have consumed me. Father, please help me to be a better Christian who is not obsessed with the flesh but with Your glory. . . ."

I prayed for almost thirty minutes, finishing up my prayer with a hearty, "Amen." It was echoed by a female voice behind me.

"Alison," I stammered in surprise. I looked up at my bride-to-be, who was dressed in a flowered church dress and matching hat. She must have let herself in with the key I'd given her. "How long have you been there?"

"Long enough to know that we need to talk."

She sat down on the sofa solemnly. I swallowed hard, studying her face as I pushed myself up from the floor. I wasn't sure how much of my prayer she'd heard, but there was no doubt she'd heard enough for me to be concerned. Alison was a good woman and we shared many interests, but because of her size and weight she was insecure about my love for her. The last thing I wanted her to hear was me testifying to the Lord about lusting after flesh.

"Talk about what?"

"About us," she said flatly, patting the cushion beside her. "Now sit."

Hesitantly, I walked over to the sofa and did as I was told. I placed my hand on her thigh then stared in her pudgy but cute face, hoping to soften the mood with my eyes. Alison was a large woman, probably a size 20 or more, but her size didn't matter to me, because she had a heart of gold. I'd never met any woman who could make me laugh the way she did. We were both into watching sports, and we could talk about almost anything. Even more importantly, she was just as devoted to the Lord, if not more than I was. In my eyes, she was the perfect woman, and the only woman I'd ever even considered taking as my wife.

"You've been thinking about sex again, haven't you?" Her voice was calm but demanded an answer. I lowered my head in shame, unable to give her a reply. Alison, like me, was not a virgin, but had taken a premarital vow of celibacy when she accepted Christ into her life.

"Brent," she said, putting a finger under my chin and lifting my head. I avoided eye contact, even though this time when she spoke her voice was softer. "Brent, please, baby, look at me. I know it's hard, and I understand. I have the same urges and feelings that you have. I love you, Brent."

I turned my eyes toward her. Without a word, she placed her hand on mine and leaned forward. She kissed my lips gently, and instinctively, I kissed her back. I was shocked when her tongue parted my lips. Alison and I didn't French-kiss because we both agreed that it was lustful and would probably lead us down the road to breaking our premarital vows. I broke the kiss in protest, but she grabbed my head and forced her lips back on mine, sucking the air from my lungs as her tongue explored my mouth. For a few seconds, I savored the kiss and my hands roamed her large, soft body, but then I broke it abruptly. What we were doing was wrong.

"Alison! What's gotten into you?"

She grinned wickedly as she removed her hat, closing the gap between us. I'd never seen her like this, and the insatiable look of lust on her face made me move a foot back on the sofa. "You've gotten into me, Brent. I love you, I want you, and we don't have to wait anymore." She took my hands and placed them over her breasts. When I realized what she was doing, I pulled them back and moved another foot away.

"Alison, I can't . . . we can't . . . this is wrong. We made a vow to God. The Lord says . . ." I went to reach for my Bible, but she brought my hands back to her breasts.

"I know what we promised God, Brent. But ours is a good God, a merciful God, a forgiving God, and I'm sure He'll forgive us if we break our vow this one time. We only have a week before our wedding, and you need this. We both need this."

She reached into my lap, massaging my penis through the thin material of my pants before unzipping my fly and pulling it out. She stared for a moment, then looked up at me and smiled one last time before lowering her head. A warm wave of pleasure overcame me as the words, "Lord, please forgive us," quietly escaped my lips.

It was a little after 9:00 the next morning when the smell of bacon woke me. Not long after that, Alison walked into the bedroom carrying a plate in one hand and my favorite coffee cup in the other. She was naked except for the top sheet of my bed, which she had wrapped around her large torso, and a grin that told me she'd had the time of her life.

"Good mornin'."

"Mornin'," I replied as she stepped up to the side of the bed.

"I made your favorite breakfast. I even made you homemade biscuits just the way you like them." She lifted the plate.

"I can see that." I smiled, looking over the plate like a hungry wolf before taking it out of her hand. "What's the occasion?"

"I just wanted you to know how much I love you. How much I enjoyed myself last night. You know, I never had a man make love to me the way you did last night. It was as if you knew my body better than I did. Just thinking about it gets me warm and tingly all over." She shuddered, then rubbed her arms, trying to rid herself of the goose bumps that appeared.

I lowered my head, trying to conceal an ego-driven grin. I was happy Alison was pleased with my performance, but I wasn't surprised. Ever since I first started having sex as a teenager, women had been pleased with my abilities in bed. Funny thing is, all I was doing to them was what I wanted to have done to me.

"If I'd known it was going to be like that, I would have insisted we did it a long time ago." She gave me that same wicked smile from the night before as she placed the coffee cup on the night table. I watched as she loosened the sheet, letting it fall to the ground. I stared at her soft, naked body, then shook my head as she reached for me.

"Alison, we can't do this again until we're married. Now, I think you should get dressed. We both have some praying to do before we go to service."

4

James

I pulled my UPS truck in front of Michelle's mother's house. I was nervous as hell about seeing her, so it took a good five minutes before I got out of the truck and knocked on the door. I'd asked to have my route changed after we stopped messing with each other, so it had been quite some time since I'd been here. Despite the obvious reason, I was also concerned that seeing her might bring back some old feelings like in that Fantasia song, "Truth Is." We'd had some good times in that house, but I was hoping to keep those memories suppressed. Back in the day, Michelle could make me stand at attention just by looking at me, and the last thing I needed was to find myself sexually attracted to her after all these years.

Thankfully, my concerns disappeared when she answered the door in her beat-up old sweats and hair rollers, like she had in the old days before we started fooling around. Seeing her in her less made-up state made me question why I'd ever messed around with her in the first place. She wasn't ugly by any means, but for lack of a better word, the *aura* she used to have was gone. She couldn't hold a candle to what I had at home. It's amazing what a little loneliness will do to make a man think an average-looking woman is the woman of his dreams. Of course, at the time I wasn't getting any at home, and well . . . let's be honest: Michelle was willing to do anything and everything to make me happy at the time.

"What? You gonna just stare at me or are you coming in?" she asked as if I was holding her up from doing something important. Funny thing is, if I remember correctly, she was the one who wanted to speak to me. I didn't reply, though. I just opened the screen door and walked into the living room.

"Damn, James, you gettin' fat," she spat as I walked past her.

I turned to see her staring at me with a less-than-desirous look on her face. I immediately sucked in my gut with a frown. Her smart-ass comment had not just hurt my ego, but my feelings as well. Yeah, I'd gained a few pounds since I'd seen her last—probably closer to ten or fifteen—but it wasn't as if I was totally out of shape. In retaliation, I eyed her from head to toe, lashing out in a calm yet condescending demeanor. "Thanks, Michelle. You're lookin' good too. I see you did your hair just for me. . . . Oh, and is that a new outfit? 'Cause that gray in your sweatshirt matches your black rollers perfectly."

She touched her rollers self-consciously, obviously embarrassed by my remark, but that didn't last long. "Was that supposed to be funny, James?"

I smirked, but again I didn't reply. Michelle rolled her eyes, then plopped down on the sofa with an attitude. "Well, tell me if you think this is funny." She lifted a piece of paper from the coffee table and handed it to me. I looked at it and shrugged. All it had was some math problems scribbled on it.

"What's this?"

"That is seventeen percent of the average UPS driver's monthly salary, multiplied by thirty-six months. That's what my social worker says I'll get in back child support if I take your ass to court."

"Thirty thousand dollars? Are you insane?" I shouted. I looked down at the paper again as I eased myself into the love seat.

"Children are expensive," she replied nonchalantly. "Now, if you don't like it, he's in the bedroom taking a nap. You can take him home to your wife and you ain't got to give me shit."

My stomach began to tighten up and beads of sweat started to roll down my forehead. I glared across the room at Michelle, whose smug grin was forming into a full-fledged smile. She was enjoying herself. She was enjoying herself a great deal, and my next thought was that I should get up out of my seat and knock that smile right off her face. Fortunately for her, I didn't hit women, but I was starting to understand why some guys did.

"Michelle, I don't have thirty thousand dollars, and if I did . . ."

She cut me off with a wave of her hand and an exaggerated snap of her fingers. "Relax, James. I don't want you to give me thirty thousand dollars." I let out a thankful sigh that was halted by her next comment. "But I do want eight hundred a month, plus child care."

She didn't know it, or then again maybe she did, but the reality of the situation was that she might as well have been asking for the thirty thousand, 'cause there was no way I was giving her eight hundred a month. Shit, my ceiling was two hundred and fifty, and I was going to suggest two hundred until I could get a blood test. Once again, I could hear that little voice in the back of my head asking me why the hell I ever fucked with her in the first place, especially without a condom. I still didn't have an answer, and once again I contemplated getting out of my seat and smacking the shit outta her.

"I can't give you eight hundred a month. I'm living paycheck-to-paycheck as it is." I sat up defiantly. "Besides, I don't even know if I'm the father of your son."

There, I'd said it, but now I wished I hadn't, as Michelle's honey complexion turned a crimson red. She looked like she was about two seconds from blowing a fuse.

"First of all, his name is Marcus! And he's not my son, he's *our* son."

"So you say," I replied, reaching over to the end table next to me and picking up a framed picture of a child I assumed was Marcus. He had the same chocolate-brown complexion as me, but other than that, I couldn't see any resemblance.

"Momma's baby, Poppa's maybe . . . is that what you trying to *say*?" She was rolling her head as she spoke, but I had gone there now, so I wasn't about to back down.

"Yeah, that about covers it." I placed the picture back down on the end table. "He don't look nothin' like me."

"Are you crazy?" She stood up and pointed a finger. "That boy looks like you chewed him up and spit him out."

"That boy is not my son, Michelle. At least, not until we have a blood test."

Now she looked like she wanted to smack the shit out of me. "So, what you tryin' to say, that you don't plan on helping me until you have a paternity test?"

I nodded and she walked to the door, her face twisted in aggravation. I don't know why she was so mad. She had to know I was going to ask her for a paternity test.

"You know, I was hoping you were going to be reasonable

about this, but that's all right. I'll see you in court, James. You can get a paternity test there for free. Oh, and you can believe I'm going for my thirty thousand dollars now. You still live at 214 Dunlop Avenue in Hollis, don't you? I'll make sure to have them send the paperwork to your house as soon as possible."

I stood up and we locked eyes. I'm sure we were thinking the same thing, but while Michelle seemed to be finding pleasure in her threat, it filled me with fear. The thought of Cathy waiting for me one evening at the door, holding child-support papers demanding thirty thousand dollars, turned my stomach again. "Why you doin' this, Michelle?"

"Because I don't know what else to do, James." Her eyes started to tear. "I'm a single mother with no man, a job working as a home health-care worker, and a baby to raise. I tried, but I can't do this by myself. Now, you may not know he's your son, but I do, and you're going to help me whether you want to or not. So, I'll see you in *court*."

She stood defiantly, staring at me with her arms folded and tears running down her face. For the first time since I'd arrived, I felt sorry not just for myself but for both of us.

"Are you sure he's my son?" I asked tentatively.

She stared directly into my eyes and without blinking said, "Yes, James, he's your son."

"Look, maybe we can work something out. I can try to stretch my route out longer and get a couple hours overtime each day." She gave me this so-now-you-wanna-work-things-out look. "It's gonna be tight, but I can probably scratch up the eight hundred if you let me give you two hundred a week. But I don't know about the child care. You can't get blood out of a turnip."

She gave me a skeptical look but finally nodded her head. "I can work with that for now, but when I need a babysitter, I'm calling you, then I'm calling your wife."

5

Sonny

I was in the middle of an interview with the director of human resources for UPS's Queens, New York, hub. The interview was supposed to be just a formality for me to get the job as a driver, but I wasn't so sure about that anymore. I'd had a bad feeling about the balding, overweight white man sitting in front of me from the second I walked in the room. He just had that look— you know, the look that said, *I'm interviewing your black ass because I have to, but I really can't stand niggers, so don't even think you're getting a job out of me.* Oh, he was too politically correct or just plain afraid of the lawsuit I'd slap on UPS to say something like that to my face, but he was thinking it, that I was sure of. I'd been on too many job interviews with too many racist corporate motherfuckers the past three months not to know that look. So, unless I could pull a rabbit out of my hat and convince him that I was one of those good, helpful niggers like James, my chance of finally getting a job were slim to none.

"Well, Mr. Harrison, I must admit you have a very impressive resume. A bachelor's in computer science from Virginia State University, three years IT with Sherman, and before that, ten years with Henry Schein. James was right when he said you were a very smart man."

"Thanks." I sat up in my seat. I was feeling a little more comfortable. Maybe this guy wasn't so bad after all, I thought, until he shot me an annoyed, cross-eyed look that seemed to say, *When I need your opinion, I'll ask for it.*

"Mr. Harrison, there is something I don't understand, though." He looked down at my resume and frowned. I hated this part; this was where he asked me why I hadn't been working the past three months, then I decided whether to tell the truth or to lie. "Why are you applying for a job as a UPS driver? You don't have any experience as a truck driver. You've never even worked in the delivery field." He sat back in his chair, staring at me with his beady eyes. I felt like I was shrinking before him, and the more I tried to sit up, the smaller I became. I wasn't expecting this question because James made it seem like the job was in the bag.

"I understand that I don't have any experience, but I do have the proper license and I'm very motivated. I'm extremely motivated."

"I'm sure you are, but if you were me, would you hire a guy with a computer background to drive a truck?"

Damn, the redneck had me on that one. He had used reverse psychology and it had worked. I tried to remain confident, but at that point I knew the end was near.

"All I can tell you, Mr. Weinstein, is that I wanna work for UPS, and I'm sure I can be a damn good driver." I felt like a slave begging the massa to take me out of the field and put me in the house.

"I believe you could be a good driver, but for how long? How long would you be happy driving a truck, Mr. Harrison? Six months, a year tops." He shook his head. "No, Mr. Harrison, you're not a truck driver."

"Mr. Weinstein, please, you don't understand. I really need this job."

He glanced at my resume one last time, then slid it into a folder, sighing as if he was sorry. But that redneck motherfucker wasn't sorry. He wasn't sorry at all. He'd achieved his goal. He didn't want me to have this job in the first place. Unfortunately, my stupid ass listened to James and my desperation to find a job, instead of my intuition and my wife, who, although supportive in the end, wanted me to keep my ass in Seattle. I was tempted to cuss this redneck's fat ass out before I left, but I wasn't sure how that would affect James. So instead, I stood up and said, "Thank you for your time," as if he'd done me a favor.

"Sit down, Mr. Harrison," he ordered, and the only thing that went through my mind was, *No he didn't!* At that point, I'm sure he could see the contempt on my face, so he rephrased his demand. "Mr. Harrison, would you please sit down?"

I took a deep breath and did like he asked. Why, I don't know. Slave mentality, I guess.

"Mr. Harrison, I basically promised James I'd give you a job as a driver, but after looking at your resume, I just can't do it."

That motherfucker had the nerve to smile. I pushed myself out of my chair. He'd already made it clear he wasn't going to hire me. I wasn't about to let him ridicule me further. "I think you made that pretty clear the first time."

"Mr. Harrison, I have one last thing to say, and after that you can leave."

The second I walked out of the UPS building, I took a deep breath, wiping away a single tear as I dialed my home phone. Jessica answered on the second ring, and the first thing that came out of her mouth was, "Did you get the job?" There was no "Hello," no "Hey baby," not even a "How did it go?" None of that. Just a straight-to-the-point "Did you get the job?"

"Well . . ." I replied rather solemnly, but before I could answer, she cut me off.

"Oh, God, don't tell me you didn't get the job, Sonny." Her voice cracked with concern, and for a second I was afraid to answer.

"No, hun, I didn't get the job as a driver," I replied, but all I could hear was her breathing. "Jes, you still there?"

She finally responded, her words even sadder than before. "What are we going to do?"

"We're going to celebrate," I told her with excitement.

"Celebrate? Celebrate what? Being broke?"

"No, my new job as a UPS computer analyst."

"New job? Computer analyst?"

"That's what I said."

"But you said you didn't get the job."

"I said I didn't get the job as a driver, but that's only because they wanted to offer me a job as an analyst."

"You got the job?" she mumbled happily.

"That's right, baby, so pack your bags, because James hooked us up and we're moving back to New York."

"You got the job?" she repeated, like she still didn't believe me. I knew she'd been concerned about me being out of work, but I never knew just how much until now. I guess that's why she allowed me to come to New York and interview. She was afraid that if I didn't, I might not get a job anywhere.

"Yes, baby, we got the job."

"Thank God," she said, and the relief in her voice made me smile. "So when are we moving? Oh, my God, I've got so much to do."

"I'll be back in about a week or two. I've gotta find us a place to live and get a few things straight here. Do you think you can get everything ready to go by the time I get back?"

"Sweetheart, you can count on it," she replied, in a voice that assured me the job would be done.

6

James

Brent, Sonny, and I were at Madison Square Garden. By halftime the Knicks were getting their butts whipped by Shaquille O'Neal and the Miami Heat. That was okay, though. The night was still young, and after the game we were going to head over to Hooters to celebrate Sonny's new job and Brent's last few nights as a bachelor. I tried to arrange a big shindig at a strip club with all of our friends, but Mr. Born-Again Brent nixed that idea a couple of nights ago. I had to twist his arm just to get him to let Sonny and me take him to Hooters.

Despite his holier-than-thou protest during the week, Brent had been in high spirits from the minute we picked him up and headed to the game. I think he was a little more excited about the whole Hooters thing than he wanted to admit. I guess that's how it is when you're going to be married in less than twenty-four hours. You wanna see someone else's titties one last time. You don't necessarily wanna touch 'em, but you do wanna see 'em. Then again, even for an old married guy like me, a beer and some titties sounded pretty good. Who knows, I thought, maybe if we were lucky and he drank enough beer before the end of the game, Brent might let us take him to a real strip club.

I turned to Sonny, who as usual had his cell phone glued to his ear, talking to that bubble-butt, gold-digging wench he called a wife. Damn, I couldn't stand that bitch. It seemed like she was calling every half hour on the hour since he got into town just to see what he was doing. I felt like grabbing his phone and saying, "He's at a basketball game, bitch! Same place he was half an hour ago when you called. Damn! Give the brother a break so he can watch the game."

I didn't blame her as much as I blamed Sonny, though. We

were all dedicated to our women, but I'd never seen anyone as whipped as him. He was mesmerized by that oversized ass of hers. He acted like he was a dog on a leash and she was his master. I was convinced that anything she said, he'd do, and that included jumping off the Brooklyn Bridge. I was starting to get heated just thinking about it, so it was a good thing my cell phone began to ring before I opened my mouth.

I reached in my pocket and hit the talk button without looking at the caller ID. A big mistake, I soon found out.

"James." It was Michelle, and a wave of anxiety came over me when I recognized her voice. I was supposed to drop off $200 by her house earlier that afternoon, but my route had more packages than I anticipated, and I ended up doing more overtime than I expected. In my haste to get home, shower, and pick up the fellas, I completely forgot about it 'til now.

"I got your money," I assured her.

"Good, but that's not why I'm calling."

I hesitated before speaking, and I could feel both Brent's and Sonny's attention turn to me. "Then why are you calling?"

"I need you to babysit your son."

From the tone of her voice, this was not a request, it was a demand. I turned my back and spoke low so Brent and Sonny could barely hear me. "Michelle, I can't babysit tomorrow. Brent's getting married."

"Who said anything about tomorrow? I need a babysitter now."

"Now?" I snapped, glancing at my friends.

"That's right. Now," she snapped back. "I gotta be at work by nine o'clock and the lady that usually watches him is sick. I can't afford to miss work."

"What about your mother? Why can't she watch him?"

"My mother's down South, James. She's been down there taking care of my grandmother for the last three months. I don't know when she's coming back." It almost sounded like she was pleading.

"Michelle, I'm sorry, but I can't do it tonight. I'm already in Manhattan. In order for me to get there by nine, I'd have to leave now."

There was silence on the line until she spoke in an ominous, threatening tone. "Look, James, I don't have time to argue with you. Now, I need you to babysit, so you might as well get your ass up and come on back to Queens!"

"I heard you the first time, Michelle, so you don't have to yell. But like I told you the first time, I can't do it tonight. I'm busy."

"Oh, is that right? . . . Well, is your wife at home? 'Cause if you can't watch him, I'm damn sure gonna ask her."

All of a sudden my head began to hurt. Michelle had a way of pushing my buttons like no one else. "Don't go there, Michelle," I said angrily.

"No, James! Don't you go there. I told you before, I'm not playing with you. This ain't no game to me. I will call your wife. So, what's your home number again? Oh, yeah." She repeated the digits. I'd never heard anyone sound so serious, and it scared the hell out of me, especially when she continued. "Now, she don't go to bed early, does she? 'Cause it'd be a shame to wake the sister up when all you gotta do is come over here and babysit."

"Aw'ight. Look, let me call you back in five minutes. I'll see if I can arrange something. But I'm gonna call you, so don't do nothin' stupid until then." I hung up the phone and turned to my friends. "Guys, I got a problem."

7

Sonny

I'd been on the phone with my wife during most of the game, making arrangements for my return to Seattle and our move to New York. We'd decided to rent a house with an option to buy somewhere in Long Island. It would have to be near the Queens border, so I could see my friends. I was thinking someplace like Valley Stream or Elmont, where they still had some black folks and the schools were good.

I loved New York, especially Queens, but I was not about to subject my kids to the New York City public school system. I knew I wouldn't be able to afford to send my kids to private school. James sent both his boys to private school and it was costing him damn near as much as his mortgage payment. I'm sure he wouldn't be able to afford it if Cathy didn't work. I wasn't about to ask Jessica to get a job. She'd been a stay-at-home mom so long, just the thought of going to work would probably give her hives. So, my goal was to get my kids in some decent schools and still be able to afford to own my own home in New York someday.

While my wife and I were working out the details, I heard James shouting into his own phone, "I got your money!" He had this strange look on his face, like whoever he was talking to had him terrified.

"Hun, let me call you back," I told my wife.

I hung up the phone and turned toward James, who was now trying to hide his conversation. What the hell was going on, I wondered, and who the hell did he owe money to? James wasn't the type to gamble, and if he needed to borrow some money, I'm sure he would have gone to Brent. That's what I would have done.

I made eye contact with Brent, who seemed just as puzzled by James's strange behavior as I was.

When James finished his conversation, he turned to us, looking defeated. "Guys, I got a problem."

"What's up?" Brent asked, his voice filled with concern.

James lowered his head and whispered, "I can't hang out tonight. I've gotta go take care of something."

"Excuse me," I said in disbelief. "You can't leave. You're the one who insisted we all go out tonight. Did you forget the man's getting married tomorrow?"

James turned to Brent. "No, I didn't forget, and I'm sorry, Brent, but something's come up. It's important. I've gotta go back to Queens."

"Back to Queens for what?" I stared at my friend. This wasn't like him. James didn't keep secrets from us. If anyone, I was the one who kept the secrets.

It took a while for him to speak, but when he did, I was even more confused. "I gotta go babysit."

"Babysit? Babysit who? What's going on, James?" If you think I was annoyed, you should have heard the irritation in Brent's voice.

"It's a long story."

"Well, then, give us the short version," I demanded. I continued to stare at him in amazement. The brother couldn't even look at us.

"I really ain't got the time. I gotta get back to Queens before nine, so I don't piss her off." He tried to stand up, but I placed my hand on his shoulder and pushed him down. He glanced at Brent, then at me. I think he finally realized he wasn't going anywhere without giving us an explanation. A full explanation.

"Okay, okay, but you've gotta promise not to tell anyone. Not even your wives. If this gets back to Cathy, my marriage is over." He glared at us both, tight-lipped, waiting for our reply.

"Don't worry, James. We're not gonna say anything. Are we, Sonny?" Brent's eyes moved to me.

"Nah, bro, you ain't got to worry. Shit, we got your back. You know that." This whole thing was starting to get interesting. The only time I'd ever seen James act all secretive like this was when he was fooling around with this girl named Michelle a few years back, but to my knowledge, that was over and done with. Besides, if he was messing with her or anyone else, he would have told me. Or so I thought.

"Y'all remember that girl, Michelle, that I used to see a few years back, don't you?"

Oh, my God, he is fucking her again.

"Who could forget her? For a skinny girl, she had one of the *phattest* asses I've ever seen." Brent didn't seem to know what we were talking about, so I used my hands to emphasize my statement. "Come on, Brent, you know her, the redbone with the big ol' ba-dunk-a-dunk. Damn, how could you forget her? It ain't like James had a thousand affairs."

Brent finally nodded as if a lightbulb had just gone off in his head. "Ohhh, yeah, I remember her. The girl from your UPS route, the one you almost left Cathy for, right?"

"Mm-hmmm, that's her. But I wasn't going to leave Cathy for her or anyone else."

"No, but you're about to leave your best friend's bachelor party to babysit her kid, aren't you?" I asked in disgust. "You just couldn't resist that big ol' booty, could you?"

"Why are you always classifying women by their asses?" Damn, ol' boy had it pretty bad. He was even defending her honor.

"Some people remember faces, James. I remember asses. Now stop trying to change the subject. You messin' with her again, aren't you?"

"Nah, I ain't messing with her, Sonny." James had a little attitude to his voice now. "But she says I'm her baby's daddy."

There was a brief, shocked silence as his words registered.

"What did you say?" Brent asked, the disbelief in his voice and on his face.

"I said, she says I'm her baby's daddy."

"Oh, shit," I mumbled, clearing my throat as I sat back in my chair. There was another moment of painful silence before Brent and I asked, "Are you?" in unison.

James shrugged his shoulders, giving us the lamest answer we could possibly hear. "I really don't know."

I jumped out of my seat, pointing my finger in his face. "What you mean you don't know? How the fuck you don't know? Did you fuck her without a raincoat?"

All he did was nod, and I went off on him again.

"Oh, my God! What the fuck is wrong with you?" I was about two seconds away from putting my foot in his ass.

"Sit down, Sonny," Brent ordered. "Let the brother explain."

"Explain! There ain't no explanation for this, Brent!"

"I said, let the man explain. Other people are trying to enjoy the game."

I looked around and everyone in our section was staring at me. So I did as Brent asked, folding my arms and staring angrily at James. I was disappointed in him, really disappointed. He was the one who always had his shit together.

"You're right, Sonny. I should have never slept with her without a condom, but hindsight is twenty-twenty. I just have to deal with the consequences now."

"So, did you have some type of blood test or something?" Brent asked.

"Nah, I asked her for a blood test, but she threatened to tell Cathy about the baby if I pushed the issue."

I unfolded my arms. "That's 'cause the baby ain't yours. Can't you see she's trying to trap you? That's why she don't want you to have a blood test. That's what these young girls do." I was so heated, you would have thought she said it was my baby.

"Yeah, but what am I supposed to do about it? She told me if I don't pay her child support and babysit, she's gonna go to Cathy."

"Fuck it. Let her tell Cathy. But I wouldn't give that bitch shit!" I told him adamantly.

"He can't do that and you know it, Sonny." Brent chimed in like he was Johnnie Cochran defending his client.

"Why the fuck not?"

"Because Cathy will divorce me," James said, "the same way your wife would divorce you if you showed up with a baby by some other woman." *Yeah, right,* I thought to myself. *My wife's not going to divorce me if I come home with a child out of wedlock—she's going to castrate me.*

"But that baby ain't yours, man," I protested.

Brent shook his head. "Have you listened to a word the man's said? He's not sure if he's the father himself, so why should you be?" I didn't have an answer for that.

"Look, you guys enjoy the game and Hooters," James said with finality. "I gotta go babysit."

"Keep your head up, bro. We're gonna figure a way outta this for you, man," I told him with certainty.

"The only way out of this is to keep this crazy bitch happy so she doesn't go bothering my wife. And that's exactly what I'm going to do."

Brent grabbed his arm. "The only way out of this is to put your faith in God and pray on this."

James looked him in the face and said, "I've been praying, Brent. I'm just waiting for God to answer my prayers."

8

Brent

"I love you, Mr. Williams."

"I love you more, Ms. Hendy . . . I mean, Mrs. Williams." I smiled as I said it. I was sure my bride-to-be was smiling.

We'd been talking on the phone for about twenty minutes. I was lying on my living room sofa about to take a shower, change into my pajamas, and go to bed in anticipation of tomorrow's big event. After the game, I'd gone to Hooters with Sonny at James's request, but I still couldn't believe he actually left the game to babysit a kid he wasn't even sure was his. Lord, I hoped Cathy never found out about this. Not having James around kinda spoiled the rest of the evening for Sonny and me. We didn't even stay fifteen minutes at Hooters before deciding to leave. When I got home, I prayed, then I called Alison to say good night.

"Mrs. Williams. Lord knows I love the sound of that," Alison said. So did I. It was hard to believe, but this time tomorrow we'd be on our honeymoon on Paradise Island in the Bahamas. We were planning on trying to have a baby right away. Both Alison and I loved kids, and we both wanted at least two. I wanted to be a dad more than anything in the world.

"Me too. I can't wait to show you off as my wife."

Alison was quiet for a moment before she said, "Brent? Can I ask you something?" Her tone lost its excitement.

"Sure, baby. What is it?" I sat up.

She never asked a question. It was more like a statement, a confusing statement at that. "You don't have to do this if you don't want to. I'll understand if you wanna back out."

I pulled the phone from my ear, staring at it before resting it back against my head. "Huh? What are you trying to say?"

"I wanna know if you really wanna marry me. Are you sure you're not just doing this because you feel sorry for me?"

How could she be questioning my love? Maybe she was just having last-minute jitters, but her comment caught me off guard and left me feeling insulted. "Why would you ask me that? You know I love you, Alison. Have you ever even seen me look at another woman?"

"No, but I see the way they look at you. They all want you, Brent, even the married ones. How long are you going to want me, with all of them waiting in the wings for us to fail?"

"Until death do us part," I answered, confused by her sudden lack of faith in me.

"I hope so, Brent, because sometimes I think that you could do better. That you're just settling with me, and I don't want you to settle."

"I'm not settling, Alison. I love you."

"But why? Why me? I'm black as hell, I'm damn near forty, and I weigh over two hundred fifty pounds." Her curse caught me by surprise. "The only thing I got going for me is my Indian hair."

"You're the woman I fell in love with, so all the rest of them don't matter. And I don't give a darn if you weigh two *thousand* pounds. I love *you*, Alison, for the woman you are inside. I don't care about that superficial stuff. I want you to be my wife."

"That's all I wanted to hear," she answered, sounding more like herself again. "'Cause once we walk down that aisle, I'm never giving you up. And I mean never."

"I don't want you to give me up. Alison, you're the woman I wanna grow old with."

She let out a thankful sigh. "I love you too, Brent, more than anything in the world."

"Good, then we still have a date to meet at the altar tomorrow?"

"I'll be there," she assured me.

We chatted for a few minutes longer, then said our final good night before hanging up. I took a shower and got ready for bed. I thought about calling James to see how things were going with the babysitting, but before I got to the phone, there was a loud knock on my door. I jumped out of bed.

"Who is it?" I asked as I went to the door.

There was no answer, so I pulled back the curtain on the window beside the door. I did a double take, letting go of the curtain when a figure I recognized turned toward me. There was another knock on the door, and this time I opened it with a sense of excitement and fear.

Jackie Moss, my church's sexy organist, walked into my house. There was no question in my mind that Jackie was intoxicated, but even drunk, Jackie's presence had a way of warming my heart and chilling my soul. It had been obvious from the first time we met that there was a mutual attraction between us. I've got this thing for green eyes, and Jackie's were the greenest I'd ever seen.

"Jackie, what are you doing here?" I couldn't help but stare.

Ignoring my question, Jackie strolled over to my living room bar, taking out two glasses and filling them with Hennessy, then offering me one. It almost fell to the floor in our exchange.

"You're drunk?"

"Uh-huh. I wouldn't be here unless I was."

"So, why are you here?" I asked again.

Jackie gulped down the entire glass of Hennessy, giving me a look that told me everything I needed to know and more. "I came here to get you to cancel this ridiculous wedding. You can't marry fat-ass Alison Hendy."

"Why?" I snapped, not happy about the insult to Alison, "because you're jealous?"

Jackie laughed. "Whether I'm jealous or not doesn't matter. The whole congregation is laughing at you, Brent."

"So, let them laugh. What are they going to say when Alison and I are still together forty years from now?"

Jackie frowned. "Brent, you're the most handsome man in the church. People like you and I aren't supposed to get married."

"How can you say that? You're married."

Jackie placed the glass back on the bar and approached me. "That's exactly why I'm telling you that you shouldn't. You don't really love her."

"I do love her, Jackie. She's everything I ever wanted in a woman."

"Please. Then why are you looking at me that way? You can't even take your eyes off me. You know it's me you really want."

I tried to look away, but the truth is the truth. I did want Jackie. I'd never met anyone so attractive, so perfect, but my mother always warned me that if something seems too good to be true, it usually is. In Jackie's case, Momma's words rang truer than ever, because my true soul mate was already married—to a prominent member of our church. In another place and another time, our fates probably would have been different. I'm sure it was the Lord who intervened and forced First Lady Wilson into introducing me to my bride-to-be, Alison. If she hadn't, Jackie and I would have probably started an affair that would have rocked the church. And that was something I would never do.

"Sometimes what you want isn't necessarily what you need," I said. "I'm sorry, but I will not give in to lust. I love Alison, and I'm going to marry her."

"You don't love her. Not the way you could love me." Jackie stepped up and kissed me like I'd never been kissed before. My entire body began to tingle and blood was rushing to places it shouldn't have been. I was so turned on it took everything I had to pull myself away.

"That's where you're wrong, Jackie. I do love her. Maybe not in the physical sense like you're offering, but in an emotional and spiritual sense that will last a lifetime. Now, I think you should leave."

Jackie grinned at me wickedly. "Do you really want me to leave, Brent?"

I was hesitant, but I nodded.

"Okay, I'll leave. But not before I give you your wedding present."

"What wedding present?"

"This one."

Before I could respond, Jackie's lips were pressed against mine and a warm, Hennessy-flavored tongue parted my lips and began to explore my mouth. The alcohol taste didn't bother me at all, and we kissed passionately for a good ten seconds. This time, I couldn't hold myself back. Believe it or not, it was Jackie who ended our kiss abruptly with a grin. "Now, that's a present I'm sure you'll carry with you throughout your marriage. Feel free to share it with your new wife anytime you like. I'll see you tomorrow at the wedding."

And on that note, Jackie strode toward the door and walked out.

9

James

It was late and I was watching Ving Rhames play the new Kojak when my cell phone rang. The caller ID had my home phone number on it, and I immediately turned the sound up and switched the TV from Kojak to BET, where music videos were playing. I was hoping to give my wife the impression I was at a strip club. I know what you're thinking. Why the hell would I want my wife to think I was in a strip club? Well, it's a hell of a lot better than telling her that I was at my former mistress's house babysitting the son she said was mine.

"Hello?" I raised my voice, trying to speak louder than the 50 Cent video on the TV.

"James, honey, it's me!" she yelled back to make sure I heard her.

"Hun, you're gonna have to speak up. I can barely hear you with this loud-ass music."

"What time are you coming home?"

"Three, four, depending on if we decide to go to a diner. We just got to the club about an hour ago. We're not doing anything, Cathy, just looking, honest."

"I know. I'm not tryin' to bitch. I just wanted you to wake me up when you come home."

"Wake you up for what?" I didn't like the sound of that. Cathy tried to act like she wasn't, but my wife was a jealous woman . . . a very jealous woman. She was always snooping around my shit, checking my phone, my pockets, and my car. She never found anything because I wasn't doing anything, but you'd be surprised by the coincidental shit that got me in trouble.

"You'll see."

"Come on, Cathy. What you gonna do, give me the sniff test again?" I laughed, but I was only half-joking.

"No, baby, I'm gonna give you the hardness test, so be prepared to stick your plug in my socket. You got a problem with that?"

A smile crept up on my face. No, I definitely didn't have a problem with that. We hadn't had sex since the night Michelle sprang the news on me about Marcus being my son, and I was in definite need of some stress relief.

"No, ma'am. I don't have a problem with that at all. Matter of fact, I'm about ready to blow a fuse right now."

"Well then, I'll see you when you get home. Don't forget to wake me up." Now that's what I was talking about. I couldn't wait to get home.

I hung up the phone and turned the TV down just as Marcus walked into the room, wearing a Pull-Up and dragging a blue stuffed bunny behind him. Believe it or not, this was the first time I'd seen him, other than a picture or the quick peek in his room when I arrived.

On my way in, Michelle had rushed out the door to a waiting cab. "He's asleep and he shouldn't wake up before I get home around four, but if he does, take him to the bathroom then give him some juice in his Lion King sippy cup. He'll go right back to sleep after that," she said over her shoulder. "Oh, and the dog's in the laundry room. Let him out in the backyard to do his business if he starts to whine." Ain't that a bitch? Not only was I babysitting, but she had me dogsitting too.

"Mommy! Where's my mommy?" Marcus was on the verge of tears.

Suddenly, as I stared at him, a chill ran through my body. This had all just seemed like a bad dream, but now here was this kid, in the flesh, needing, wanting, and crying. Up until now, I'd pretty much convinced myself that there was the possibility that I was Marcus's father, since I was at the scene of the crime, but not the probability, since I wasn't the only one she was having sex with. I mean, damn, we'd only had sex without a condom that one time.

Now that Marcus was standing in front of me, I finally got a good look at him and saw that there was some resemblance to me and my people. He wasn't a dead ringer like my sons, James

Jr. and Michael. They looked just like me. Ain't no denying those two. Marcus, maybe he could be my son, but I still thought he looked more like the other guy Michelle was screwing. She'd admitted to me once while we were dating that she went raw-dog with her boyfriend Trent almost every time.

Either way, I was in no position to stand up to Michelle and insist on a DNA test. Things at home were going too well between Cathy and me to take any chances. If there was the slightest chance he was my son, I didn't need any drama, especially from Michelle. That girl would take the phrase "baby mama drama" to the next level.

"What's the matter, little man?" I tried to rub his head.

He stared at me for a few seconds, obviously confused. The tears began to run down his face. "I want my mommmy!" he wailed.

I took a deep breath because there was no bigger pain in the ass than a child who wanted his mother. I tried to warn Michelle of this before she left, but she wasn't hearing me. She swore up and down that he'd sleep through the night and wouldn't get up 'til daylight.

"I know you want your mommy, but your mommy had to go to work. She'll be home soon, okay?" I smiled at him, but he wasn't going for it.

"I want my mommmy! I want my mommmy! I want my mommyyyyy!" he screamed, each time louder than the first. He was about two seconds away from a full-blown meltdown, but I'd been through this same thing with my boys. I knew what to do. I was going to bribe him.

"Hey, Marcus, you want a lollipop?" He shut up immediately, nodding his head, although tears were still running down his face. "Well, if you want a lollipop, then you gotta stop this crying, man."

He sucked back tears and wiped his face with his shirtless arm. I smiled, reaching in my pocket and pulling out three Tootsie Roll Pops I'd purchased on the way over for just such an occasion. Before I could even ask him which color he wanted, he grabbed the red one out of my hand, ripping off the waxed paper. I smiled as he shoved it into his mouth.

Works every time, I thought. I never met a kid who wouldn't take a bribe. All you have to do is find out his weakness. With some kids it's candy, others it's TV. I've got a nephew who won't shut up unless you give him a dollar.

I picked him up, placing him on my lap. "Do you know who I am?"

He nodded his head repeatedly as he sucked on his lollipop. "You my daddy!"

I almost dropped him off my lap, I was so stunned by his reply. I don't know what I was expecting him to say, but it wasn't that. "Who told you that?"

He jumped down and headed toward a love seat across the room. Then he climbed up on it, pulling a photo album off the end table and on to his lap. He started flipping pages like he knew what he was doing and I walked over to investigate. About ten pages into the album he stopped, pointing at a picture. "Mommy and daddy," he said in his rather cute child's voice before pointing to another picture and repeating the same words.

I took a good look at each picture, and to my surprise, each photograph had a picture of Michelle and me at various times during our relationship. I was surprised she kept those pictures and even more surprised that she showed them to her son. Now, if you ask me, that shit was low. She'd already had junior here brainwashed that I was his dad. I wondered, how long had she been showing him my picture? Not that it mattered. The damage was done now.

I started to walk to the kitchen. "Come on, little man, let's get your Lion King cup and get you some juice, so you can go back to bed and I can think."

I swear, I'd barely turned my back for two seconds when I heard Marcus sputtering and choking. I rushed back into the living room and there he was, laying sprawled out on the floor, gagging, with his hands near his throat. My heart was doing summersaults in my chest as I dashed across the room and grabbed him.

"What's wrong?" His lips were turning blue and he gagged. I immediately turned his back to me. In one swift movement I delivered the Heimlich maneuver, and the lollipop spewed out of his little mouth. Relieved, I had to choke back my own feelings. What the hell was I thinking about? Giving him that stupid lollipop almost killed him. Without thinking, I held Marcus close to my chest to calm both him and myself. His little heart was trotting like a racehorse and so was mine. After Marcus caught his breath again, he began crying in deep gasps.

"It's all right son, it's all right, Daddy's here. You're going to be all right," I said in a soothing voice. I thanked God Cathy had made me take a CPR class at the Y when our boys were infants. When he finally calmed down, I said, "Here. Let's go get your juice."

"I wanna play with Majesty," Marcus protested between hiccups. As if on cue, the dog began to bark from the laundry room.

"Okay. I'll let you play with Majesty or whatever his name is for a little while, then back to bed you go."

After Marcus drank his juice and went to the toilet, he romped around with his little mutt until he dozed off in the middle of the floor. I picked him up and carried him to his bedroom, feeling something stirring in my gut. Marcus had his arm wrapped snugly around my neck.

I laid him down in his twin bed and shook my head. Lord, what if something had happened to him while he was with me? I don't think I could've lived with that. He was a good kid, even if he wasn't my son. And if he was my flesh and blood and died . . . dear Lord, I didn't even wanna think about it.

10

Sonny

"Ladies and gentlemen, please raise your glasses one more time and join me as I wish my best friend, Brent, and his lovely bride, Alison, farewell before they depart on their honeymoon."

Cheers and clinking glasses echoed throughout the Westbury Manor reception hall as Brent and Alison took center stage. I handed the microphone to Brent so he and his bride could say their final good-byes, then slipped into the crowd to check in with my wife. It had been one of the most emotional wedding ceremonies I'd ever been to. I don't think there was a dry eye in the place after Brent and Alison recited from memory their very personal vows. If that wasn't enough, the Westbury Manor reception hall looked like something out of a magazine, and the food they served tasted like it came from a five-star restaurant. Add in DJ Smooth, arguably the best old-school DJ in Queens, and you had the best wedding I'd ever been to, including my own. I'm sure the whole affair set Brent and Alison back a pretty penny.

After maneuvering my way through the crowd now surrounding the Williamses on the dance floor, I found an empty table toward the back of the hall. I sat down, pulled out my cell phone, and dialed my wife. We talked for about fifteen minutes and I told her about the wedding. She was jealous, of course, and wished she was there, but said nothing could tear her away from packing up our belongings so we could move them to New York. Jessica was excited about our move. She probably asked me fifteen times a day when I was coming home to move them out.

"Excuse me, sir. Can I have this dance?" a warm, sexy voice purred just as I hung up the phone.

I looked up to see the woman who took my virginity, my high

school sweetheart, Tiffany Boyd. She was still as pretty as they come, with her smooth bronze skin highlighted by a large dimple on her right cheek. She'd gained a little weight over the years, most of which ended up around her hips, and of course you know I didn't mind that, being the ass man that I am.

"It's been a long time, Tiffany. I heard a rumor that you married crazy-ass Kareem." I started to laugh but stopped when I saw her expression.

"Crazy is right," she said as she sat beside me. That man put me through hell before I divorced him."

"Oh, wow, I'm sorry to hear that."

"So am I, but he's out of my life now." She smiled, changing the subject. "So, speaking of rumors, I heard you were dead."

"No, I'm still alive and kicking." We both laughed.

It's funny how you don't think about a person for years and then they pop up and your mind is flooded with memories. Right now, most of mine had to do with sex and how Tiffany used to put it on me every night in the backseat of my father's car. Boy, did she have some good damn pussy. My dick was getting hard just thinking about it. I was glad I was sitting down so the table could cover it.

Tiffany was a year older than me. We started dating in my sophomore year of high school. She was one of those girls who never had any girlfriends and was always hanging around with a bunch of guys. Truth is, she had a reputation for being a slut, and the only reason I started to date her was because I wanted to lose my virginity.

What I didn't know was that it wasn't as easy to get in her pants as everyone said. Oh, she wasn't a virgin, but you could count the guys she'd been with on one hand. I found out later that many a brother had lied on their dicks when it came to her, including my boy Brent. Let him tell it, all you had to do was buy her an ice-cream sundae or a shake from Baskin-Robbins and take her for a walk down by Roy Wilkins Park, and she'd do all the rest. I must have bought twenty-five sundaes and another thirty shakes before I finally got some, and even then, she didn't initiate it. Funny thing is, by the time she did give me some, I really liked her and didn't give a damn what her reputation was. From that point on, we were boyfriend and girlfriend, an inseparable pair. That is, until she graduated and joined the Navy without telling me.

"How you doing, Tiffany? You're looking good." My eyes were fixated on her hips. Deep down, I wanted to ask her to turn around so I could see her ass.

"Thanks." Her dimple got deeper. "You're not looking so bad yourself for a dead man."

"You know what they say. Embalming fluid helps preserve your youth." I rubbed my hand across my smoothly shaved face. We both cracked up, laughing.

"Oh, Lord, Sonny, you still crazy. You know that?" She was still chuckling.

"Yeah, and you're still the prettiest girl at the prom. Did you know that?"

Don't ask me where that came from, because I don't have a clue, but neither one of us was laughing anymore. We were staring at each other, our eyes doing all the talking, reminiscing about what quite possibly was the greatest night of either of our lives. I loved my wife more than anything in the world, and when she married me she made me the happiest man in the world, but the happiest night of my life would always be the night of Tiffany's senior prom.

The lights in the hall got dim when the DJ announced that Brent and Alison had just left the building and he would only be playing three more songs. As if it were scripted, the next song he played was "Endless Love."

"Remember this?" Tiffany finally broke our silence.

"How could I ever forget our song?"

"So, can a sister get a dance or what?" She placed a hand on her hip.

"Sure," I told her as I stood, trying my best to use my tuxedo jacket to hide my erection.

I thought about Jessica and the kids back in Seattle. Like I said earlier, I'd never cheated on my wife before, but dancing wasn't cheating, so I didn't feel any guilt. Tiffany led the way to the dance floor, and for the first time, I saw that bodacious ass of hers. It looked just like a Georgia peach in that tight-fitting dress, and my dick got just a little bit harder.

When we got on the dance floor, Tiffany wrapped her arms

around my neck and placed her head on my shoulder. She was so soft and smelled so good that I just wanted to squeeze her and pull her in close, but I resisted. I didn't want her to feel my bulging manhood up against her dress. I wanted to believe she wouldn't mind, but the last thing I needed was to get slapped on the dance floor at Brent's wedding.

"I love this song," she whispered, snuggling her head up against my neck. She pulled me in a little closer, and I'm sure she could feel what was going on down below. "Whenever I hear it, I think of you and the prom. That was the best night of my life."

"Mine too." I couldn't see her face, but I was sure she was smiling from the sigh she let out. She pulled me in closer and my stuff slid right up against the soft mound between her legs.

"You've got me feeling like we're in high school again, Sonny." I rubbed my hands against the skin where her dress was open in the back. "I'm starting to feel like it's the prom all over again." I didn't reply. I was too busy enjoying the pleasure of our bodies rubbing up against each other.

"That was the first time I ever spent the entire night with a man."

"For me that was the first night for a lot of things," I whispered.

"I'll never forget that night. That was the first time you ever went down on me."

"You know, I had to read a book to find out what to do."

"What's the name of that book? 'Cause there's a lot of men that need to read it. You were the absolute bomb." Now I was blushing.

"It's called *The Joy of Sex*."

"Oh, it was a joy, all right." She reached behind and moved my hands lower. I stopped them at her waist, opening my eyes to see who might be looking. I wanted to feel Tiffany's ass, to massage it with my hands, but I was afraid someone might see me. Fortunately, most of the guests had left shortly after the bride and groom, and everyone on the dance floor was preoccupied. I slowly guided my hands below her waist, feeling the soft globes of her perfectly round backside.

"That's not too much for you to handle, is it?" she teased. "She's a little bigger than she used to be back in the day."

"Nah," I replied, my hands continuing to roam. "You don't have to worry. I can handle it. I like 'em big."

"Good." She pulled me in closer and our two-step became a flat-footed grind.

We danced like that for at least one more song without a word being said, and I was starting to feel woozy. I hadn't had more than one or two glasses of champagne throughout the night, but I felt like I was drunk. I'd heard of people getting sex-drunk, but I'd always thought of it as an urban myth until now.

I think Tiffany was just as intoxicated as I was because the way she was grinding up against me, I wouldn't have been surprised if she was close to orgasm.

"Sonny," she whispered halfway through the third song.

"Yes?"

"My kids are with my ex-husband tonight. I was wondering if you'd like to come home with me."

I lifted my head and looked in her eyes. I would have gone anywhere with her at that moment. "Yeah, I'll go home with you," I replied without any hesitation.

I bent down to kiss her, but the music stopped and the lights came on before our lips could meet. We stepped apart, but it was hard because we were still drawn to each other. I tried to position my rock-hard manhood in my pants so it wouldn't be so conspicuous, while Tiffany scrambled to push down her hiked-up dress. We got ourselves together just in time, because her girlfriend called her from the door like she was her mama, and on top of that, James was headed our way.

"I'll meet you in the parking lot. I gotta get rid of my friend," she said.

"No problem. Looks like I'm gonna have to do the same."

She stepped toward me as if she wanted a kiss, then stepped back when she glanced at her friend. "I'll be outside," she mouthed then walked toward the door, switching her ass just for my benefit. I couldn't wait to get her out of that dress.

"Hey, is that who I think it is? Is that your ex, Tiffany?" James pointed and we both watched her walk away.

"Yeah, that's her," I said nonchalantly.

"Man, she's sure got a nice ass." He laughed. "Bet you wish you could get some of that again."

"Yep, that'd be nice." We stepped outside. I took out a pack of cigarettes from my tuxedo pocket. James caught me smirking as I placed one in my mouth.

"What's going on, man? What are you up to?"

"Who, me?" I pointed at myself, grinning innocently.

"Yeah, you. What were you two talking about?" James obviously sensed something, but I don't think he understood the full magnitude of what was going on.

"She wants me to go home with her tonight." I lit my cigarette, my eyes still glued on Tiffany's behind.

James laughed. "Get the fuck outta here. She does not!"

I gave him a very serious look. My words were condescending. "Okay, if you say so."

James studied my face. "Oh, shit. You're serious, aren't you?"

"Serious as a heart attack."

"Just like that. After all these years, she just walks up to you and asks you to sleep with her?"

"Well, we did dance first."

He stared at me a moment, then finally said, "Daaaaaamn, women are bold these days."

"It's the world we live in, bro. Look at how they treat Brent. Get used to it."

"So, what'd you tell her? You gonna do it?"

I took a long drag of my cigarette, then exhaled as I answered his question with another question. "What would you tell the woman with the best coochie you ever had in your life if she offered you some?"

I grinned smugly, smoking my cigarette as he contemplated my question. After a few seconds, he smiled, reaching in his wallet. He pulled out a condom and handed it to me. At that point, we both knew his answer.

"Don't make the same mistake I did. But don't do anything I wouldn't do." He patted me on the back, and I actually stuck out my chest with pride.

"Don't worry, I will . . . and a whole lot more." I took another drag of my cigarette and started walking toward the door to get my coat.

"Hey, Sonny? What about Jessica?"

I stopped and turned toward my friend. "What about her? What she doesn't know won't hurt her."

11

James

Cathy and I were on our way home from Brent's wedding when we got stuck in a terrible traffic jam on the Cross Island Parkway. Her head was on my shoulder and I was holding her hand as I drove. I think she fell asleep about ten minutes into the drive, although she made overtures before we left the reception that she wanted to make love when we got home. I didn't have a problem with that at all. Matter of fact, it made me contemplate the question Sonny had posed to me before he left to sleep with Tiffany.

What would you tell the woman with the best coochie you ever had in your life if she offered you some?

As a man who wants to be honest with himself, I had to admit that I'd probably take her up on the offer. Thank God, unlike Sonny, the best coochie I've ever had belonged to my wife. Yeah, I cheated on her with Michelle a few years back, but I wasn't proud of it, especially with all this craziness with her claiming I was her baby's daddy. However, it wasn't because of the sex that I strayed from my marriage. It was because we lost our connection as friends and we stopped talking to each other. Don't get me wrong. There was a sexual connection between me and Michelle, but it would have never happened if Cathy and I hadn't stopped being friends.

When we finally pulled into the driveway, it started to rain hard. Despite the dreary weather, Cathy woke up smiling seductively, and it was obvious what was on her mind. She guided my hand to her crotch, pulling up her dress, and I could feel the heat through the thin material of her lace thong.

"I'm so wet," she whispered.

I began to rub between her legs gently, and a soft moan escaped from her mouth as she rested her head back on her headrest.

"I want some, James. I want some bad." She moaned again just as my fingers found the little button she called her "spot." She closed her eyes and enjoyed my smooth, easy touch for a few seconds. "You know you owe me from last night."

We hadn't had sex last night as we had planned. When I got home from babysitting Marcus, Cathy had been in a deep sleep, and to be truthful, I was glad. I was too mentally drained to do anything, especially after Marcus almost choked to death on that lollipop. All I wanted to do was go to sleep and forget.

"So, you gonna give me some or what?" She reached over to grab my manhood and I stopped her with my free hand.

"I don't know, Cathy. I'm a little tired," I teased.

"Tired?" If looks could kill I'd be dead. "Well, you better go inside and drink a cup of coffee or something, 'cause I need some. I ain't had none in over a week. And you know how I am when I ain't had none in a while." She forced her hand free from my grasp and it landed in my lap. She had a smile a mile wide when she felt the rock-hard pipe under my tuxedo pants. "Now that's what I'm talkin' 'bout."

The rain let up for a few seconds and Cathy immediately released my manhood and reached for the door.

"Come on now, James," she whined, suggesting I wasn't moving fast enough. "I told you I want some."

"Aw'ight, boo, I'm coming." I reached for my door and she smiled, rushing out of the car. "I'll meet you upstairs. I wanna take a shower and put on something sexy." She sounded giddy as she ran to the front door ahead of me.

When I got in the house, the sound of running water floated down the stairs. I slid out of my tuxedo jacket and was about to slip off my cummerbund when the phone rang. "I got it," I yelled up the stairs, reaching for the phone. As usual, I checked the caller ID. The number was unavailable.

"Hello."

"James?" I almost pissed on myself when I heard Michelle's voice. Instinctively, I covered the phone, tilting my head and listening to make sure the shower was still running.

"What the hell are you calling my house for?" I hissed into

the phone. Threats were one thing, calling my cell phone was another, but I couldn't believe she had actually dialed my home number again. This chick was getting on my nerves. "I told you about this shit."

"Don't be screaming on me, James. I tried to call you on your cell phone, but you didn't answer." She was right. I'd cut my ringer off for the wedding ceremony and had completely forgotten to turn it back on.

"This better be important, Michelle, and don't even think about asking me to babysit. You already told me you don't have to work tonight."

"I don't want you to babysit, James," she said coldly. "I need you to go to the twenty-four-hour Walgreens on Guy Brewer and get me some Children's Tylenol. Marcus has a fever."

"You gotta be kidding. *You* go get it!" I knew I sounded belligerent and unfeeling, but this girl was going too far.

"You know I ain't got no car and it's raining outside. I'm not taking my baby out in the rain. He's sick already."

"I'm busy, Michelle. Don't you have some dude who can help you? Damn, you know you need a man."

"Very funny, James. And no, I ain't got nobody to help me. You my help! So stop trying to avoid your responsibility."

Suddenly, the upstairs bathroom door opened. I looked up and Cathy was at the top of the stairs with only a towel wrapped around her. I don't think she had a clue who was on the phone or what we were talking about, but I panicked. I dropped the phone on the floor, and by the time I got my shit together, Cathy was headed down the stairs. I scrambled to pick it up.

"Sweetheart, you don't care if I don't wear a nighty, do you? It's only going to come off once we get started."

"Whatever you want to do, hun," I told her quickly. "Just get your fine ass up the stairs so we can do it." Thank God she stopped halfway down the steps. I placed the phone on my ear and it was dead.

"Okay." She stared at me suspiciously. "Who's that on the phone?"

"Aah . . ." I glanced at the phone, wishing it wasn't in my hand. "It was Sonny, but we . . . we got disconnected."

"What did he want?"

"Ah . . . his rental car broke down on the Conduit. . . ." I couldn't even finish my lie because the phone rang again.

Cathy gave me a disappointed look that was about to become an angry look. "You're not going to pick him up, are you, James?"

"Not until I put you to bed properly, baby. Sonny's just gonna have to wait. I promise."

"Good, now hurry up and get your friend off the phone. Momma wants some lovin'." She turned around and walked back up the stairs while I quickly walked toward the kitchen.

"Hello?"

"Why'd you hang up on me?" Michelle snapped.

"I didn't." I was trying to remain calm.

She raised her voice even louder. "Yes, you did."

"Look, I don't have time to argue with you. It was an accident. I dropped the phone by accident."

"Whatever." I could almost see her neck rolling on the other end of the phone. "So, are you gonna bring me some Tylenol for your son?" I hated it when she called him my son.

"Yeah, I'll be over there in a few." I tried to think of a lie to give me more time. "I'm waiting for my wife to come home with the car." I hung up the phone, then hit the talk button again. When I heard the dial tone, I placed the phone on the kitchen table. Now if she called back, she'd just get a busy signal, I told myself as I walked toward the stairs to take care of my wife.

12

Sonny

I was following Tiffany back to her apartment in Queens, still intoxicated from the effects of our dance. There was an accident on the Cross Island Parkway, so she was taking me some back way through residential neighborhoods in Long Island. About thirty minutes into our ride I spotted a sign that read: ENTERING THE TOWN OF ELMONT and I could feel my hormones start to kick into overdrive. I wasn't quite sure where we were, but I was sure that we were close enough to the Queens border that I'd have Tiffany naked as the day she was born within the half-hour. It had been seventeen years since we'd made love, but I could still remember the way she moaned and the warm, wet, velvety way she felt when I slid inside her.

Tiffany and I had a sexual chemistry like no one I'd ever been with, and it was never more evident to me than the way I felt the second we walked on the dance floor. I couldn't wait to kiss her, to touch her, and yes, to make love to her. But as Murphy's Law would have it, there were always going to be some obstacles in my way, this time in the form of a ringing cell phone.

I checked the caller ID, hoping it was James, but I knew it wasn't. It was my wife checking up on me. I was tempted to answer it and tell her I was on my way home or tired, but I never hit the talk button because I didn't want to lie. Matter of fact, when it stopped ringing, I turned the phone off completely. I'd just have to deal with the consequences in the morning. I know it sounds crazy for me to jeopardize everything I had with Jessica, but for me this was a once-in-a-lifetime opportunity.

Believe it or not, I felt no guilt until we pulled up to a stop sign and I saw a house for rent. It was a white Cape Cod with black or maybe blue shutters. It was dark, but the yard looked big enough for my kids to play in. Damn, this was it. This was the house Jessica and I had always dreamed of. I searched for a pen to write down the phone number on the FOR RENT sign, but I couldn't find one. Tiffany was now a block in front of me and I had no choice but to speed up and catch her, hoping I'd be able to remember how to get back to my family's dream house.

Ten minutes later, I pulled in behind Tiffany's car and watched her get out, swaying those lovely hips as she walked to the sidewalk. She stared at me through the passenger-side window for a few seconds, obviously waiting for me to get out of the car. When I didn't, she walked over and knocked on the window. I rolled it down and she stuck her head in, grinning.

"You coming?" I wanted to say yes in the worst way, but James's words and my reply had been echoing in my head ever since I'd seen that house for rent.

What about Jessica? he asked.

What about her? What she doesn't know won't hurt her, I had replied.

Looking back on things, I couldn't believe those words came out of my mouth. I knew it would hurt Jessica, if only because my conscience would kill me and I wouldn't be able to look her in the face.

"Get in for a minute. I have to tell you something."

She opened the door and slid into the car, no longer grinning. "What's wrong?"

"I'm married. I have a wife and kids back in Seattle. I thought you should know that." I didn't bother to tell her I was moving back to New York, because I didn't plan on seeing her once my family was here.

"I appreciate you telling me, but I figured as much when I saw your wedding band. I don't wanna take you away from her, Sonny. I just want to borrow you for a night or two."

"No, I don't think you understand. I'm happily married. I love my wife."

She gave me a strange look. "Then what are you doing here? Why did you come?"

"Honestly, I don't know. Somehow I got caught up in the moment on the dance floor and things got out of hand. You brought out things in me that I haven't felt in years. Even now part of me wants to take you inside and make love to you all night long. But

I can't, because I love my wife. She and my kids are my world, and I will not give them up for one night of pleasure, even if it's going to be the greatest night of pleasure in my life. And I'm sure it would be."

She lowered her head. "God, I am such a fool. How could I let something like this happen?"

"You're not a fool. I'm the fool for leading you on." I placed a sympathetic hand on her shoulder.

She lifted her head and turned to me, her eyes not nearly as angry as I thought they would be. "Now you're the one who doesn't understand. I'm the fool because I let you go seventeen years ago. I've had one bad relationship after another, men cheating on me, beating on me. All I ever wanted was someone to be my friend, my lover, someone who loves me. I'm the fool because I had all that in you. I just couldn't see it at the time."

I didn't know what to say.

"Go home, Sonny. Go home to your wife and your family in Seattle. But you tell her I said she better watch her back. If she ever messes up, I'm going to be waiting here in New York to step into her shoes, because she's the luckiest woman on this earth."

She leaned over and kissed my cheek, then stepped out of the car. I watched her walk to her door and thought briefly about chasing after her so we could finish what we had started on the dance floor. Instead, I turned on my cell phone and called my wife to tell her about our dream house and just how much I loved her.

13

James

It was almost forty-five minutes later when I left Cathy asleep in the house. I'd given her what I called "a sleeping pill"—two orgasms from oral sex and a quickie doggy-style from the back. That put her to sleep every time. I hated the idea of using sex with my wife to get me out of the house, but there was nothing I could do. Once again I was letting Michelle dictate the situation, and it was starting to piss me off because I really wasn't sure that the boy was my son.

In spite of the rain-slicked roads, I pulled in front of Michelle's place twenty minutes after I left my house. I was barely up the walkway when she flung open the door and grabbed the Walgreens bag out of my hand. "It's about damn time!"

"How is he?" I asked. She didn't reply, so I just followed her into the house. When we entered his bedroom, I knew something was very wrong. Marcus's arms were lying limply by his side and his eyes were glazed. I felt his forehead, and he was burning up. His skin looked dry and his lips were parched.

"Hey, little man. You aw'ight?"

Marcus gave me a weak smile. The dim light in his eyes showed he remembered me. "Daddddy," he whispered.

I didn't respond—I just turned to Michelle, who was opening the Children's Advil. I wanted to say something, but from the look on her face, it wouldn't have been wise.

"Why'd you get this? I told you I wanted Children's Tylenol," she complained.

"Children's Advil is better than Tylenol. It'll bring his fever down faster. Trust me. I've got two sons, remember?"

Michelle stopped what she was doing and turned to me as she spoke. The word "attitude" should have been written all over her face. "No, James, you've got three sons: James Jr., Michael, and *Marcus*. Don't you ever forget that!"

Our eyes locked, and my mind told me this was not a battle I could win. So, it was time to change the subject. I was starting to formulate a plan, though, and when it was all said and done, I'd have the last laugh.

"Did you take his temperature?" I asked.

"Yeah, it looked like it said 105, but—"

"A hundred and five! It can't be 105. He'd be damn near dead if it was 105!"

"I don't know. Maybe I was reading the thermometer wrong. I never had to do this before. My mama was always here." She looked like she wanted to cry.

"Where is it?"

She took the thermometer off the dresser and handed it to me. I inserted it in Marcus's mouth. When I read the red line and it indicated 101, I turned to Michelle. "We better take him to the emergency room."

"Okay. Let me give him a dose of this Advil and I'll be ready." Michelle grabbed up Marcus's jacket and a blanket to throw over his head.

I opened my eyes to the bright lights of Jamaica Hospital's waiting room and the annoying sound of Michelle's agitated voice calling my name. I'd dozed off about twenty or thirty minutes ago and now all I wanted to do was close my eyes and go back to sleep—something Michelle was not about to let me do, from the scolding look on her face. Why the heck was this girl so mad at me all the time?

"Wake up, James." Michelle kicked me lightly.

"I'm up," I snapped, moving my feet to my right side so that she couldn't kick me again.

Absentmindedly, I scanned the waiting room, thankful that I didn't see anyone I knew. It would be just my luck that one of Cathy's friends would walk into the waiting room and see me with Michelle. I checked my watch. I'd been gone from my house over two and a half hours. All I could do was pray that Cathy would sleep through the night and not notice I was gone, but the way things were going in my life, I was expecting her call at any moment. I needed to get my behind home.

"What'd the doctors say? Is Marcus going to be all right?"

I didn't have a clue as to what Marcus's condition was because I'd been forced to stay behind in the waiting room after they called his name. Can you believe that after sitting there for an hour and fifteen minutes, they still wouldn't let me go with Michelle, because only one parent was allowed in the examination room during treatment? What I didn't understand was why they hadn't rushed him straight into the examination room in the first place. When the nurse took his temperature, she had it at 102. Recently, there'd been quite a few cases of West Nile virus in the news, so I was more worried about the little guy than I let on. Especially when I remembered that I'd seen a dead bird in Michelle's driveway the other day.

"It's an ear infection. The doctor says he's going to be all right."

I let out a sigh of relief. "My kids have had ear infections before. They're really no big deal as long as he doesn't have them on the regular."

"I'll be able to take him home once the fever breaks," Michelle said.

"Thank God. How long do they think that's gonna be?" My face didn't hide the fact that I was ready to leave. As far as I was concerned, I'd done my good deed. Hell, I'd gone beyond the call of duty. I'd brought her the children's Advil, taken her to the hospital, and stuck around for a few hours.

"I don't know. The doctor said it could be twenty minutes, it could be a couple of hours."

"A couple of hours?" I glanced at her, shaking my head. "Michelle, I can't stay here a couple of hours. Do you think if I gave you cab fair you could . . ."

She raised her hand to stop me from talking. I was sure she was about to tell me some shit like, "Hell no, you can't leave. I ain't about to take my baby home in no cab," but to my surprise, she didn't say anything like that.

"Go on home, James. I got money for a cab." She actually looked sincere.

"You sure? I don't want any trouble, Michelle."

She nodded, giving me a slight smile. "Ain't gonna be no trouble, James. I know you gotta be home before the sun comes up." She bent over and kissed my forehead.

"What's that for?"

"That's for being a good father. I know I was tough on you, but I appreciate what you did."

"Ms. Jones?" We both turned toward the voice and an Indian man in a lab coat approached us. "It looks like your son's fever has broken. You can take him home."

Both Michelle and I smiled. "Thank you, doctor," I said. The doctor walked back to the examination area and Michelle turned toward me. "I understand this isn't a perfect situation for you, James, but all I want you to do is treat my son the same way you do his brothers. I don't want no more, no less. You think you can handle that?"

"I just don't want any drama, Michelle."

"Neither do I. I just want you to be a father for my son."

"Then that's what I'll be. All you gotta do is work with me." And I meant what I said.

14

Brent

From the time we stepped off the plane to the second our limo pulled in front of our hotel on Paradise Island in the Bahamas, Alison was in awe. She looked like a child on her first trip to Disney World. I'd completely forgotten that she'd never been out of the country before, let alone gone to a tropical paradise. She was so excited that she was pointing, holding her breath, and testifying all at the same time. It was truly a blessing just to watch her as she admired the postcard beauty of the island's palm trees and blue-green waters.

"Hey, look over there." I wrapped my arm around her and pointed to our hotel.

"Lawwd have mercy, is that our hotel?" She started shaking and waving her hands in the air like she'd just been struck by the Holy Ghost. I had to admit I was pretty impressed myself. We were staying at the Atlantis Casino Resort on Paradise Island. The hotel was just as inviting as the brochures had said it would be. It was truly a sight to behold.

Once we got out of the limo, we spent about a half-hour in the lobby, admiring what could only be called an aquarium. Whoever designed the place and came up with the name Atlantis hit the nail right on the head.

We followed the bellman to our room. After I tipped him for bringing up our suitcases, to Alison's surprise, I picked her up in my arms and carried her 250-pound frame over the threshold. Now, I'm not saying it was easy, and I almost dropped her, but I'd been lifting weights at the gym in preparation for this moment. I wanted to make our honeymoon special for her, and I think I was on my way to a good start. Of course, I couldn't wait to put her down once we got in the room, and I'm sure I pulled a muscle slightly in my back, but the look of pleasure on her face was worth any amount of pain I might have received.

"Oooh, Brent. You're something else." She threw her arms around me and gave me a deep kiss as she pulled me on the bed. "I love you, Mr. Williams. I love you so much."

"I love you too, Mrs. Williams," I murmured between kisses.

Alison tried to take off my shirt. I was sure she wanted to make love, but I resisted. I wanted to build things up before we made love. I wanted our lovemaking to cap off the most wonderful day of our lives.

"How about we go take a walk on the beach?" I suggested.

"Oooh, Brent, that sounds so romantic." Alison squealed.

"Good, then come on. Let's unpack these bags and get our bathing suits on."

Alison smiled her agreement, but then a reluctant, self-conscious look came over her face. "You know what? I don't think that's such a good idea. Why don't we just stay in the room?"

"Stay in the room? Alison, I know you wanna make love, but we've got all night to do that. We're on a tropical island, sweetheart. Don't you wanna walk along the warm beach with the sun on your back and a Bahama Mama in your hand?"

"Not if I gotta wear a bathing suit, I don't." She sat on the bed, pouting. "Did you see how skinny those women were, standing by the pool?"

"Yeah, and?"

"I don't look like them in a bathing suit, all right? I'm not going to go out there and embarrass you, Brent."

"Embarrass me how? I don't want those women. I just want you. Beauty is in the eye of the beholder, Alison, and you're beautiful to me. Why do you think I married you? Now, go on and get in your bathing suit. I'm going to get my trunks so I can take a walk with the prettiest woman on the island, my wife, Mrs. Alison Williams."

Looking a little less tense, Alison went into the bathroom. She came out sporting a black-and-white sarong wrapped over a one-piece black bathing suit, and I swear she looked twenty pounds slimmer. She had a white-and-black scarf wrapped around her hair, which gave her a sassy look.

"Mmm, mmm, mmm, now what were you worried about?

'Cause those girls by the pool ain't got nothin' on you." I walked over and kissed her.

The beach was crowded with women wearing what looked like G-strings more than bikinis. Some were even sunbathing with their tops off, but I didn't pay them no mind. I was very happy with who I was with. Although some of them were with their men, the majority of the women seemed to be like the sister in Terry McMillan's *How Stella Got Her Groove Back*. They were there with their girlfriends, and they were on the prowl. A few of them even tried to holler at me when I went to get Alison and myself some drinks from the beachside bar, but I made it very clear that I was with my wife and that they didn't have nothin' for me that she didn't have more of.

With drinks in hand, Alison and I strolled along the beach. At first she seemed a little self-conscious, but as we continued to walk, I held her hand and she became more comfortable. I'm not going to lie, there were more than a few people staring at us, especially the sistahs, but whenever they stared, I just pulled her in closer.

"Brent, I know we never put a time on it, but I wanna have a baby right away."

"Sounds like you been talking to First Lady Wilson again."

"We've had a few conversations. But that's not why I wanna have a baby right away. I love you, Brent, and I just want a piece of you inside."

I smiled. "I love you too, Alison, and I can't wait to have a child with you."

"Good, because I didn't bring any kind of protection." We both laughed. "I wanna have a house full of babies for you. Four, maybe even five kids."

"Wow, are you sure? That's a lot of wear and tear on your body."

She let go of my hand and wrapped her arm around my waist. "I don't care what it does to my body. I just wanna make you happy and be the mother of your children. You know, sometimes it's hard to believe you've never had children before."

I stopped walking and turned to my wife, wrapping my arms around her. "I've always loved children, Alison. I just never met a woman I wanted to have them with until I met you." I kissed her gently and she smiled.

"Brent, I love you so much. Do you know that?"

"Yes, I do, but make sure you show me how much you love me later tonight."

"You ain't said nothin' but a word. Everyone on this island's gonna know my name when I get finished with you tonight." Alison squeezed my butt, then kissed me passionately. When I opened my eyes from our kiss, there were two black women in their twenties staring at us like we were in a freak show. I was about to say something to them, but Alison beat me to it.

"What y'all looking at? You ain't never seen a woman kiss her man and squeeze his butt?" The women didn't say anything to us, but Alison's words snapped them out of their trance.

"What I wanna know is how much she's paying him," one of the women whispered under her breath to her friend, who laughed. She forgot water carries sound well, and we heard every word.

"What!" Alison shouted. I'd never seen her react to anything so aggressively. "I know you ain't accusing me of buying my man. You know what? Y'all gonna make me forget I'm saved out here." Alison kicked off her sandals, then snatched off her earrings as she headed toward them. I grabbed her arm and both girls took off back the way they came. "That's right, he's fine, ain't he? And he's all mine! All two hundred and seventy pounds of me." She struggled to get free. "Let me go, Brent. Let me go!"

"No, sweetheart, forget them," I pleaded. It took a while, but she finally calmed down. "You all right, baby?"

"Yeah, I'm all right, but I'm not gonna let these skinny B-I-T-C-Hs ruin my honeymoon anymore. I'm sorry if they can't find a good man, but God blessed me and answered my prayers when He sent you to me, and I'm not going to be ashamed of that blessing anymore."

"Well, all right. Praise the Lord," I told her as we held hands and walked back toward the hotel. From that moment on, Alison's whole demeanor changed, and she was no longer happy to be with me, she was *with* me, and God help anyone who might get in her way.

She was so happy, all she did was chat about our future family. She'd already picked out biblical names for our children: Michael, John, Mary, Moses, Peter, and Eve. We'd raise them in the church, and not only would they be good Christians, but they'd also be good people like their mother and father.

We ended up eating dinner at a small hotel café on the beach. Don't ask me how many Bahama Mamas I had, but they snuck up on me. By the time the sun went down and the hotel lights came on, I was officially drunk. I think Alison was too because she pulled her chair up close to mine and started nibbling on my ear in public. It was quite obvious to anyone who walked by exactly what she had on her mind.

"Baby, can we go back to the room? I've got an itch that needs to be scratched and I need to use your scratcher." She guided my hand along her smooth, thick thigh, probably hoping that it would find its way between her legs.

"Sounds like somebody I know is ready to start working on that baby," I teased.

Alison couldn't contain her grin as she whispered, "Mmm-hmm, and if we don't get it right the first time, we'll keep trying until we do."

I finished off what was left in my glass, then led my bride back to our room to consummate our marriage. We kissed and touched the entire way. If we hadn't been in a hotel, I'm sure there would have been a trail of clothes leading to our room. Once inside, Alison slipped into the bathroom to change into something a little more comfortable while I slipped out of my bathing suit and fell backward onto the bed.

As I waited for her to come out, I realized there was one major problem. I was a lot drunker than I wanted to admit, and as a consequence, my penis was limp as a wet noodle. I'd been like this before when I was drunk, and I'd always ended up getting embarrassed. The one thing sisters did not wanna hear was that you couldn't get it up for them even if you were drunk. They always made it seem like not being able to make a man hard was as bad as losing a breast or having a hysterectomy. It made them feel like they were less than a woman, like they weren't sexy anymore. Matter of fact, I pissed this one sister off so bad I honestly think the experience was the reason she turned gay. The last thing I wanted to do on my honeymoon was kill my new wife's already fragile self-esteem.

At first I thought maybe I'd pretend I'd passed out from the alcohol, but I decided against it because it wasn't fair to Alison, who deserved a night of pleasure. Then I remembered something James used to say when we were in college. "When in doubt, eat her out." So, that's what I was going to do. I was going to give Alison more oral pleasure than she'd know what to do with.

A half-hour later, Alison was squirming around on her back, enjoying the aftereffects of her second orgasm. She was huffing and puffing like she'd just run a marathon and when I lifted my head, she begged me to put it inside. I gave her a drunken smile and shook my head.

"I'm not ready for that yet," I told her, lowering my head. I had a special technique when it came to oral sex, a technique that had every woman I'd ever slept with willing to put aside our differences and jump into my bed on a moment's notice. You see, unlike most guys, I knew how to find a woman's clitoris. I also knew how to take my time getting to it. Soft, moist kisses around her inner thighs were always welcomed, in addition to slow, wet licks around her lips. Then and only then do you go for her clit, and when you do, you suck on it like a nipple. At the same time, you enter her with your finger, curling it upward until you find her G-spot. Using the same rhythm as your tongue, you go to work until she or her orgasm stops you.

"Oh, God, Brent baby, please, please, I can't take no more." Alison grabbed my head and almost gave me whiplash, she pushed me back so hard. I gave her about three seconds to rest, then tried to lower my head again. She stopped me by covering up her stuff with both hands. "No more, I can't take no more," she pleaded.

"Can't take it, or you're just too tired?"

"Both!"

I pretended as if I was trying to get at her again and she squeezed her legs. "Well, let's take a break, then."

"But what about you?"

"Don't worry about me. I'm just here to please you. When you get yours, I feel like I got mine. Besides, I'll wake you up later."

"You sure? I thought you wanted to try and have a baby tonight?"

"We will. The night's still young and baby, you're tired. Get some rest and we'll pick up where we left off in a couple of hours." I kissed her, then turned her on her side so I could wrap my arm around her as she slept. *Couple hours, my behind,* I thought. After coming three times like she just did, I wasn't going to have to worry about her until morning.

Alison was snoring in less than ten minutes, but I, on the other hand was wide awake. For some reason I couldn't sleep. My mind kept drifting back to the night before my wedding. I still couldn't get the sweet taste of Jackie's kiss off my lips. I loved my wife, but that Jackie did things to me that I couldn't even begin to explain.

"Brent, honey, are you okay?" Alison's words snapped me out of my drunken daydream, but I hesitated, asking myself a few questions before I answered hers. Why was she asking me if I was okay? Did she know I was thinking about Jackie? And if she did know, how the hell did she figure it out? Was I that obvious?

"Yeah, I'm okay, why?" I finally replied.

"Because you keep rubbing your stuff up against me. It's kind of hard to sleep when your man's rubbing his hard penis up against your butt."

Hard penis, I thought, adjusting my hips. Alison was right. My dick was rock-hard and I owed it all to Jackie. "I'm sorry, baby. I didn't even realize I was doing that."

"It's okay. I don't know why you just didn't put it in before. I know you needed some release." She rolled completely on her stomach, then reached for my manhood, grasping it gently. "Oh, my . . . I didn't know it was like that. Why don't you put it in? I think we'll both sleep better after we consummate our marriage." I moved on top of Alison, wondering what she'd do if she knew the real reason why my stuff was so hard.

15

Sonny

I'd been up since six o'clock in the morning, cleaning the house I'd rented for my family. I'd gotten lost a few times trying to find it again the morning after I'd been following Tiffany and spotted it. When I finally found the house, I copied the number from the sign and called it from my cell phone. The guy on the other end was real cool. His name was Bernie, and he came right down to the house from his office to show me the place. I was impressed. The house had three bedrooms and two baths, plus it had recently been fully renovated and painted. I knew my wife would love it because she had always said she wanted an updated kitchen, and my kids, well, they were going to lose their minds when they found out their new home had a swing set. So, after a short negotiation, Bernie and I agreed on a lease-purchase deal.

I'd been staying with my brother while I was in New York, but once we signed the papers and I gave Bernie a check, I started to sleep in the house on a blow-up mattress. I wanted to get the place ready. I only had a week or so before I had to start my new job. Now all I had to do was get on a plane back to Seattle, rent a truck, and pack up my family so we could make the long drive back to New York. I know it all sounds overwhelming, but I was excited. Things were finally starting to go my way.

There was a knock on the door, then a familiar male voice yelled, "Anybody home?"

"Yeah, come on in. I'm in the family room," I shouted.

I could hear the screen door shut, then James walked in, followed by a little boy who looked to be about the same age as my three-year-old daughter, Kerri. James was supposed to take me to the airport, but I wasn't expecting the little boy, and he kind of caught me off guard. He must have been that girl Michelle's kid, but why the heck was he with James?

"Nice place you got here, Sonny." James grinned, nodding his approval as he offered me his hand. I took it, pulling him in close.

"Thanks, bro. I just hope Jessica likes it." I let go of his hand and we both turned our attention to the little boy standing next to him.

"So, who's this little man?"

James placed his hand on the boy's shoulders, giving me the *we'll talk later* look as he introduced us.

"This is Marcus. Marcus, this is Mr. Harrison. You can call him Uncle Sonny."

"Hey, Marcus. How you doing, man?" I stuck out my hand and he slapped it hard. "I'm good. Are you really my uncle?"

I chuckled, not knowing how to answer him. "Well . . . you see . . ."

"Yeah, he's your real uncle," James cut in. "Hey, why don't you go out and play on that swing set while Uncle Sonny and I talk?" James pointed to the sliding glass door leading to the backyard, and Marcus took off.

"So, now you're claiming him, huh?"

James gave me a *fuck you* look as he walked toward the sliding glass door, which Marcus had left open.

"Don't look at me like that," I chastised. "You're the one who wants him to call me Uncle Sonny, so you must be claiming him. I don't blame you, though. He does look like you."

"I ain't claiming nobody." James closed the door, staring at the boy as he went down the slide. He turned to me. "And he don't look like me . . . does he?" It almost sounded as if he was pleading with me to agree with him. I didn't have the heart to tell him the truth, so I gave him a vanilla answer.

"A little, but hell, you could say he looks like me too."

"Better you than me," he mumbled. I walked over and put my hand on my friend's shoulder. The way he watched that little boy reminded me of the sparkle he had in his eyes as we watched his and Cathy's sons play Little League in the park last weekend. That sparkle told me how much he really cared. He opened the sliding glass door and shouted, "Marcus, don't swing so high. You might fall and hurt yourself."

"Okay, Daddy," the boy yelled back, and he smiled.

"Daddy? You're letting him call you Daddy already?"

James's smile disappeared. "What else is he going to call me?"

"How 'bout James? You're starting to get attached to him, aren't you?" I asked.

"Yeah, I am. He's a good kid, Sonny."

"How 'bout finding out if he's yours first? Or is there something you haven't told me?"

"Look, Sonny, I wish I knew whether he's really mine or not, but I don't. The problem is, Marcus never asked for this shit. He's the real victim in all this, not me. All he wants is a man in his life. So, until I find out the truth, he's my son."

"That all sounds good. And I'll be sure to vote for you if you run for daddy of the year, but you need to get yourself a paternity test." I couldn't believe he hadn't gotten one already. Letting this kid call him Daddy. He must have been outta his mind.

"I know. I was looking them up on the Net. But they're expensive. I don't have any cash to spare right now, and I'm not getting one from the court or worse, on one of those talk shows. You know that's how Michelle found out her boyfriend wasn't Marcus's father? She went on the *Two Sides to Every Story* show."

"Get the fuck outta here. She went on TV and got caught out there?"

"Yep."

"Dammmmn, now that's what I call triflin'."

"Don't I know it?"

"Speaking of triflin', where is his mother? Why you got him so early in the morning, anyway?"

"She had to work some mandatory overtime, so I had to keep him this morning." James sighed. "I'm supposed to take him to her after I drop you at the airport."

"I gotta give you credit, brother. Ain't no way I'm getting outta bed to go across Queens to get him, then come back across Queens over here to Long Island to pick me up, then go back across Queens to LaGuardia Airport."

"I didn't have to go across Queens to get him. I had him last night too." James's voice went low, as if he really didn't want me to hear his explanation, but I heard every word.

"What?" I was in disbelief. "You bullshitting me. How'd you get away with that? I know you didn't bring him home."

"Hell, no. Are you crazy? I spent the night at Michelle's house."

"And Cathy didn't say anything?"

"Nope. She thought I was out with you last night. And around three, when Michelle called talking that mandatory overtime crap, I called and told Cathy I was over here and I was too drunk to drive home. I needed her to pick me up. She wasn't about to get out the bed, get the kids dressed, and come get me. I'm safe as long as I get my ass home before the boys' baseball games at noon."

"Man, you got some shit with you." I laughed.

"It ain't like I wanna lie to my wife, Sonny. I just think I would hurt her more if I told her the truth."

"I hear you, man. What she don't know won't hurt her."

"Exactly. I'm just afraid of the day she finds out the truth."

"I'm afraid for you," I chimed in.

He glanced at his watch. "Look, not to change the subject, but it's getting late. We keep putt-putting around and we're not gonna be able to stop for breakfast, and Marcus and I haven't eaten."

"Neither have I."

"So, you ready to go?" I nodded and he opened the sliding glass door to tell Marcus to come inside.

"Why don't you put my bag in the car? I just have to call my wife and let her know I'm on my way to the airport." I pointed at my luggage, but James didn't move. "What?" I asked.

"You one henpecked dude, you know that?" He picked up my bag and headed for the door, followed closely by Marcus. "I'll meet you in the car. Come on, Marcus."

I ignored him, reaching for my phone and dialing my home number.

"The number you have dialed is not in service. No further information is available," a recording informed me.

"What the fuck you mean, no further information is available? That's my fucking home phone. Somebody's gonna tell me something," I cursed. I dialed the number again, this time using speed dial. I was hoping I'd made a mistake when I punched in the number.

"The number you have dialed is not in service. No further . . ." This time, I didn't let the recording finish. What the hell was going on? It was impossible that our phone could be disconnected. I gave Jessica all the household bills to pay right before I left two weeks ago.

I was starting to get a little angry at Jessica, but then I cooled down. It was my fault for not putting the bills in the mail in the first place. The frustrating part was that it was only six in the morning on the West Coast, and the telephone company wasn't going to be open for another three and a half hours. Jessica would probably go crazy if she couldn't contact me before I got on the plane.

"Hey, Sonny?" James yelled. "You got a delivery man." I walked outside, still confused over the phone call, to see a uniformed man standing in the driveway.

"Is this 44 Lawrence Street?" he asked.

"Yeah, it is, but I'm not expecting any packages."

He looked down at his clipboard. "Does Sonny Harrison live here?"

"I'm Sonny Harrison."

"Well, then I have some packages for you. Where should I put them?"

"I don't know. Bring them inside," I told him, then looked to the sidewalk, where I saw a half-dozen large cardboard boxes. As I watched him carry them into the house, I wracked my brain, but couldn't think of any explanation for what could be in these boxes.

I checked the return address on one of the labels: SONNY HARRISON, 44 LAWRENCE STREET, ELMONT, NEW YORK.

"Hey," I called to the driver, "I didn't send anything to myself."

"Sir, I just bring the boxes to the address on the label," he answered without turning to face me. He was too busy unloading another five boxes from his truck.

After he left, James came in the house. He must have strapped Marcus in his car seat because the boy wasn't following behind him this time.

"You ready?" he asked.

"Yeah, just give me one second. I wanna see what's in these boxes." I tore open the first box. My computer equipment was neatly packed in this one. Perhaps Jessica was sending some of our stuff ahead so we wouldn't have the truck so loaded down when we made the move from Seattle. That was smart, I decided, but I was still going to get on her about the phone not being paid.

There was a letter taped to one of the boxes. I ripped it off, thinking I would read it at the airport since we were starting to run a little late, but something made me open it. My heart nearly stopped when I read the enclosed letter.

Dear Sonny,

I packed up all your stuff and put it into these boxes, so there's no need for you to get on a plane to come back to Seattle. And if you do, that's on you, because there's nothing here for you. Me and the kids are gone. I know what you're thinking. Why is she doing this to me? But deep down inside, you know exactly why I'm doing this. You need to learn how to treat a woman, Sonny, and stop taking advice from those low-rent friends of yours. I hope you enjoy being back in New York with your friends. The three of you deserve each other.

Please don't try to find us, Sonny. We're moving on with our lives. And if you don't understand what that means, let me make it very clear: It's over. I don't love you. I haven't in years. I was just playing along until I could have my freedom.

Your ex-wife, Jessica
P.S. I sold the car and took all the money out of the bank, so there is really no need for you to come back.

"Oh, no, not my 'Vette," I mumbled.

"Sonny, what's the matter?" I could hear James's words, but I couldn't answer as I read the letter again. I think I was in shock. This shit had to be a joke of some kind. "Sonny, what's the matter?" This time James was shouting.

I handed him the letter, then ran to the front door. Jessica was probably playing a trick on me. She probably flew in this morning and was waiting outside the house to surprise me. Knowing James and Brent, they were probably in on it. But when I looked outside, nobody was there. I pulled my cell phone out and dialed my home number. I got that stupid recording again and almost threw my phone across the room.

"She can't do this to me, James. She can't just up and leave me and take away my kids."

His response was anything but supportive. "I told you she wasn't no good. She's been a gold-digger since you met her. And who the hell she think she's calling low-rent?"

"No, man. It's got to be a mistake. I gotta get home. Somebody could have kidnapped her or something."

"Sonny, be real. Do you think a kidnapper would take the time to pack up all your shit and mail it to you? She probably had some other man on the side the whole time. Just was waiting for you to leave so she could make her move."

I wanted to grab him by the head and scream, "Nooooooo!" at the top of my lungs, but instead I said, "James, she's never cheated on me. I'm sure of that. And there is no other man, aw'ight?"

"But—"

"James, I don't wanna hear it, okay? Just take me to the airport."

"Okay, but don't say I didn't warn you."

16

Brent

Alison and I left Paradise Island more in love and devoted to each other than when we arrived. I'd never enjoyed a vacation as much as I enjoyed my honeymoon. We'd been close before our marriage, but now our relationship was more tightly bonded on a spiritual and emotional level. We prayed together, ate together, slept together, and woke up to pray again together. I'd never felt closer to anyone than I did to her, and that included my boys, Sonny and James. She was no longer just my girlfriend or even my wife, she was my new best friend, and we had no secrets— except for the one I kept. And as far as that was concerned, I made a promise to God that I would not break my marriage vows and fall into the temptation of lust with Jackie Moss or any other vixen who might try to come between me and my wife.

But promises to God or not, the devil was always going to throw out his temptations, and I was going to have to be strong. I once read somewhere that the road to hell is paved in acid-laced roses, very appealing to the eyes and nose, but as dangerous to the touch as a cobra's bite. Well, that was the first thing I thought of when Alison and I stepped into the baggage claim area of LaGuardia Airport, and instead of the bishop and the first lady being there to pick us up, it was Jackie Moss standing by the carousel in front of a baggage cart. The first word that flashed across my mind was *Trouble*, and that was *Trouble* with a capital T. Jackie was looking sexy as hell in a navy-blue pin-striped suit and a tight-fitting, pale-blue designer shirt. It took all the resolve I had not to think naughty thoughts.

"Hey, Jackie, it's good to see you." Alison grinned, wrapping her arms around our church organist. Jackie did the same to

Alison, winking at me over my wife's shoulder. I didn't say anything, just stared, hoping Jackie could somehow read my thoughts of contempt.

"It's good to see you too, Alison. How was your trip?"

Alison gave Jackie a smile and an exaggerated sigh. "Ohhh, Lawd, I don't think I've ever seen such a beautiful place. It was like heaven on earth, simply magnificent. Oh, and the company wasn't bad either, if you know what I mean." Alison nudged Jackie with her elbow.

"Well, good, good." Jackie's attention turned to me. "How about you, Brother Williams? Did you enjoy your honeymoon?"

I wrapped my arm around my wife. "I don't think I could have gone with anyone else and had such a good time." I bent down and kissed my wife, making sure my lips locked with hers longer than our usual peck. When I broke the kiss, Jackie was looking in the opposite direction. Hopefully that would get my message across.

"So, where are the bishop and first lady? I thought they were picking us up."

"The bishop couldn't make it, so I volunteered to pick you up." I closed my eyes, resisting the urge to shake my head at Jackie's nonsense. I had a bad feeling about this because I couldn't remember Jackie volunteering for anything at church.

"Everything all right?" Alison asked.

"Ms. Alison, I've got some bad news." Jackie paused, and I wasn't sure if it was for dramatic effect or if things were really that bad. "First Lady Wilson is in the hospital. The bishop took her in the other day because she'd been having some pain in her lower abdomen, and they had to keep her. It doesn't look good."

Alison put her hand over her heart and gasped. "Oh, my Lawd! What do you mean, it doesn't look good?"

Once again, with all the thespian flair of a Shakespearean performer, Jackie's green eyes rolled back, head shaking in pity. "Cancer . . . The first lady has pancreatic cancer. She's going to die, Ms. Alison. The doctors say she only has about six months to live."

Alison threw her hands up in the air, closing her fist, as if imploring God to turn back the angel of death. She and Charlene Wilson were thick as thieves, and I'm sure this news must have hurt like it was her own sister. I couldn't imagine how I would feel if I'd just gotten the news that James or Sonny were stricken with cancer. Knowing me, I'd probably fall to my knees and beg the Lord to take me instead of them.

"You all right, baby?" I soothed her, easing my arm around her shoulder. I held my wife tightly as she broke down and wept. Jackie was studying my face each time I looked over Alison's shoulder. I tried to ignore the stares, but I was drawn to those green eyes as I tended to my distraught wife. "Baby, it's going to be all right."

"I need to go to the hospital," Alison insisted. "I've got to see Charlene. I've got to be there for her, Brent. She's always been there for me."

"I know you do, honey. As soon as we get home, I'm going to drive you over there. What hospital is she at, Jackie?"

"She's at Saint Joseph's. It's on the way to your house. Why don't I drop you over there now, Ms. Alison? Then I can drop Brother Williams off at your house with your bags. He can get his car and come back and get you later. That way you can spend more time with the first lady."

Alison nodded her head, looking up at me. "That makes a lot of sense. What do you think, Brent?"

What I thought was just what I suspected in the first place, that this whole thing was all a ruse for Jackie to spend some time alone with me. It angered me that Jackie would purposely put me in this position, and trust me, it was done purposely.

"I don't know, Alison. We don't wanna put Jackie out. Why don't we just go home and I'll take you to the hospital?"

Jackie flashed me a coy smile. "Nonsense. You're not putting me out at all. It's times like this that we have to help each other. That's what being good Christians is all about. Isn't that right, Ms. Alison?"

"Mm-hmm. Jackie's right, Brent." Alison was giving me little or no recourse. So on that note, it was settled. I just hoped my wife—and I, for that matter—didn't live to regret it, because Jackie was like the apple the serpent offered Adam and Eve—so tempting, yet one taste could destroy everything.

It didn't take long for us to get our bags and find Jackie's Lincoln Continental in the airport parking lot. I opened the front door for Alison to get in, but Jackie put a quick halt to that by opening the rear passenger-side door.

"Why don't you sit in the front, Brother Williams? You're going to be sitting there once we drop Ms. Alison off at the hospital anyway. No need to be moving around like we're playing musical chairs." Jackie turned to my wife, politely blocking her way to the front of the car. "Don't you think that makes sense, Ms. Alison?"

Alison shrugged. "It really doesn't matter to me. I just want to get to the hospital and see Charlene."

"That's the most important thing, isn't it?" Jackie smiled, ushering her into the backseat and shutting the door.

I glanced at Jackie, who was now walking around the car to the driver's side. *What the hell are you up to?* I thought as our eyes locked. I hated moments like this because somehow Jackie always managed to make me smile. It was those eyes, those damn beautiful green eyes. They were the reason for my weakness. Whenever I looked in those eyes, I just couldn't be mad at Jackie anymore, but that still didn't mean I was going to break my marriage vows.

I got in the car and Jackie followed suit. Five minutes later, we were on the Grand Central Parkway, and I was nodding my head and clapping my hands as I sang along with Kirk Franklin's new CD. I loved me some Kirk Franklin. Unfortunately, I must have been so into his music that I didn't notice Jackie's spider-like fingers inching their way across my seat and into my lap. When I did realize what was going on, I immediately took hold of Jackie's hand and removed it from my crotch. I glanced at my wife, who didn't seem to notice what had happened because of the large luxury seats of the Lincoln Continental. This only brought a smile to Jackie's face, who tried it again.

"Will you stop it?" I shouted. I swatted Jackie's hand so hard that it made a loud smacking sound.

Jackie yelped. "Ouch!"

"What happened?" Alison sat up and looked over the seat. I didn't say a word, but Jackie's quick thinking saved the day.

"Your husband had the nerve to smack my hand because I was trying to change the CD."

I turned toward my wife and Alison glared at me, looking embarrassed. "Brent, you know better than that. You're a grown man, and this is not your car, and that is not your CD player."

"It's okay, Ms. Alison. If he likes the CD so much, he can

have it." Jackie flashed a grin at my wife and I lowered my head. I didn't think it was possible, but Jackie was making me sick. Thank the Lord that a few minutes later we pulled in front of the hospital.

I got out of the car and opened the door for Alison. She gave me a peck on the lips and I told her I would be back shortly. When she was out of sight, I stuck my head into the car and told Jackie I needed to get something out of my bag in the trunk.

Jackie popped the trunk, then stepped out of the car. I took all our bags out.

"What are you doing?"

"I'm catching a cab home."

Jackie frowned. "What? Why?"

"You know why, and you know what you're doing."

"Oh, what am I doing?" Jackie asked in a mocking tone, looking down at my crotch.

"You just don't get it, do you? I love my wife." I started walking toward a cab that was letting off some passengers.

"I know you do, but you love me too. You can run, Brent, but you can't hide. I'll see you in church on Sunday. Oh, and just in case you're wondering . . . I won't be wearing anything under my robe."

17

Sonny

The damn plane couldn't fly fast enough to get me back to Seattle. I had to find out what the hell was going on with my family. I still had Jessica's letter in my hand. I must have read it a thousand times, trying to decipher every last word she'd written. I'd been second-guessing myself and every decision I'd made since we'd met seven years ago, but I still couldn't come up with a reason why she might do this to me and our family. Jessica knew how much I loved her. Not only did I tell her every day, but I showed her in ways other guys never would. Deep down inside, I still wanted to believe this was all a sick joke.

After my plane landed, I ran straight through the baggage claim area to the exit for the cab stand. I didn't give a damn about my luggage. I'd get that later. Once in the cab, I gave the driver my address and told him to step on it. Of course, you know I tried to call my house again, but I still got that recording. I even tried to call my landlord, Mr. Hopkins, to see if he knew what was going on, but he didn't answer either. For the next fifteen minutes, I stared blankly out the window. When we pulled in front of my apartment, my hands started shaking so badly I couldn't pull out the money to pay the driver. I was scared, more scared than I'd ever been in my life, but that fear was overridden by my desperation to see if my family was still in our home.

I did have a glimmer of hope when I started up the walkway and spotted my Corvette in my assigned space. In her letter, Jessica had written that she'd sold my prized possession. There was a good chance that if the 'Vette was there, Jessica was just calling my bluff so we wouldn't move back to New York. She might have been the one who suggested we move back East, but after all, she did despise James and Brent. She felt they were bad influences on me. Unfortunately, the feelings were mutual. My friends had never liked her, especially James, and now his preaching was sounding more and more like prophecies.

When I stepped in front of my apartment, I heard voices coming from behind the door. I couldn't make out what was being said, but I distinctly heard both a man's and a woman's voice, and I felt my heart sink. My mind had been clouded ever since the delivery man dropped off my shit along with that Dear John letter. It wasn't cloudy anymore, though. Suddenly I had clarity, and the only thing that was going through my mind was that Jessica had a man in my house and I was going to kill her. No, I was going to kill both her and the man.

I reached for my keys to open the door, but thankfully common sense prevailed. I walked away from the door and headed to my car. Oh, don't get me wrong. I was still gonna kill both of them. Jesus Christ himself couldn't stop me from doing that. But I wasn't about to rush in there with my bare hands to do it. For all I knew, that fool in there with her could have been a karate expert, or even worse, some type of thug with a gun. I had to go in there prepared.

I opened the trunk of my Corvette and pulled out the spare as quickly as possible. Underneath it was a wooden box I'd been hiding for years. No one knew it was there, including Jessica. I took out the box and tucked it under my arm, then placed the spare back where it belonged. I got in my car, looking around to make sure no one was watching before I opened the box. Inside it was a black nine-millimeter semiautomatic handgun with two fully loaded clips.

I stared at the gun, wondering how the hell things had come to this. I'd been a good, faithful husband. Yes, I liked to look at women's asses, but I'd never strayed, even when it came to Tiffany last week. I guess Jessica never really knew how much I loved her. Well, she was about to find out.

I pushed one of the clips into the gun, then pulled back the hammer, sliding a bullet into the chamber. I stuck the gun into my belt, then covered it with my shirt as I stepped out of the car. I walked briskly back to my apartment and waved nonchalantly to my landlord, who was calling my name as he parked his car. I didn't have time to deal with Mr. Hopkins. I had business to attend to.

I stood at the door and pulled the gun out of my pants. I still couldn't make out the conversation behind the door, but at this point, I really didn't care. Surprisingly, I was a lot calmer than I would have thought. I hated the idea that things had come this far, but I loved Jessica, and if I couldn't have her, nobody would. I took out my key and quietly stuck it in the door as I went over my plan in my head.

The plan was to surprise Jessica and her friend, possibly even catch them in the act of intimacy. I was going to shoot the man first because brothers were always trying to play the hero. Jessica I wasn't worried about because she was only five-five, a hundred and thirty pounds, so if she jumped bad, I could take care of her with one hand. Once I shot the dude, I'd make Jessica explain to me where things went wrong between us, then I'd take one last look at that phat ass of hers before blowing her away. Once that was all said and done, I'd go in the kitchen, grab a cold beer, and chug it down. I'd then sit down at the table with a pen and paper and write my last will and testament. I wasn't about to explain myself or my actions. I'm sure anyone who found our bodies would be able to figure that out. I just wanted to make sure my kids went to Brent instead of my trifling-ass brother or Jessica's parents. I knew he and Alison would take care of them like they were their own. When I finished writing my will, I'd probably smoke one last cigarette before sticking the gun into my mouth and pulling the trigger.

Turning the knob slowly, I pushed the door open. The short, stout brother sitting on the sofa watching *my* TV didn't even notice me as I crept up next to him. The first question that came to my mind was, *What the fuck did she see in him?*

"You're a lot fatter than I expected," I told him in a low, even whisper. I had the gun pointed at the side of his head.

"Oh, shit. Please don't kill me, mister," he pleaded. He shut up when I pushed the tip of the gun against his head.

I couldn't help it. I laughed when I saw a puddle forming on the leather sofa and realized he had pissed on himself. "Damn, you a nasty motherfucker." I continued to laugh, but stopped abruptly when I remembered it was my couch he had pissed on. "Do you know how much this sofa cost?" He didn't say anything, and I didn't have time to dwell on stupid shit that wouldn't matter in ten minutes. Besides, piss stains on the couch weren't half as bad as the stains his brains were going to make when they splattered on it.

"Where is she?" I demanded.

"In the bathroom." I couldn't believe he hadn't attempted to move out of that lake of pee he was sitting in.

"Call her."

He hesitated, so I pressed the gun harder against his head. That got him talking. "Honey?" he croaked. "Honey, come here for a minute."

Who the fuck was he to call my woman "honey"? I wanted to pull the trigger right then and there, but I didn't because I wanted Jessica to see him die.

We both watched the bathroom door open, and to my surprise, it wasn't Jessica who stepped out, but a tall, brown-skinned woman in her early thirties whom I'd never seen before. What confused me even more was that she was wearing the silk robe and slippers I'd bought for Jessica on Mother's Day. I think it took a few seconds for her to realize what was going on, but when she did, she screamed. I didn't give a damn about her screaming. I just wanted to know what the hell was going on. And where was my wife?

I motioned with the gun for the woman to sit down next to the man, then I moved in front of them. Out of nowhere, she hopped up off the sofa, feeling her pants. She looked at her ass, then the man. "Did you pee on yourself?"

"Yeah, he did," I said with a laugh. The woman rolled her eyes, shaking her head as she moved to a dry spot on the opposite side of the sofa.

"Is there anyone else here?" I moved the gun from him to her, then back to him.

"No, just us," the man replied as he began to beg for his life again. He actually started to cry. "Please, mister, you can have everything we got. Shit, you can even have her. She don't suck dick, but the pussy's pretty good. Just don't hurt me, man."

"You trifling, punk-ass little bitch!" the woman shouted. "I don't suck your dick 'cause it's so small I can't hardly find it. Mister, will you shoot this motherfucker, please?"

I laughed. These two were like a comedy act. Only problem was, I didn't have time to catch the show.

"Where is Jessica?" I demanded. Suddenly forgetting their little disagreement, they stared at me as if I was insane. I lifted the gun, moving it back and forth between them as I asked my question again. "Where is Jessica?"

"She's gone, Sonny." I glanced over to my right, and standing in the doorway was my landlord, Mr. Hopkins. He took a few steps toward me with his hands up.

"Gone where, Mr. Hopkins?"

He shrugged his shoulders. "I don't know, Sonny. All I can tell you is, she had two young men with her yesterday when she gave me the keys. She said they were her brothers."

"Mr. Hopkins, Jessica doesn't have any brothers."

He took a few more steps. "I'm sorry to hear that, but now that you mention it, Jessica did seem awfully friendly with one of those young fellas." He put out his hand. "You need to give me the gun, Sonny. You're scaring these nice people."

I'd forgotten about them. "These nice people are trespassing. And I think they know something about where my wife is." I pointed the gun at the man, who started to cry again.

"No, you're the one who's trespassing, Sonny. As of yesterday, this apartment legally became theirs."

"How? My lease isn't up 'til the end of the month. I still got twenty days plus my security deposit."

"Jessica gave up tenancy, so I gave her the security. I guess you forgot the apartment was in her name. If I remember correctly, you insisted on that."

I let out a long breath. This had to be a nightmare.

"If she gave up tenancy, why is all our furniture still here? Damn, she didn't even take down one picture."

"The lady who used to live here sold us everything in the apartment for twenty-five hundred dollars, and that included her car," the woman snapped out boldly. She was no longer funny. She was starting to piss me off.

"Twenty-five hundred dollars! That car's worth twenty thousand dollars." I felt like I was going to be sick. I had rebuilt that car from the ground up.

"Well, it's ours, and we got a bill of sale and a signed title, so we ain't giving it back." She must have forgotten I had a gun, she was running her mouth so much. I pointed the gun at her head. I don't think her coward-ass man forgot, though.

"Look, man, she don't speak for me. As far as I'm concerned, you can have my half of the car. Just don't shoot me, aw'ight?"

"You one pussy-ass nigger, Darin, you know that?" she shouted at her husband. "Shoot him, mister. Please shoot him. I'm Catholic, so I can't get divorced. But if you shoot him, I'm a free woman and I swear I won't tell." That crazy-ass wench almost sounded sincere.

"Give me the gun, Sonny." Mr. Hopkins lit a cigarette, and I wished I had one.

"You still haven't told me why, Mr. Hopkins. Why would she do this? Why would she give up all her stuff?"

"Give me the gun, Sonny, and let's go have a drink. I'll explain what I know down at the bar."

"What about them? They gonna call the cops?"

Mr. Hopkins looked at the couple. "No, they're not gonna call the cops. Not if they want the next couple of months' rent free, they won't. Am I right, Mrs. Brown?"

"How many months?" the greedy woman asked.

"Three," Mr. Hopkins replied in an annoyed grumble, and the woman smiled. "Now, come on, Sonny, give me the gun. I think we both need a drink."

After a few seconds, I dropped my shoulders and handed him the gun. Then I walked over to the wall and took down my family portrait. We walked out of the apartment to the sound of the couple fighting over the piss puddle on *their* new couch.

18

James

"Hey, Michelle, you got any beer?"

"I don't know. Look in the fridge. I'm trying to get dressed," she shouted from her bedroom. "Next time you come over here, you need to bring your own damn beer."

I got up from the sofa and frowned as I headed to the kitchen. I'd been trying to work things out between Michelle and me since we'd taken Marcus to the hospital a month ago. She wasn't making things easy, though, despite her comments at the hospital. You'd think she'd be grateful that I'd pulled myself away from my family after a hard day's work, then made up another lie to my wife to come babysit Marcus, but I don't think she gave a damn. In fact, I think she was starting to take it for granted that I'd be there whenever she needed me. I felt more like her personal slave than I did a father to her son.

This was the tenth time she'd asked me to babysit since she told me I was Marcus's father. In my heart, I still wasn't sure if I believed he was my child, but I was playing the happy camper until I could get a paternity test. In the meantime, I was stuck as Michelle's all-too-often babysitter. What was supposed to be a once-in-a-while thing was starting to get out of hand quickly. I didn't know how much longer I could take this shit, or how long it would take before Cathy started to get suspicious. So far she hadn't questioned my late-night excuses for leaving the house, but it was just a matter of time.

As I went into the kitchen to grab a beer, I passed Michelle's room and did a double take. She was standing in front of a mirror, putting on her makeup. Her hair had been recently done in a light-brown curly weave, and she was wearing a short black miniskirt, heels, and a black halter top. Her outfit left nothing to the imagination, and she looked more like she was going to the club than to work.

"Do you mind?" she snapped, closing her bedroom door.

"Sorry," I told her.

I continued into the kitchen, wondering if the door being open and the dramatic way she closed it might have been her way of flirting. Why else would she be wearing something sexy like that if she had to put on her uniform in a minute to go to work? It didn't matter what she wore; I wasn't interested. And without giving it another thought, I went and got a beer and some chips from the top of the fridge so I could sit down on the sofa and watch some TV.

About ten minutes later, I hollered down the hall to let Michelle know she was running late for work. She didn't answer, but pranced out of her bedroom, spinning around like she was on a DKNY runway and Donna Karan herself was taking the pictures. She'd changed her outfit too. This time she was sporting a pair of red skintight hip-huggers with a matching Baby Phat halter top and six-inch stilettos. I had to admit she looked damn good, even as I wondered why the hell she was dressed like that to go to work.

"How do I look, James?"

"You look aw'ight," I told her nonchalantly.

I'd been through this game with her when we first started messing around a few years back, so I wasn't about to start complimenting her on her appearance, no matter how good she looked. Last thing I needed was for her to start getting the wrong idea about us. I was there because I had to be, and anything else was out. It was not that kind of party.

"What do you mean aw'ight? I don't look good?" Michelle pivoted on one foot and put a hand on her hip. She expected an answer right away. When I didn't give her what she wanted, she spun around and walked back to her bedroom. "You know, I think I'm going to wear my black leather pants. I'll be right back."

"You better chill with your little fashion show or you gonna mess around and be late for work."

Again she didn't reply, but five minutes later she emerged in a pair of tight black pleather pants and the black halter top she had on earlier. She looked absolutely hoe-ish, and there was no way I could see her going to work wearing that. Then again, maybe she had a training class or something.

"How about this? Now, this looks good, doesn't it?" Michelle sauntered past me, then twirled so I could get the full effect. Once again I didn't respond, but I did look at my watch.

"What time you gotta be at work?"

She stared at me silently for a few seconds. "Why?"

"'Cause it's nine o'clock. Don't you have to be to work at nine?"

There was hesitation in her eyes.

"I ain't going to work tonight," she spat, the look on her face finishing the sentence with, *Mind your own damn business.* What she forgot was the fact that me sitting there made it my business.

"What? I don't believe this shit." Something inside me began to churn and the words "stupid ass" felt like they were being written on my forehead. I didn't even like how my voice was beginning to sound—like the voice of a chump. I was starting to get pissed. "If you ain't going to work, then what the hell am I doing here?"

"You here to babysit," she said as if it was law and I didn't have any say in the matter.

"Oh, really? So while I'm babysitting, where you think you goin'?"

"I don't think anything. I *know* I'm going to the club with my girls. It's ladies' night at the Q-Club. They're having male strippers and everything." She was grinning like a Cheshire cat, and all I wanted to do was knock that smile right off her face.

"I thought you said you needed me to babysit while you were at work, Michelle."

"Well, you thought wrong. I told you I needed you to babysit. I never said anything about going to work." She actually had the nerve to laugh, and I was one step closer to knocking the shit outta her.

"Well, if you're going out, you better find a babysitter, 'cause I'm outta here." I stood up and started walking to the door, but she jumped in front of me.

"Where you think you're going?" Michelle was in my face, her finger stabbing at my chest.

"Home to my wife and children," I told her bluntly. "I gotta get up at six in the morning for work. I don't got time for these games."

"You're not going anywhere until I get back from the club." She lifted her finger until it was about two inches from my nose. "Don't piss me off, James. I was planning on coming home early, but I could stay out all night."

"I don't give a damn when you come home. I'm not going to be here." I took a step toward the door and she took a step to block me. When I tried to get around her again, she stepped in front of the door so it would be impossible for me to open it without physically moving her. I didn't want to lay my hands on her, because they might take on a life of their own and do things I'd vowed I would never do to a woman.

"Get outta my way, Michelle."

"I said no! Now, you gonna babysit tonight so I can go out, or I promise you I'll make your life a living hell."

"You think you haven't already? Now move, damn it!" She folded her arms defiantly and I took a step closer. I really needed to get out of there before I hurt her. She was pulling something out of me that had never surfaced before, and the funny thing is, I really didn't care. Yes, I knew if I hit her I'd end up in jail, but I was starting to think it might just be worth it.

"Why, so you can go home to that bitch of yours?"

"You calling my wife a bitch?" I could feel myself start to hyperventilate, the muscles in my neck and shoulders bulging. At the same time, my hands were now balled up into fists. There was no doubt in my mind that things were about to become physical. I think Michelle sensed it because without saying another word, she stepped out of my way. "Tell Marcus I'll try to call him tomorrow," I said.

She sucked her teeth and rolled her eyes, which made me smile when I walked out the door. I'd finally stood up to her. I felt like a prizefighter who'd been getting his ass whipped the entire fight but found a way to knock out his opponent in the final round. It felt good to finally win one. I was going to have to be sterner with Michelle in the future. She wasn't the type you could reason with. You had to tell her how it was going to be. Now that I looked back on it, I wished I had stood up to her on day one.

"Hey, James," Michelle shouted after me. "You might wanna

hear this before you go home." I turned to see her standing on the walkway about fifteen feet from my car. She was grinning so wide, I knew something bad was about to happen.

"What do you want, Michelle?"

"Oh, nothing. . . . I just thought you might wanna hear what I'm about to tell your wife." She flipped open a black cell phone that I hadn't even noticed was in her hand. My heart almost stopped when she started pushing numbers and raised the phone to her ear. "Hello, Mrs. Robinson, you don't know me, but my name is Michelle, and—"

She never finished the sentence. Within seconds, I had knocked the phone out of her hand and the two of us were scrambling on the ground, trying to get it. I never hit her once, but when it was all said and done, I had her pinned to the ground with my body, and the cell phone was closed in my hand. Despite being on what you might call the losing end, Michelle was laughing her ass off.

"What the hell is so funny?"

"We used to wrestle just like this back in the day, when you had to go home and I'd take your keys because I didn't want you to leave, remember?"

Yeah, I remembered all right. After we wrestled, we'd always ended up making love again before she'd let me leave. I looked in her face, and for the first time since she'd told me Marcus was my son, the glow was back. We stared at each other for a few seconds without saying a word. I don't know if it was the fact that we'd just finished wrestling or what, but I had this crazy urge to kiss her, and I'm sure she would have reciprocated if I had. I brought my lips closer to hers as I considered going forward with my urge. I knew if we kissed, we were going to end up in bed doing all the freaky shit men do with their mistresses that they won't do with their wives. And that was the trap: the kinky shit, shit I wanted to do with Cathy but was too afraid to ask, that had you coming back again and again for more.

I lowered my lips even closer to Michelle's, but before I pressed them against hers, I thought, *Why can't I ask Cathy to do the kinky stuff Michelle would do? After all, she is my wife. That's why we're married.* And on that note, the glow was gone and I had no more desire for Michelle. I pulled my head back and pushed myself off her. I could tell from her expression she was disappointed, but she didn't say anything.

Just then, her phone rang, and we both knew it was Cathy calling back.

"So, I guess I'm going to the club now, huh?" I nodded and she said, "You better let me answer it, because she's just gonna keep calling."

I took a leap of faith and handed her the phone.

"Hello?" I watched as she listened, praying she wasn't going to do anything stupid. "Yes, I'm sorry about that, Mrs. Robinson. I must have dropped the signal. Like I was saying, you don't know me, but my son is in the same grade as your son, James. I was wondering if you could tell me who to call to get him in the Little League."

19

Sonny

I was staring at the family portrait that I'd taken from the wall of my apartment when I left with Mr. Hopkins. Tears were falling from my eyes as all kinds of memories of my wife and kids flooded my mind. We had a good family, and I'd been racking my brain trying to figure out what went wrong. Was I that bad as a husband and provider? How could she do this to me? She'd stripped me of my dignity and literally left me with nothing more than a few boxes and the shirt on my back. I'd never been so humiliated in my entire life. That was okay, though, because after tonight, when it was all said and done, the pain might not be gone, but I'd be able to move on with my life.

Straightening out the portrait of my family, I took out my lighter and flicked it on, turning it up until a two-inch flame came out. I kissed each of my kids before placing the portrait under the flame. I took one last look at Jessica, and a tear rolled down my face until I could taste it.

"I'm sorry," I whispered as I watched my family go up in smoke, "but what I need is closure."

From that point on, I sat back in my seat and waited for her to come out of her office. Fifteen minutes later, like clockwork, she walked out of the building and headed for her car. She was wearing a navy-blue suit that was very professional, but it couldn't cover her large behind, and every guy she passed was breaking his neck to look at it. I'm not going to lie, it pissed me off the way they were looking at her, and I didn't calm down until she got in her car.

Once she pulled out of the parking lot, I hung back a few cars as I followed her. There was no need to be all up on her and make her notice me. I'd known where she was going before she even got in the car. After all, I had been following her for almost two weeks without her knowledge, and she was, if anything, a creature of habit. I still couldn't believe I hadn't caught her with a man yet. Then again, that was probably a good thing because I would have lost it right then and there. It was hard enough trying not to approach her these past two weeks. When she pulled in front of the school, I parked about a block and a half away so I could see her car with my mirrors but wouldn't attract any attention. The last thing I wanted was for some observant parent to start talking to school officials about the suspicious white cargo van that seemed to show up around the same time every day the after school program let out.

The kids were in some type of fancy after-school program where she had to go inside to sign them out. How she could afford to pay for private school and an after-school program on a receptionist's salary I don't know, but I made a mental note to find out.

About five minutes later, she drove past, never even looking my way. I didn't pull out behind her because it was Thursday and I knew she'd be headed to the supermarket. I happened to know a shortcut that would get me there at least five to ten minutes before she arrived, so I'd be waiting when she got there.

Just as I predicted, I was parked and waiting for her when she pulled into the underground garage at the supermarket. It looked like today was the day I'd finally execute my plan, because she'd parked right where I wanted her to. I gave her a minute for her and the kids to leave the parking garage and go in the store, then I jumped out of the van, hurrying after them. I was getting pretty good at this sleuth shit, because once they doubled back and came down the same aisle where I was, but they never even noticed I was there following them. It's amazing what a hat and some sunglasses can do to change your appearance. I'd thought about confronting her when she was in the supermarket, but there were too many people around for what I had planned. I watched her and the kids fill up a shopping cart for about thirty minutes, then slipped back to the parking garage when they headed toward the register.

Once inside the parking garage, I glanced at my watch. I had about five minutes to get my plan into action, so I headed straight for my van. I got in, ditching the disguise before I searched for an empty parking space between the entrance of the garage and her car. The hard part was finding a space she'd definitely pass. Luckily, just as I started to search with the van, a car pulled out of the perfect space and I backed into it. Immediately, I shut off the van and unlocked the hood. I checked my watch again. *Two minutes to go*, I thought, as I stepped out of the van and stretched. Every muscle in my body felt like a rubber band, I was so nervous.

Please, God, don't let me get caught, I prayed.

I walked around to the front of the van and lifted the hood. When I spotted her and the kids entering the garage, I took a deep breath, bending over the van so my head was underneath the hood like I was trying to fix something. A few seconds later, I could hear the kids running around, but I never lifted my head up from the engine, even when I heard her yelling at them a few feet away.

"Damn it, Tony, didn't I tell you to get your butt over to this cart?"

Patience, Sonny, patience, my boy, I kept telling myself. *She's almost there.*

By this time, she was close enough for me to hear the cart and see the kids' feet. Once I saw her feet, I purposely backed into her cart.

"Ah, shit, watch where you're going," I growled angrily.

"Oh, I'm sorry, mister." It took a few seconds for her to recognize me, but when she did, her jaw dropped as if she was frozen in time. I would have paid good money to know what was going through her mind at that exact moment.

"Sonny? What are you doing here?" she whispered, grabbing the boy by his collar. I didn't say a word, but a huge grin crept across my face. I'd gotten the exact reaction I'd been looking for, and her look of surprise said it all.

"Didn't think you'd ever see me again, did you?" There was a long pause between my words. I rested my hand against a pole, blocking the path to her car.

"No, I can't say I did." She smiled, snapping out of her haze.

"It's good to see you again, Tiffany."

"It's good to see you again, Sonny." She let go of her son and walked over to give me a hug. I held her tight, keeping the embrace for a little longer than she expected. When I finally let her go, she stared at me, looking confused. "What are you doing here? I thought you lived in Seattle."

"I did, but things have changed in the past few weeks." I turned toward the van, pulling the hood down with a look of frustration. "My wife left me for another man. I just returned from Seattle today. That's why I'm driving this raggedy rental van that just broke down." I kicked the car tire.

"I'm sorry to hear that, Sonny." She wasn't really sorry, which was evident from the smirk that was slowly taking over her face.

"Are you sorry about my marriage or the van?"

"Both."

"Then why are you smiling?"

"Let's just say . . . because I'm happy for me," she admitted. Her hesitation was probably because the last time she spoke boldly to me, things didn't work out the way she had planned. But what she didn't know was that this time, I had planned this out very carefully.

I turned my attention to her children. "So, who is this handsome young man and beautiful young lady?"

"I'm sorry. These are my children, Tony and Nikki. Say hi to Mr. Harrison, guys."

They both waved, reminding me of my kids.

"So, if your van's broke, can I give you a lift somewhere?"

You can give me a lot more than that, I thought, as my eyes drank in her figure.

"Only if I can take you and your kids to Chuck E. Cheese first."

Both kids jumped up in the air. "Please, Mom. Please, please, please!" they screamed, and she nodded.

And there it was in a nutshell. My plan had worked. Yes, I could have gone about bumping into Tiffany a lot of different ways. Hell, I could have just gone to her house; I knew where she lived. But anyone who knows anything about women knows the key to their hearts is always through their children. If you can win over her children, then getting her to love you is easy. So now I was on the path to doing what I'd planned. I was moving on with my life the best way I knew how. I was going to replace one family for another. That way, I could finally have closure.

20

Brent

It was Sunday, the Lord's day, and the first day I'd seen my wife for longer than a couple of hours since we returned from our honeymoon. Oh, she was sleeping at home, but after work she'd rush straight over to the hospital to visit with the first lady, then over to the bishop's house to make his dinner and lunch for the next day. Now, going to see the first lady every day was all right with me. I mean, the lady was dying, and you can't get back lost time. But this cooking the bishop's meals stuff was out, especially since I was home alone eating TV dinners and spaghetti out of a can. Don't get me wrong, I knew the bishop was an important man and he had to eat, but he had three or four hundred women in the congregation who would love to cook his meals. Why the heck was it my wife's responsibility? That question was the main reason Alison and I were arguing in the church parking lot before we went in for Sunday service.

"Brent, I promised Charlene I'd do it. Besides, the bishop loves my cooking and he's got to eat."

"I don't care, Alison. Your husband loves your cooking also, and he's got to eat too. Now, you tell the first lady you can't do it. Matter of fact, if it will help, tell her I said you can't do it. There are plenty of women in the church who can cook the bishop some good meals."

"But Brent—"

I cut her off. "But nothing. You think I don't know what this is all about? You and the first lady ain't slick." She gave me this *What-are-you-talking-about?* expression. "I know what you're up to. I know you don't want any women in that house." Her silence confirmed my suspicions. "You two don't give the man any credit, do you? He loves his wife, Alison. She doesn't have anything to worry about."

"I know that, Brent, but Charlene said . . . Brent, I promised her. I can't go back on a promise."

"What about the promises you made to me? I guess those don't mean anything. Maybe I should talk to Lisa Jackson or Sydney Wilson about cooking for me. I'm sure if I told them that you were too busy to cook my meals, they'd be happy to volunteer."

Alison's face lost all expression. She knew that Lisa and Sydney had been after me from the start. Sydney didn't even come to our wedding because she was so upset by our marriage. Alison was also intimidated by their high-fashion looks and slim bodies.

"You wouldn't," she challenged, but it was obvious she was scared.

"Why not? A man's got to eat. Isn't that what you just told me?"

"Brent, don't do this. Don't twist my words. Charlene is sick."

"So am I, Alison. I'm sick of you not being home. I didn't get married to sit at home alone. I told you when we got married that I wanted a family. I thought we were going to try and have a baby right away."

Her voice warmed up as if for the first time she realized what was wrong. "We are, honey. It's just that she's my friend and she's sick. Wouldn't you want her to be there for me if the shoe was on the other foot?"

"No—I mean, yes. But I wouldn't want her cooking my meals, and I'm sure the bishop wouldn't allow it. Now, you can visit her every day, but when visiting hours are over, I want you home. Don't get me wrong, but it's been two weeks since . . . well, you know . . . and I miss you." I gave her the look.

I know how this sounds, but it wasn't really the sex that I missed. It was the affection, the camaraderie. Shoot, I just missed my wife and best friend. But if she was willing to come home if she thought it was all about the sex, then that's what I'd let her believe.

"Ohhhh, baby, I'm sorry." Alison almost looked ashamed, like she was just realizing she might be at fault here. "But you know what? As soon as we get home from church today, Mama's going to cook your favorite dinner, then take you upstairs and put it on you in bed. I think tonight's as good a night as any to make a baby." She leaned her head on my shoulder in a gesture of affection.

"Alison, that sounds great, but it's not just about that. I just want my best friend back."

"I never left, baby. You'll see." I took her hand and we kissed passionately until we were interrupted by a knock on my window. When we looked up, we saw several of our fellow church members laughing at us.

"Hey, you two lovebirds, this is a church, not a motel. Get a room!" Everyone standing outside our car laughed as Shorty, the church's new youth minister and church clown, cracked one joke after another until we stepped out of the car, blushing.

"I'm gonna get you for this, Shorty," I told him with a grin as I slapped his hand.

"You can try, Brother Williams. You can try."

I can't speak for Alison, but I couldn't stop blushing, even when we entered the church, because after Shorty, the next person I saw was Jackie, who was wearing a long choir robe. My mind was flooded with one thought and only one thought. Was Jackie wearing anything under that robe?

Bishop Wilson preached a good sermon about how your marriage should be like a threefold card. If you put God first, then your spouse, then yourself, you will have an enduring, Christ-centered marriage. Although I was listening to the bishop speak, I couldn't concentrate. I tried to focus on the sermon, but my mind kept coming in and out as I stared at Jackie's robe. Every so often, Alison would nudge me.

"Baby, you all right?"

I nodded. My mind kept wandering, though. All I could think about was Jackie playing that organ and wearing that robe with no clothes under it. When the choir sang Donnie McClurkin's song "We Fall Down (But We Get Up)," Jackie soloed and the church went wild. There were people dancing and shouting, and a few were even being struck by the Holy Ghost. Even First Lady Wilson, who was out of the hospital for Sunday church service, stood up, waving her uplifted hand back and forth, shouting, "Hallelujah, hallelujah," over and over again.

From behind the organ, Jackie gave me a smug look of satisfaction, then a wink, as if to say, "If I can do this to them, what do you think I can do to you?"

Suddenly, I felt hot, and I was beginning to sweat. I adjusted my tie and tried to fan myself, but the sweat just kept rolling down my face. How could I be in the house of the Lord feeling like this, lusting after someone else's mate while I sat next to my own? I felt my penis begin to expand, and I had to fight hard to keep an erection from going full-flag.

"That was beautiful, wasn't it?" the bishop asked when the performance was done. The congregation responded in a chorus of "Amen."

"Now, I'd like you to open your Bibles to . . ."

"Brother, it's time." I almost jumped out of my skin and out of the pew when I felt someone tap me on the shoulder. When I glanced in the aisle, Deacon Walls was standing there next to me.

"Huh? Time for what?"

"It's time to take up the collection."

"Oh, yeah, I'm sorry, Deacon. I'll be right there." The deacon walked away and I turned to Alison. "I'll be back."

Alison nodded approvingly. She was so proud that I was starting to make the moves to become a deacon of the church. I adjusted myself under my suit jacket and carried the Sunday program in front of my bulge. As I passed the collection basket along each row, the swelling in my pants went down, and I purposely avoided looking in the direction of the choir. The last thing I wanted was to be passing the collection plate and have someone spot the tent in my pants. I could just hear the whispers behind Alison's and my back now.

After I passed the collection basket up the right side of the pews, Deacon Walls, Deacon Rogers, and I went into the finance office behind the sanctuary with the church's treasurer, Deacon Alexander. I felt a real sense of pride collecting the money. As a commodities broker, everyone knew I handled money well, and they were even talking about appointing me the next church treasurer when I became a deacon in a year or so.

I left the deacons to count the money and headed to the small unisex bathroom in the back of the church before heading back to my seat. When I finished my business and opened the door, Jackie was standing in front of me.

"What do you want?" I demanded.

"I want you. Haven't you figured it out yet?" Jackie's hands reached out and began to roam my chest, but I quickly removed them.

"Stop it. We're in the church. What's wrong with you?"

"Nothing a little some of this wouldn't help." Jackie grinned, reaching for my groin.

I stepped out of reach. "Will you stop? Don't you have an organ to play?"

"I sure do, and if you would stop moving around, I'm going to play it like a flute."

Like the other day in the car, I was starting to get fed up with Jackie's behavior. Common sense told me it was time to go back to my seat before someone overheard what was being said and misconstrued it. I started to walk away.

"Hey, Brent," Jackie called.

I knew better than to turn around, but I still did it. "What?"

"This." Jackie was standing in the entrance to the restroom. In one swift motion, Jackie had turned around and the robe was lifted up to expose two perfectly round brown globes. I wanted to avoid looking, but my eyes wouldn't listen to my brain.

"I told you I wouldn't be wearing anything under my robe. How do you like my assets?"

Of course I didn't answer, but the truth was, I liked Jackie's assets. Matter of fact, they were now permanently ingrained in my memory for those occasional times I needed help getting it up for my wife. I hurried back to my seat, grinning like the little boy who'd just seen his first copy of *Playboy*. The memory of that first peek was a secret a boy would keep with him for the rest of his life. I felt the same way about Jackie's ass. I'd never tell anyone, but I'd always remember.

21

Sonny

I was staring out the window of the Coconut Grill restaurant in Manhattan as I waited for Tiffany to show up for dinner. It was directly across from the Beacon Theater, where we were supposed to see Tyler Perry's new stage play. With that all being said, I was about to walk out of the restaurant because Tiffany was an hour and thirty-five minutes late for dinner, and the play had started five minutes ago. I called both her house and her cell phone several times, but only got her voice mail, with no returned calls. It was hard for me to believe that she'd stood me up, though, because I'd talked to her when she got off work and she was very excited about dinner and the play. She loved Tyler Perry's DVDs and kept telling me how happy she was because this would be her first live show. She even went as far as to make arrangements for the kids to stay with their father for the night, so you know it was going to be on when we got back to my place.

I decided to give her cell one more try, but the phone just went straight to voice mail again. I really didn't want to leave, but sometimes you just have to face facts. Tiffany, like Jessica, had fucked me! Who knows? Maybe her ex came over and made her an offer she couldn't refuse. Despite what she had told me, I knew she still cared about him. Why else would she keep his old love letters and pictures in a box in the back of her closet? Of course, I'd taken care of that by depositing the box in the nearest Dumpster when I left the night I found them. I don't think she'd noticed yet that they were missing, or at least, she hadn't confronted me about it.

Damn, I thought, *she was supposed to be different. She was supposed to love me unconditionally.*

"Sir, can I get you another Heineken while you wait?" The waitress snapped me out of my thoughts. I glanced out the window, hoping and praying that Tiffany would be walking up to the building or standing in front of the theater, but that was only wishful thinking.

"Do you mind if I ask you a question about women?"

The waitress nodded.

"If someone doesn't show up for a date, are they trying to send you a message?"

The waitress gave me a sympathetic smile. "It depends. Things happen sometimes that aren't planned. Does she have children? Maybe her kid got sick." Damn, I never even thought about her kids.

I gave the waitress an inquisitive glance. "But no matter the excuse, shouldn't she have at least called?"

"Definitely. If she didn't call, she didn't give a . . ." She didn't finish her sentence, but I got the point. She was right, Tiffany didn't give a shit.

I lowered my head. "Thanks for the advice. I guess I gotta go kick someone to the curb . . . if she hasn't already kicked me to it first." I stood up, reached into my pocket, and pulled out a twenty-dollar bill, placing it on the table. I wasn't sure how much a beer cost in that joint, but I'm sure it was considerably less than the twenty dollars I left. "Oh, by the way, keep the change."

"Thanks, mister," the waitress replied with a grin. "Next time you need some Oprah-type advice, come on by. I read all of Dr. Phil's books."

I wanted to laugh, but I was just a little bit too angry. I really thought Tiffany cared about me. I walked out of the restaurant, checking my watch as I lit a cigarette. She was now officially an hour and fifty minutes late. I felt like a fool. She'd dissed me, and there was nothing I hated worse than disrespect. I was going to have to reevaluate our relationship, and it looked like we were finished.

I was about to hail a cab when I heard Tiffany shouting my name. I ignored her, chuckling pitifully as I raised my hand to flag down a driver. If she'd shown up ten minutes earlier, I would have been upset about her missing dinner but still been happy to attend the show, although I would have purposely complained about being hungry the entire time. But this wasn't ten minutes ago, and we'd now missed almost a half-hour of the show. She shouted my name again, this time pressing her horn like she'd lost her mind.

"Sonny! Sonny!"

I glanced in the direction of her voice. She was getting out of her double-parked car and heading my way, looking flustered, and actually, kind of beautiful, with her hair windblown and cheeks all flushed. She was wearing a red silk dress with an asymmetrical hemline, which showed off her beautiful thighs. I'm sure it complemented her ass, too, but that was beside the point. Right now, I was pissed. But I don't think she noticed when she approached me.

"Sonny, where you going?"

"Where am I going? I'm going home." My voice was dripping with attitude, while her voice sounded exhausted.

"Home? But I thought . . ."

I turned and pointed my finger at her. "You *thought*? Like I *thought* you would call if you were going to be late. I *thought* you were going to be here two hours ago. And I *thought* you were different." She just didn't understand. I cared about this woman so much I actually had to fight back tears.

"Sonny, don't be like that. I am different. You know that. You don't know what I've been through trying to get here. Kareem . . ." She laid her hand gently on my upper arm and I backed away, gesturing for her to leave me alone.

"Save it, okay? I really don't wanna hear it. You could have told me that when you called." I spoke with bitter contempt. "Oh, that's right. You didn't call, did you?"

"I know. I'm sorry. I couldn't find my phone. I think someone stole it."

"Oh, that's a convenient excuse. Why didn't you use a pay phone or your house phone?"

She stared at me sadly. "I don't know your number. It's in my phone."

"What, you don't know my number by heart?" How could she not know it after three weeks of dating? "We talk almost three times a day."

"I don't know anybody's number by heart. Whenever I lose my phone, I lose contact with half the people I know."

"Are you trying to say that you want to lose contact with me?"

"No, Sonny, that's not what I mean. You act like you have my number memorized."

"I do." I recited her digits while she stared at me, looking stupid.

"Sonny, you're making way too much of this, baby."

I couldn't believe she just said that. "Is that what you think? That I'm making too much of this? You're two hours late. We missed the show, and you didn't even have the common courtesy to call me." I started to walk away and she followed me like a little kid. "You know what, Tiffany? Brent and James warned me about you. You ain't any different than Jessica." I resumed my search for a cab. "Taxi!"

"Damn it, Sonny! Why won't you just listen to me?" She reached up and grabbed my arm, trying to pull it down, and I angrily jerked it back up in the air.

"Get the fuck off me," I growled, staring at her as if I was about two seconds from smacking the shit outta her.

"Go ahead. Hit me. I can take it. It won't be the first time a man hit me for no reason. At least then maybe we can talk civilized and you'll let me explain." I froze for a second. Either she had a legitimate excuse for being so late or she was crazy as hell. I'd never had a woman tell me to hit her before. Just the thought of it snapped me back to reality. I lowered my hand.

"I'm not going to hit you. I just want you to leave me alone."

"Why? What are you afraid of, Sonny? All I wanna do is tell you why I was late. If you don't wanna listen for me, do it for my kids. They love you, Sonny, and so do I."

I folded my arms and stared at her silently. Did she mean it? Did she really love me, or was she just saying that because she thought it was what I wanted to hear? I looked in her face and she looked sincere. I wanted to believe her so bad. I wasn't sure what the truth was, but it was the mention of the kids that truly softened me. Besides, I was curious about what type of excuse she was going to come up with for being late. Whatever it was, it had better be a good one, because I had promised myself that I would never again let Tiffany or any other woman disrespect me like Jessica did.

"Aw'ight, I'm listening."

Tiffany's face crumpled as she took a deep breath. "Well, for starters, Kareem wouldn't watch the kids. I tried to find a babysitter, but I couldn't, so I had to take them with me."

"Take them with you? What are you talking about? Where are the kids?"

She pointed at her car. "In the backseat."

"The backseat? You're joking, right?"

She shook her head. I walked over to the car and peeked in. She wasn't lying at all. The kids were there, sound asleep. I turned toward her, suddenly feeling like shit. All I had to do was let her explain, but in my stubbornness, I wanted to believe she would do me wrong.

"I'm sorry I didn't wanna listen." I spoke very softly.

"That's okay. I know how it must have looked. Can we go home now?"

She tossed me the key, then got into the passenger seat. I opened the driver's-side door and slid into the car.

"Why wouldn't Kareem watch the kids? He ain't seen them since we started dating."

She hesitated as if she didn't want to talk about him, but if I had anything to say about it, she was going to. I cleared my throat, giving her the look.

"It's my fault. He just gets me so mad. I should have never told him," she said sadly.

"Told him what?" I tried to conceal the jealousy in my voice, but I'm sure she could hear it.

"He asked me where I was going, so I told him, on a date—"

I cut her off. "Why'd you tell him anything? He's not your man. I'm your man."

"I know you're my man. And I don't know why I told him, but once I did, he started trippin'."

"Trippin' how? He didn't put his hands on you, did he?" I was starting to breathe hard. If he touched her, I swear to God he was a dead man.

"No, but he tried to tell me that I was moving too fast and that he couldn't condone me dating this soon after we divorced, so he wasn't watching the kids."

I was now fire hot. "Moving too fast? Condone? Who the hell is he to tell you anything, much less what he condones? That son of a bitch can kiss my ass."

"He's just jealous, Sonny. When I left him, he told me I'd never find anyone else who would love me the way he did. Well, I found you, baby, and he's just jealous that I'm happy."

"You know I never liked Kareem," I snapped angrily.

"I know that. I don't like him either, but he's my kids' father. What am I supposed to do?"

"You could always take out a life-insurance policy on him and have him killed."

She laughed. "I already have a policy on him. But I couldn't get lucky enough to find someone to kill him."

"Yeah, you never know," I said with a smirk.

"Let's stop talking about Kareem, okay? Let's just make up for the time we missed tonight and try to enjoy what's left of it." She reached over and took my hand, kissing it gently. "I love you, Sonny."

I glanced over at her, then looked at the kids in the rearview mirror. "I love you, too, but if we're going to be together, we're going to have some ground rules. You got it?"

"Yes, I got it." She smiled at me.

"I'm serious, Tiffany."

"So am I, Sonny. I'm happy for the first time in years. I don't wanna blow this. Now, take me home so I can show you just how serious I am."

22

Brent

So there I was, only six weeks after my honeymoon, waiting in Bishop Wilson's office for him to counsel me on my marriage. Why was I there? Guilt, I guess. I hadn't been able to make love to Alison without fantasizing about Jackie in almost three weeks. That's not so good when you're trying to make a love child. Unfortunately, after seeing Jackie's exposed rear, my wife just didn't do it for me anymore. Not to mention the fact that Jackie was putting more and more pressure on me each week. I loved Alison and I knew that if I wanted to remain married and have a family, something was going to have to give. This thing with Jackie had to stop before the fantasies and constant flirting became reality.

To pass time as I waited for Bishop Wilson, I studied the plaques on his office wall. In addition to his many accomplishments, he also held an M.F.C.C. in Guidance and Counseling. Not that I even knew what that meant, but I guessed it meant he knew what he was talking about. Cracking my knuckles, I vacillated. Should I stay or should I go? I almost got up to leave. Perhaps I should've talked to Sonny or James about the whole situation, but I didn't.

There are a lot of things I never told my two friends, and there were certain things I couldn't tell anyone except God. Anyhow, since I got saved, Bishop Wilson and the first lady had been like family to Alison and me. I guess that's why I was waiting for him. As the head of the church, he was as close to God as anyone I knew. They say you should go to the elders of the church when you have a test of faith. Well, I was definitely having one. This problem with thoughts of lust and adultery didn't seem to want to go away.

"Are you waiting for me, Brother Williams?" My thoughts were interrupted by Bishop Wilson as he walked into the office.

"Yes, sir, Bishop. I was hoping we could talk."

"Sure. Let me get out of this robe and I'll be right with you." I turned around and watched him put down his briefcase, take off his robe, and sit down at his desk. I detected a note of sadness, but he was still holding his head up high as usual. The bishop carried himself with the regal air of a king, and I felt both humbled and ashamed to be in his presence.

"So, how's Alison? I saw her at the hospital last night, but I really didn't get to speak with her." He sat back in his chair and rocked a few times as he listened.

"She's doing fine, Bishop. She's busy as heck, though, between working, going to see the first lady, teaching Sunday school and trying to take care of me. I don't know how she does it."

"Yeah, these church women are something else." The bishop smiled. "I remember about a year ago, when Charlene was a little stronger, she had about thirty different hats. Lord, what I would do to have those days again."

"So, how is the first lady doing, Bishop?"

"Oh, she's doing about as well as can be expected." A sad look crossed his face. "I'm hoping to get her home from the hospital soon, but she's still rather weak."

"Yes, Alison told me. If there's anything I can do, please let me know."

"You and Alison have done more that your fair share. Tell Alison I appreciate how she comes to the hospital every day and sits with Charlene. She's in a lot of pain, but you know what a trooper my wife is."

I nodded my head. "She certainly is, Bishop. I believe she can beat this thing."

"That, son, is entirely up to the Lord." He bowed his salt-and-pepper head in my direction. "Now, Brent, what brings you here? A handsome newlywed like yourself shouldn't have a problem in the world." He gave me this piercing look, his distinguished voice sounding like a cross between James Earl Jones and Barry White.

I scratched my head. "I wish that was true, Bishop. Heck, I don't even know where to start."

"Well, let's start with you. How's your relationship with God?"

I lowered my head. "I wanna say my relationship with God is good, but I can't."

The Bishop stroked his beard. "Why's that?"

"Well, to be honest"—I paused as I thought about the consequences of my words—"there's someone else in my life other than my wife."

The Bishop sat up in his chair, and it was obvious he was a little stunned. He gave me a solemn look before he spoke. "Are you having an affair, Brother Williams?"

"I don't think I would call it an affair, Bishop, but I'm afraid it could go down that road. That's why I'm here."

"What exactly do you mean by going down that road? Have you slept with this person?"

"No! No, I've been celibate since I got saved . . . that is, until Alison and I got married." I felt a twinge of conscience when I remembered the one lapse in our vow of celibacy, the week before our wedding, but we were now man and wife, and it wasn't the problem at hand, so there was no need to confess this to the bishop. "No, it's just that this person brings out something in me that no one else can. It's hard for me to explain, but any time this person is around, I have thoughts of lust."

"Well, during every marriage, people are faced with lust and temptation, but you've got to get past this. Can I ask you something?"

"Sure."

"Obviously you've known this woman since before you got married. Why didn't you pursue her instead of Alison?"

"I did—until I found out that Ja—umm, I mean, the person I was pursuing is married too."

"I see. Well, that definitely wouldn't have worked." He cleared his throat before speaking. "Well, Brent, you know, I'm tempted by women every day in the congregation. I just make sure I don't allow myself to get into a compromising position. I don't even counsel female members by myself. Has she put you in any compromising position?"

"Yes. Every time we see each other." I put my head down in my hands. I saw a vision of the passionate kiss the night before my wedding, Jackie's hand reaching across my lap on the way home from the airport. Last but not least, I visualized what I'd seen under Jackie's gown. Good God! "Bishop, if you could have seen what was going on two Sundays ago right here in the church, you might have passed out."

"In my church?" I could tell by the look he gave me that he was disappointed, and from that point on, I could no longer look him in the eyes. "Is this a member of my congregation we're talking about?"

I nodded my head glumly.

"Who is it?"

"I'd rather not say. But what I will say is that it's a prominent member of the church who's married to another prominent member of the church. And both should remain nameless."

The Bishop's voice sounded stern. "Tread lightly, young fella. Something like this could ruin more than your marriage. You don't know these church folks like I do. They're not all Christians like they portray themselves to be."

"That's another reason why I'm here." I looked up with miserable eyes, then shifted in my seat. There was nothing I could say.

"Do you love Alison?"

I gazed up at him. "Yes, sir, I do."

"Do you want your marriage to work?"

"Yes, Bishop, with all my heart."

"Well, the Bible speaks of temptation and lust. We have to learn to yield not to temptation and we have to keep our thoughts off lust. The desire leads to the action sometimes. In Matthew 5:28, you know Jesus said to look at a woman with lust in your heart is the same as to commit fornication or adultery."

I nodded, feeling guilty. How many times had I seen Jackie's green eyes float in my mind just before I exploded inside of Alison? So although technically I hadn't committed adultery, in my heart I knew I had.

The bishop was quiet for a while. "Let's go to the scriptures and get the Biblical view on the matter of adultery."

I turned my empty palms upward. "I didn't bring my Bible."

"I have an extra Bible here."

The Bishop handed me the Bible from his bookcase. For the next thirty minutes, we went over different scriptures and he had me read them out loud. But one stuck in my head.

"Exodus 20:14."

"You must not commit adultery."

"Do you know what the scripture, IF YOUR RIGHT HAND OF-FEND THEE, THEN CUT IT OFF, means?"

"No."

"Well, it means, get rid of any person or practice that causes you to sin. Sin cuts off God's blessings to you."

Finally, the Bishop got down to his counseling business. "So don't put yourself in any compromising situations with this woman, and work on building your relationship with your wife."

"I will."

"Are you and Alison giving each other the marital due?" The Bishop gave me a grave look. I felt embarrassed to talk about what went on in our bedroom with him, but I nodded. "I know this sounds nosy, but you'd be surprised at the number of young couples who are not sleeping with each other then wondering why affairs slip into their relationship. So, how often are you and Alison intimate?"

"Not enough for me, but we're going to do something about that. After all, we are newlyweds."

"Well, good. Keep doing that. Don't let temptation come be-tween you." The bishop took a deep breath.

"I'm sure you're a man of integrity, Brent. I watched all the women in the church run after you, but you kept your head. I watched you have a Christian courtship with Alison after you were saved, and I know you will do the right thing."

I stood up and shook his hand. "Maybe you're right, Bishop. Everything will work out. I'll be careful."

"Young man, just pray whenever the devil tries to overpower you."

Although I sounded firm and resolved, inside I felt as shaky as Jell-O. I understood what the scriptures said, but that didn't stop me from thinking about Jackie. I knew I needed to be strong. I had to stop fantasizing about Jackie when I was in bed with Alison. I would have to say "freeze" whenever my body thought about Jackie. My mind knew it wasn't right. If I could just get my body to agree with what my mind thought.

Straightening my shoulders, I made a new resolution. I made up my mind that no matter what Jackie threw at me, I was passing. No, my marriage wasn't going to end before it even got started.

23

James

It was a little after four in the morning when I pulled into my driveway with my headlights turned off, praying to God that Cathy was asleep. There wasn't a light on in the house as I eased around to the back door, so I was feeling pretty safe. I quietly let myself in, then slipped off my shoes in the kitchen. From there, I tiptoed up the stairs like a cat burglar, making sure not to make one stair creak. When I reached the top, I stubbed my toe on one of the kids' toys and went into mini-convulsions to keep from hollering. I was in so much pain, tears were coming out of my eyes, but I never made a sound. When I got the pain under control, I crept into my bedroom.

I couldn't make out more than the outline of her body, but it looked like Cathy was asleep on her side of the bed with her back to me. Now it was just a matter of getting into the bed without waking her up. One leg at a time, I slowly climbed in, trying not to make a sound. As I eased the covers around my neck, I sighed thankfully. God had answered my prayers, and now all I had to do was slide my pants off and go to sleep for the three hours before my alarm clock went off.

But there wasn't going to be any sleep for me tonight, because out of nowhere, there was movement from Cathy's side of the bed, and without warning, her end table light came on. The bulb's brightness stabbed at my eyes like a thousand pins, making me pull the covers completely over my face to protect them. When my eyes finally adjusted to the light, I was staring at Cathy's aggravated face. I hadn't seen her look like this since she tried to kick me out a few years back. Her face was flushed and her eyes were red, like she'd been crying for hours. There was no doubt in my mind that she knew I'd been gone, which meant I was in trouble. I clutched the covers up around my chin, trying to hide the fact that I was still dressed.

"Where the hell you been?"

"I didn't—" Cathy didn't even let me finish my lie before she reached down and snatched the covers off me.

She glanced at my clothes. "Now, I asked you a question. Where have you been?"

"Huh?" I was thinking about telling her I went for a walk.

"Don't *huh* me, James Robinson! You ain't hard of hearing. I said, where the hell have you been? I've been blowing up your phone ever since I heard your car pull out the driveway five hours ago."

Let me rephrase what I was thinking before. I wasn't in trouble; I was in big trouble, because there's no such thing as a five-hour walk, especially since she heard me taking the car.

"Ah . . . ah . . . well . . ." What I was trying to do was get my lie together, to think it through so it would sound legit, but under this kind of pressure it was hard. The longer I waited to answer, the more heated Cathy seemed to get. Then a lightbulb went off in my head. Sonny. I'd blame it all on Sonny. Cathy would believe that since Sonny was always getting himself into trouble. But after seven years of marriage, she was on to that one before I even got the words out of my mouth.

"And don't even try that 'I was with Sonny' crap, 'cause I called him. He said you were on your way home four hours ago, and I don't even believe he was with you then. I'm surprised he didn't try to warn you that I called. Anyway, it don't take four hours to come from his house. It only takes fifteen minutes. So where the fuck were you?"

Sonny probably did try to warn me, but I'd left my phone in the car to charge while I was babysitting Marcus. Stupid me, I never even checked to see if I had any calls. Well, there was always Brent. Now that he was married, Cathy would never call his house this late.

"Oh, and I called Brent too. He and Alison were at home in bed like married people are supposed to be, so don't even go there either."

"I wasn't gonna say that."

"Then what were you going to say?"

I stared at her dumbfounded for a few seconds because I was

just plain stuck. I knew I had to tell her something. I just didn't have any idea what it was. When I didn't answer her question fast enough, her eyes began to fill up with tears. She shook her head like I'd already given her an answer and it wasn't what she wanted to hear. Slowly, tears fell from her eyes, until her face was covered with salty streams.

"Who is she?" she sobbed.

"Huh?"

Her voice became more serious and she was gritting her teeth. "Who is she?"

I'd never felt so trapped before in my entire life. I loved this woman more than I loved myself, and I wanted to tell her the truth, but sometimes the truth is more painful than the lie. I looked at Cathy and I could see the pain I'd caused her spread across her face. I knew I had to do something, but the only thing I could think of was to play dumb.

"What are you talkin' about?"

"What am I talking about? Don't you play stupid with me, James Robinson. I wanna know who she is. And please don't tell me it's someone I know." I tried to put on a confused expression, like I didn't have a clue, but that only set her off. She reached down and grabbed the clock radio, throwing it at me. I batted it away with my arm, but if I was a second slower, it would have broken my nose.

"Hey, what's wrong with you? Stop it!" I yelled as she grabbed a coffee cup and flung it across the room. This time I ducked, and the cup ricocheted off the wall, hitting me in the back of the neck.

"I'm not stopping shit until you tell me the truth. Who the fuck is she?"

She reached for the lamp, and I grabbed her arm, throwing her on the bed. "I said, stop it! I'm not messing with anybody!"

"You're a liar," she cried, then began swinging her hands at me like a maniac. "I know you're cheating on me, James."

Before I could deny it, she hit me in the head, and God only knows where I found the control not to hit her back. "No, baby, I swear I'm not."

She hit me again and I held her arms, pinning her to the bed.

"Damn it, Cathy, stop it! I swear to God I'm not doing anything." She was struggling to get free.

"If you're not doing anything, why you sneaking out in the middle of the night?" She continued to struggle. "You don't think I noticed you've been gone all the time? You've got more excuses to be out this house than you do to be in it. If there's somebody else, just tell me! Just tell me so I can move on with my life."

"Cathy, I swear to God I'm not cheating on you."

There was a quick knock on the door, then light from the hallway flooded the room as my oldest son, James Jr., pushed open the door. I was praying that Cathy wouldn't continue her wild tirade with our son in the room.

"Mom, you okay?" he murmured, sounding scared and confused. I immediately let go of her wrists, as I watched my son staring at her tear-drenched face. "Mom, you okay?" he repeated. I was surprised when Cathy didn't answer him.

"She's fine, Jay-Jay. Go back to bed, son," I said firmly.

He ignored my command, walking closer to our bed with a raised voice like he was a grown man. "I was talking to Mommy." His voice softened. "You okay, Mom? Why you crying?" For the first time since he was born, my son challenged my authority. It was like taking a shotgun blast through the chest, because at that moment, I could feel my son's hatred, and I couldn't blame anyone but myself.

"Get off of her!" he shouted.

That was it. Whether I was to blame or not, I was not going to be disrespected by my eight-year-old child. I was about to get up and slap the taste out of his mouth. He knew I didn't play that shit. At that point, Cathy took over as only a mother could, putting aside her anger at me to protect my relationship with my son.

"It's all right, Jay-Jay. Mommy's fine. Daddy and I were just playing. Now go to your room like Daddy said."

My son glanced at me with disdain as he wrapped his arms around his mother's neck, whispering, "Okay, but if you need me, I'm in my bedroom."

I watched him walk out of the room like he didn't have a fear in the world, and the only thing that came to mind was that he was just like me.

"Get off of me," Cathy snapped as soon as he was gone. I let her up from the bed.

"Do you know what he asked me yesterday?" Tears welled in her eyes again.

"No." I closed my eyes, awaiting her response.

"He asked me, 'Are you and Daddy getting a divorce?'" Cathy stopped talking for a second as her voice cracked. She swallowed back her tears and continued. "He's old enough to remember what it was like when we had problems before. He adores you, James, but he knows something's wrong. You didn't even go to their games on Saturday. You never missed a game before."

I felt like shit. "I'll go talk to him." I stepped off the bed and she grabbed my arm.

"I think you need to talk to me before you talk to him."

She gave me that look again. I didn't want to go through what we just went through before, so I pleaded a little more humbly. "Baby, I ain't been with nobody. You gotta trust me."

"Trust you? Why should I?"

"Okay, I didn't want to tell you this, but . . ."

Cathy sat up, looking at me with those big, innocent doe eyes. "Tell me what?"

"You really wanna know where I've been?"

"Yes." She nodded slowly. "I wanna know."

I wanted to tell her to be careful what she asked for, because the truth is a double-edged sword, so it can cut you from two directions. But if she wanted the truth, I'd give it to her. I was tired of lying, and even more tired from being up all night and fighting with her. It was time for the truth. Besides, it couldn't get any worse. She already thought I was fooling around. Which was worse, me having an affair now or me having a kid out of wedlock? I guess I was about to find out.

I reached out and took her hand. I was surprised that she let me touch her, although she looked like she was holding her breath as she waited for me to speak.

"Cathy, before I tell you this, I just want you to know how much I love you and our boys."

"We love you too, James. Now tell me what's going on."

"Damn, I don't even know where to start." I heaved a deep sigh. "We're behind on the mortgage, Cathy. And I know you don't like it, but I took on a second job, driving for an escort service at night to get us caught up." I just couldn't do it. I was so close to telling her the truth about Michelle, but I lost my nerve when this lie popped into my head. I used to drive female escorts around when Cathy and I first met, but she put a stop to it right after we got married. With that history, it wasn't so far-fetched for her to believe that I'd started driving again.

Apparently the lie was a good one, because she no longer looked concerned about me cheating; she looked scared to death about the mortgage. I was glad she never looked at the bills.

"How did this happen?"

"Thank your boy Mayor Bloomberg and his new tax assessment. Because of him, our mortgage went up three hundred dollars a month."

"How far behind are we?"

"Well, we were three months behind, and they were about to put us into foreclosure before I took this second job, but now we're just two months behind." I knew the word "foreclosure" would be enough to make her forget about her suspicions. Once the lie came to me, it was easy to keep spinning the false tale.

"Thank God. We're not going to lose this house, are we, baby?" Now I was "baby" again.

"No, we're not going to lose the house. Not if I can help it. But I am going to have to continue to work some late nights. I know you don't want me driving for an escort service, but it's the only fast money I know how to make."

"Don't worry about me. You just do what you gotta do to save our house. If I have to, I'll get a second job too." Cathy started to cry again, and I felt like such a dog, especially when she scooted over and put her arms around me.

Oh, the web we weave when we practice to deceive, I thought. As soon as I told that lie, I knew I was going to have to tell another lie to cover it, but I couldn't bear to tell her about Marcus. I wanted to stop lying, but I just couldn't break her heart like that. How could I explain that I'd been with another woman while we were having problems, and conceived a child outside of our marriage? There were just no mitigating circumstances or excuses for that. When we first separated, Cathy and I had been going to counseling, trying to repair our marriage, and I'd still chosen to pursue the affair with Michelle. Cathy believed we were well on our way to happiness again, and this would seem like a mockery of all that she held sacred.

24

Brent

"Look, man, I gotta get out of here. Cathy's cooking fried chicken, and you know how much I love her fried chicken." James smiled contentedly as he folded the check I'd given him and placed it in his wallet. We'd just spent the last hour talking about and even doing a little praying about his situation with Michelle. I'd known the guy for over thirty years, and I'd never seen him look this depressed, so I felt obligated to help him both spiritually and financially. I'd given him a check so that he could finally put this whole paternity thing behind him. Maybe finding out the truth would give him some peace of mind. I just hoped it was the truth he was looking for.

"I wanna thank you for this, Brent."

"Not a problem," I replied as he gave me a grateful hug.

"Tell Alison I said hi."

"I sure will." I walked him to the door and he hugged me again.

"Call me when you get your results."

James nodded as he walked out the door. "You'll be the first to know. I'll see you at church on Sunday."

"I'll be looking forward to it."

I closed the door and walked into the kitchen to fix myself a frozen dinner. It was a little after seven in the evening, and Alison wouldn't be home from visiting the first lady until some time around 8:30, or 9 o'clock. Now that I thought about it, I should have asked James to call Cathy and see if I could join them for some of that fried chicken. Cathy wasn't a gourmet in the kitchen like my wife, but she could fry the heck out of some bird. Well, hindsight is 20/20, I decided, as I pulled out a potpie and turned the toaster oven up to 350 degrees. Just then, the phone rang, and I wondered if James had left something behind.

"Hello."

"Brent?" It was Alison.

"Hey, honey, what's up? You still at the hospital?"

"Yeah, we're about to bring the first lady down to the chapel. There are too many people in the room and even more in the lobby. The entire women's choir showed up to see her after rehearsal, so the bishop asked the hospital chaplain if it was all right for us to have a service in the chapel, and he said yes."

"Y'all having a service? Maybe I should come on down there."

"No, you stay right where you're at. It's a women's devotional service for the first lady. I don't need you showing up and working up all these women. It's bad enough I've got to look at them gawk at you on Sunday. Besides, I want you to set the table for two. I've got a little surprise for you."

"A surprise? Don't tell me." I was smiling from ear to ear. "You're pregnant?"

"No, baby, I'm not pregnant yet," she replied sadly. "But that is something we need to work on when I get home. I know I'm ovulating."

"So . . . what's the surprise?"

"Did you eat yet?"

"No, I was just about to put a potpie in the oven."

"Well, I'm glad I caught you because I just sent someone over to The Rib Shack to bring you some of those ribs you like so much."

"Some Rib Shack ribs? Praise God, that sounds good." I shoved the potpie back in its container, then into the freezer. I loved me some Rib Shack ribs. The meat just falls off the bone. "Who you got bringing them over? Don't tell me it's that crazy Shorty."

"No, I haven't seen Shorty tonight, so I sent Jackie." My heart almost missed a beat.

"Jackie? Jackie Moss, the organ player? Now, that is a surprise." This was more than just a surprise, it was an unwelcome one. "Ah . . . you know, honey, that's not necessary. I'm actually kind of tired, and by the time Jackie gets here, I will have eaten my potpie and gone to bed. So go on and tell Jackie I said some other time."

"I can't. I gave Jackie the money almost half an hour ago. Your food should be there any moment."

Of course, you know at that exact moment the doorbell rang. I closed my eyes, praying Jackie would behave and respect my marriage. I didn't have much faith in my prayer being answered, though. Maybe I should have just told Alison about the advances Jackie had been making on me. What better way to stop your wife from sending her rivals to your bed than to make sure she knows who her rivals are? I actually considered telling her for a minute, but realized it would be impossible. Telling Alison that the spouse of a church trustee was relentlessly pursuing me would end up causing a whole lot more drama than I was already having fending off Jackie's advances. Besides, in a way, I was just as guilty as Jackie because I sometimes enjoyed the attention and couldn't control my attraction.

"Brent, are you still there, honey? Is something wrong?"

"No honey, nothing's wrong. I just hear someone at the door. I think Jackie's here."

"All right, then. Go eat your dinner so you can get some rest. I'll be home after a while. I love you, Brent."

"I love you too." She hung up the phone as the doorbell rang again.

I slowly walked to the door, hesitating before I opened it. Once again, I closed my eyes to pray, but a vision of Jackie's exposed rear end waiting for me on the other side of the door flashed into my mind. My eyes flew open. That was not the thought I wanted to have as I opened the door. Not if I wanted to make it through dinner without getting myself into trouble.

I opened the door and as usual, Jackie was looking good and smelling good.

"Hey, Brother Williams, your wife asked me to bring you some dinner."

I was surprised by Jackie's formality. Usually when we were alone, I was addressed by my first name or some endearing term. I stuck my head out the door, assuming there must be a church member lurking behind Jackie or sitting in the car, but there was no one.

"I know. She called." I stood there trying to avoid Jackie's piercing stare. That is, until I realized Jackie wasn't staring at me at all.

"Well, can I come in? The food's going to get cold. I've got potato salad, macaroni and cheese, collard greens, corn bread, and two pound of ribs. Oh, and peach cobbler." I stepped aside and Jackie walked by very nonchalantly, without even looking my way. I was confused. This wasn't the same aggressive Jackie that barged into my house so many times before and mooned me in the church two Sundays ago. No, this Jackie seemed more laid back, more subdued, more down to business, and maybe even uninterested in me. "Where would you like to eat?"

"How about over there?" I pointed to the dining room.

Jackie nodded, leading the way. Lord knows I tried, but I couldn't keep my mind or my eyes off Jackie's ass. It was as if there was a LOOK AT ME sign plastered on both cheeks. Jackie caught me looking too, dead to rights, but instead of that arrogant you-know-you-want-me smirk I was accustomed to, I got nothing. No reaction at all, just a, "Where are the plates?" And believe it or not, that bothered me. It bothered me a lot.

A few minutes later, Jackie was taking the dishes out of the breakfront and setting the table while I opened a bottle of wine. My dinner companion brought another confused look to my face by declining anything stronger than wine. On Jackie's last visit, my liquor cabinet had been raided within minutes. I was glad we avoided that because hard liquor made Jackie much more aggressive.

Once the table was set and the wineglasses were filled, we sat down to bless the food and eat dinner. The meal was uneventful, mostly small talk about church gossip and politics. I have to admit, I really enjoyed myself. I got a chance to see a side of Jackie that I'd never seen before, and as far as I was concerned, we could have talked all night. Not only was Jackie sexy, but she was also surprisingly intelligent. There was one part of the meal where things got a little hot, though, and I'm not even sure if Jackie was aware of it. You see, Jackie had a way of eating ribs that was more like fellatio than consuming food. Just watching those lips nibble on those ribs and suck the juice out of those bones had my manhood standing at attention. By the time we finished our meal, I was sweating.

I was so sexually aroused that I actually thought about making a move. Probably the biggest reason I didn't was because something inside told me that Jackie and Trustee Moss had found some common ground in their relationship. I came to this conclusion because Jackie hadn't made one move toward me. I was actually upset when we were sitting in the living room and finished off the bottle of wine, because Jackie suggested it was time to leave. That, of course, was the last thing I wanted. Reluctantly, I walked Jackie to the door. Believe it or not, the thought of asking for a good-night kiss came to mind, although I wasn't brazen enough to open my mouth and do it.

"Brent, there's something you should know," Jackie said softly, looking up at me. This was where I expected Jackie to tell me about working things out with Trustee Moss and that we couldn't see each other outside of social events.

"What's that?" I leaned over so that I could smell Jackie's hair.

"I'm going out to dinner on Friday night at Umberto's." Well, that solidified it for me. I knew they were going to work things out because Umberto's was Jackie's favorite restaurant.

"I'm happy for you, Jackie. I'm sure Trustee Moss is happy about it too."

"You don't understand. I'm not going with the trustee." My back straightened up, and Jackie looked at me with what could only be described as a guilt-ridden face.

"If you're not going with Trustee Moss, then who?" I held my breath as I waited for an answer.

"Jonathan Wilcox." The name rolled off of Jackie's tongue like a love song and stuck in my throat like a slimy piece of okra, making me want to gag.

"Jonathan Wilcox from the choir?"

Jackie nodded, and I was speechless for a few seconds. I couldn't stand whiney behind Jonathan Wilcox, and I'm sure that's one of the reasons Jackie was dating him.

"Jonathan Wilcox is a sissy boy," I pointed out, still trying to conceal my mounting jealousy.

"No, he's not a sissy," Jackie snapped defensively. "He's a nice young man."

"Young is right. He's a kid! What is he, twenty years old? I thought you didn't like younger men."

"He's twenty-four, and unlike some men I've been interested in, he appreciates me." Jackie smirked as if a naughty thought had just come to mind, and I got a chill because that smirk used to be reserved for me. "He also appreciates what I can do for him."

Oh, my God, had Jackie actually done it with Jonathan? An image of them together popped into my head. The thought turned my stomach. The truly absurd thing was that Jackie and I were sitting here discussing a date, both of us ignoring the obvious fact that married people are not supposed to be going out on dates to begin with.

"What you can do for him! What the heck have you done with him?" My voice was sharp and demanded an answer. The question was, did I really want one?

"I haven't done nothin' yet. But Friday's only three days away."

"You can't be serious about Jonathan Wilcox." I started to laugh but was cut off by Jackie's very serious face.

"Why can't I? You don't want me. I've given you every opportunity to make a move tonight. Do you really think I eat ribs that way?" An image of Jackie nibbling and sucking on those rib bones popped back into my head and I immediately broke out in a sweat. "That was for your benefit. I was trying to show you what I can do with my mouth. I wanted to turn you on. I obviously failed."

No, you didn't, I wanted to scream.

I couldn't believe Jackie had purposely been sucking on those ribs to put sexual thoughts in my head. I was so weak, I fell right into the trap. And even worse, now that I'd given it enough thought, another image flashed in my head of those lips working over my penis, and it instantly sprang back to attention. I tried to inconspicuously move my hand to conceal it, but it was too late. Jackie's eagle eyes spotted it, and I knew it when both eyebrows went up.

"Mmm, mmm, mmm, what do we have here? No, don't do that. Why you trying to hide it? I'm flattered." Jackie's hands were on mine, moving them out of the way. I shuddered with pleasure and with shame as a battle raged within me. My conscience was screaming for me to stop, but the nearness of Jackie's body, the images flashing in my mind, and the fact that my wife had been spending too much time away from home all came together at that moment to overwhelm me. I'm sorry, but I could no longer control my desire.

I put my hand over Jackie's and held it on my erection. Our eyes locked, and I leaned in closer. My mouth pressed against those full, beautiful lips I'd been staring at throughout dinner and I felt the heat rushing through my body. I loved my wife, but she'd never made me feel this kind of electricity, especially with just a kiss. A moan escaped as I opened my mouth and my tongue came out to explore Jackie's mouth. As our tongues intertwined, I heard the last few faint protests from my conscience before my lust completely took control. There was only one thing I wanted now, and though it went against everything I believed in, I was ready to break my marriage vows and make love to Jackie.

"I want you," I whispered as I kissed Jackie's ear.

"You ain't said nothing but a word." It didn't take long for Jackie's jeans and underwear to slide down to the floor. "Come on, Brent, take it out. Let's see what you're working with."

A few seconds later, I was unzipping my pants as I kissed the back of Jackie's neck. I'd never felt so much passion in my entire life as I watched my lover assume the position with hands flat against my front door.

"Put it in," Jackie insisted, and I was about to oblige when a crucial thought crossed my mind. Lord, how would Alison feel if she knew I was about to make love to Jackie?

"I've gotta get a condom," I replied as I dashed into my bedroom. I may have never been as consumed with lust as I was at that moment, but I just wasn't going to be stupid.

It took me a minute to find one because Alison and I had never had a reason to use them. I finally dashed back into the living room sporting a red Trojan and ready to make love. I grabbed Jackie, who was now fully undressed, by the hips and was about to make the final plunge into adultery. Fortunately or unfortunately, depending how you look at it, that's when I saw the flash of light against my eyelids. I opened my eyes to see Alison's car pulling into the driveway, her headlights shining through the small windows at the top of the door.

"Oh, no!" I practically shouted as I pulled off the condom. My erection immediately deflated and my conscience was back, ready to kick my ass now. How could I have been so stupid? Standing here in my own house, the house I shared with my wife, getting ready to commit adultery.

"What is it?" Jackie asked.

"Alison just pulled into the driveway."

"What? Oh, my Lord. I can't get caught doing this with you."

Jackie looked as upset as I felt. Neither of us could make eye contact as we hurriedly pulled on our clothes, smoothed our hair and tried to relax our faces into casual expressions. It was too late to rush Jackie out the door before Alison came in, so we forced some small talk to make Alison think we'd just had a pleasant dinner, enjoying the food from The Rib Shack that she'd so thoughtfully ordered for me. The feelings of guilt and panic that came over me were something I never wanted to experience again. Now that I'd come so close to making love to Jackie, though, I could only hope that the memory of this close call would be enough to stop me the next time the temptation presented itself.

25

James

I was dozing on the living room couch when I heard Michelle slide her key into the lock. I sat up quickly and checked the television to see what was on. It was a boring documentary on endangered sea turtles, but Michelle was already opening the door, so I pretended to be all engrossed in watching these stupid turtles laying their eggs in the sand. I hated nature shows, so in a million years I never would have purposely chosen to watch this show. Tonight, though, I was on a mission. It didn't really matter what I was watching, as long as it bought me a little extra time at Michelle's place to carry out my plan.

Once again, she had called me to watch Marcus while she went to work. Her babysitter took off more days from work than the cast of *The Sopranos*. But I was happy to say yes this time, because I'd finally gotten what I needed to go through with my plot. I was going to get Michelle out of my life for good before things got any more complicated than they already were. Fortunately, Cathy still believed the lie about my new night job, so I was able to get out of the house fairly easily. I even left home a little early, telling her that I had to stop by Sonny's for a few minutes to give him some advice on women before I went to work. That part wasn't a lie, either. I did have to see Sonny, but not because he needed someone to talk to about his woman problems. In truth, he was holding the main ingredient I needed to execute my plan. Now it was in a box hidden beneath the couch I was sitting on in Michelle's living room.

"Hey, James," Michelle said, yawning loudly as she placed her keys on the table by the door.

I didn't turn my eyes away from the television as I grunted "Hello." Michelle was obviously annoyed by this. She marched in front of the TV, blocking my view.

"Excuse me," she said as she crossed her arms over her chest and frowned at me. "The least you could do is look at me when I walk in the room. Shoot, I know you might not like our situation, James, but I am the mother of your son. You could at least pretend to treat me with some respect."

I tried not to cringe as Michelle reminded me for the hundredth time that she was the mother of my child. I made the biggest mistake of my life when I stepped outside my marriage to mess with Michelle, and every time she said those words, I was forced to remember one more time just how stupid I'd been.

"Oh, sorry," I said, finally turning to look at her and trying hard to sound sincere. "I was just so into this show. I didn't mean to be disrespectful. How was work?"

"It was aw'ight." Michelle turned her back and noticed the show I claimed to be so interested in. "What the hell are you watching, anyway? Since when do you watch nature shows?"

"I got two—I mean three boys. They're always askin' questions about animals. I'm just trying to keep current," I explained to her. "Besides, I happen to like documentaries. Have you ever heard of these turtles? They lay their eggs in the sand, but not many of the babies survive." I pointed to the television screen, where some newly hatched turtles were running for their lives, trying to make it to the water before they were eaten by seagulls. My eyes were riveted to the screen as I tried to convince Michelle just how fascinated I was.

She rolled her eyes and went to hang up her coat. "Anyway, I'm home now, so you can go back to your precious wife."

"Actually, if you don't mind, I think I am going to stay and watch the end of this. Maybe they'll show an address where I can send a donation to help the endangered turtles." As soon as I said the words, I knew it was a mistake.

"Yeah, you can make a donation, all right, but it ain't to no turtles fund. You can donate to the care and feeding of your son. How about that? I'm sick of working all these damn hours, comin' home tired, just to spend all my money on kids' shit," she snapped. My stomach twisted, because what I wanted to do was remind her just how much I'd already saved her in babysitting alone. But I held my tongue. I had to keep the peace long enough to get her in the bed so I could go through with my plan.

"Okay," I said with a chuckle, "you're right. These little turtles will have to fend for themselves, 'cause I got a child to take care of. I'm gonna hit you off with some extra money as soon as I get my income tax back, all right?"

"You better believe you're gonna gimme something extra. I think it's time for a little increase on my weekly money anyway," she shot back. "That two-hundred-dollar-a-week shit ain't getting me nowhere."

I won't be giving you an increase if everything goes the way I plan, I thought. I was even more eager now to get this over with.

"Yeah, I know that. But let's not fight about it now, okay? You look really tired, and I wanna get back to this show. Why don't you go to sleep, and I'll just let myself out when it's over, okay?" My eyes were back on the TV screen, and I was praying she was too exhausted to continue nagging me. I almost smiled when I heard her yawn again.

"Whatever, James. Just make sure you lock the door when you go out. Oh, and Keisha won't be here Friday, so you might as well make plans to watch him then too." She didn't even wait for a response before she headed down the hallway to her bedroom.

I heaved a sigh of relief that I'd gotten at least this far, but I knew I still had a long night ahead of me. I would have to wait a while to do anything, because I had to be sure she was sound asleep before I made a move. I couldn't even change the channel from this damn animal show because if she came back in and I was watching something else, she'd know I was full of shit and kick my ass out. I sat back and watched the marine scientists trying to decide how to save the baby turtles, forcing myself to stay awake.

By the time the show was over, only a handful of babies had made it to the water, but I was too nervous to care. It was time to do what I'd come to do. I hit the mute button and listened intently. A smile came across my face when I heard Michelle snoring down the hall. She was in a deep sleep, and I was ready to make my move.

I bent down and reached under the couch to retrieve the small box Sonny had given me. When I took off the cover and removed the contents, my hands shook a little. I'd gone over the steps in my mind a million times, but now that it was actually time to go into her bedroom and do it, I was getting scared. What if the outcome wasn't what I wanted? But it was too late to turn back. I was already in a living hell dealing with Michelle and lying to Cathy, so things couldn't possibly get any worse.

I got up from the couch and tiptoed toward Michelle's bedroom, walking slowly to avoid creaking floorboards. From the sound of her snores, though, she wasn't going to wake up even if a marching band came down the hall right now. As I passed Marcus's room, I peeked in. He looked so cute and peaceful in his bed, I almost felt a little guilty. But that didn't last long. As soon as I thought of Cathy and the boys, I straightened up, gathered my nerve, and headed to Michelle's bedroom.

She was in the bed, her snores still echoing through the room. I held my breath as I crept across the room and stood beside her bed. Michelle still hadn't moved, and her mouth was hanging open so wide I could practically see her tonsils. She was out cold, and I knew it was time. I looked down to the swab in my hand and removed the protective covering. The GeneSwab DNA test had come in the mail to Sonny's house after I ordered it online. The company sent the supplies for free, and if I was successful tonight, I would get a sample of cheek cells from Michelle and send it off with $545. Within seven days, I would have the results. Of course, I was hoping they came back negative and that I wasn't Marcus's father. Sure, he was a cute kid, but I had a beautiful family at home that I was afraid I might lose when I ran out of lies and had to tell Cathy the truth. If things worked out the way I was hoping, I would find out he wasn't mine, tell Michelle to go screw herself, and never have to tell my wife a thing. Right now I wasn't ready to deal with the other possibility.

I bent over the bed, careful not to lean against it as I held the swab close to Michelle's mouth. The slightest movement might disturb her sleep, and I knew that if she caught me, I would blow my one chance at getting a DNA test from her. Besides, I didn't even want to think about what Michelle might do if she found out I still had doubts about being Marcus's father. I almost had a heart attack during the last episode when she called my wife, attempting to air my dirty secret. I didn't need Michelle losing her mind and talking to Cathy now.

As gently as I could, I placed the swab inside Michelle's mouth, willing my hand to stay steady. I touched the side of her cheek lightly, and she twitched a little. My heart took off on a race at that point, and I felt my body temperature rise at least twenty degrees. Somehow, I managed to calm myself and spin the swab slowly on the inside of her mouth to collect the cells.

The package directions said to turn it for fifteen seconds, and it felt like an eternity as I counted the seconds silently, watching Michelle for any signs that she was waking up. I felt my heart-beat slow a little as I neared the end of my count.

Twelve . . . thirteen . . . four—

Michelle's eyes cracked open a bit, and my hands flew behind my back to hide the swab.

"What the hell are you doing in here?" she asked groggily as she struggled to sit up in the bed.

"Oh, my God," I said, trying not to reveal just how scared I was at that moment. "I am so sorry I woke you up. I was just—"

"You were just what, James?" she demanded to know, now fully awake and her attitude raging.

"I just came back to check on Marcus before I left, and I don't know what happened, Michelle," I said, praying this lie would work. "I knew you were in here asleep, and something just made me want to come in here and give you a kiss good-night."

Her eyes narrowed for a second, like she was trying to process what I'd just told her, trying to decide if she believed me. I held my breath in that moment until she finally said, "Oh, okay," as if it was the most normal thing in the world for me to be coming into her bedroom for a kiss in the middle of the night.

Her eyelids fluttered a bit, and she got this look on her face that I guess at one time I might have found seductive. She was obviously waiting for me to give her a kiss now. I knew I had to oblige. Holding tightly to the swab still behind my back, I leaned in and put one hand on her shoulder. As I pressed my lips to hers for what I thought would be a quick peck, she placed her hands on my shoulders and pulled me a little closer, pressing our mouths together more firmly. Just like I had been doing before she woke up, I started counting. I figured four or five seconds of this would be enough to convince her that this was a real kiss. As I counted, I prayed she didn't open up her mouth and try to stick her tongue in mine. After a few seconds, I leaned back, separating from her embrace.

"Well, um . . ." I looked at her, unsure of how I would get out of the room without her seeing the swab.

A look of disappointment crossed her face, but she covered it up quickly with that hard attitude. "Well, um . . ." She mocked me. "I knew you was too much of a punk to actually go through with it."

"What do you mean?" I asked, squirming a little, trying to inch my way to the door now.

"Oh, please, James. You think I don't know what's going on here?"

Oh, shit. Was she about to bust me? Maybe she'd really been awake the whole time.

"What are you talking about, Michelle?" I asked, thinking I could stall her by playing dumb. Shoot, at this point, I was contemplating just running out of the bedroom with her cheek swab, grabbing the one I'd collected from Marcus before I brushed his teeth at bedtime, and bolting out the front door.

She sucked her teeth. "You think I don't know you've been wanting to get some from me ever since you started coming back around to watch Marcus?" My eyes widened as she continued. "I know your wife don't put it on you like I used to, and you know you still want it. You just don't have the balls to get with a real woman like me."

I just stood there with my mouth slightly open. I didn't know how to respond to this.

"That's okay, you don't have to try to deny it. I know what you're all about, James, and I know it's only a matter of time before you break down and come get some of this. Let yourself out and lock the damn door. I know you'll be in here again soon enough," she said with a smug smile, before she laid down and turned her back to me.

My feet wouldn't move for a second, I was so shocked that I was about to get away with my plan. "Okay then, good night," I mumbled as I backed toward the doorway. Once in the hallway, I put the plastic cover back over the swab to protect the precious DNA sample that just might put an end to my misery. I rushed to the living room, grabbed my keys along with the box that still contained Marcus's sample, and left the apartment without a backward glance.

In my car, I sat in the darkness and waited for my heart rate to return to something close to normal. Then I did a fifteen-second swab in my own mouth. I added the sample to the two that I'd collected in Michelle's apartment, closed the box, and shoved it under the seat. I couldn't wait to get to the post office as soon as it opened in the morning.

26

Brent

The sun was just starting to come up when the phone rang. I rolled over toward the nightstand and reluctantly picked it up. I had a pretty good idea who was calling, because the only person who knew I was at the Marriott hotel in San Francisco was Alison. I traveled to San Francisco about once a month on business. I loved the rolling hills and the Greenwich Village–style nightlife. This was the third day of a three-day trip, and I was positive Alison was starting to miss me. She was probably just calling to say good morning before she went to work.

"Hello?" I mumbled groggily into the receiver.

"Good morning, sweetheart. I didn't wake you, did I?" I glanced at the clock radio the hotel provided. I wasn't a morning person at all.

"No, I always wake up at sunrise," I said sarcastically.

Alison knew I hated to be awakened out of a deep slumber. I had only one rule when I was sleeping: If we don't have somewhere to be in the next hour or you're not ovulating and wanting to have sex, don't be waking me up before seven o'clock in the morning.

"Oh, my Lord, I forgot the time difference again, didn't I?"

"Yep," I said as I stretched, repositioning myself in the bed. "It's okay, though. I was kind of half-awake anyway."

"I'm sorry, baby, it's just that I've got some good news. No, I've got some great news."

"Don't tell me. . . . You just switched our car insurance to Geico." We both laughed.

"No, silly. I took a home pregnancy test this morning." My heart rate doubled as I sat up in the bed. Was this woman about to say what I thought she was about to say? Was she about to make my day in a way no woman had ever done before?

"And . . . what did it say?" I held my breath in anticipation of her reply, but it felt like an eternity before she spoke again.

"Brent, honey . . . you're going to be a daddy."

"Yeeessss!" I shouted, pumping my fist in the air.

I felt like I was on a rocket ship headed straight for the moon. Alison's words were like the sweetest love song I'd ever heard. I just closed my eyes and let that song play over and over again in my head. *Thank you, Lord, for answering our prayers.*

"I'm going to be a daddy? Are you sure?" I didn't doubt her, but I needed reassurance. I'd heard of plenty of women reading home pregnancy tests wrong before.

"Yes, honey, I'm sure. The indicator had a big pink plus sign, but I'm going to see my doctor on Thursday when you get back. Would you like to go with me?"

"Alison, I wouldn't miss it for the world." I was starting to get choked up. This was definitely one of the most emotional moments of my life. "Alison?" I whispered, then waited for a response.

"Yes."

"Sweetheart, I just wanted to say thank you."

"You don't have to thank me, Brent. You're my husband. I'm just doing what any woman would do for the man she loves. I'm giving you a child, hopefully a little boy."

Suddenly I remembered why I married her, and I couldn't hold back the tears any longer. "I don't care what it is. I just want our baby to be healthy."

"Amen to that," Alison replied. Then her voice got soft. "Brent, I love you."

"I love you too, Alison."

"Good, now you go back to sleep for a while. I just wanted you to know the good news. I'll call you later."

We said our good-byes and I hung up the phone. Alison didn't have a clue, but she'd just changed everything. "I'm going to be a dad," I said softly, my voice still full of pride as an arm reached across me and gently turned me back toward the center of the bed. "I'm going to be a dad."

"I heard," Jackie whispered, kissing me full on the lips. "I guess congratulations are in order? Why don't we celebrate by finishing what we'd started before the phone rang?"

Jackie parted my lips with a passionate French kiss, then insistently pulled me back on top of that magnificent body. We made love for the better part of an hour, but it was obvious I wasn't as into it as I had been the night before. The entire time, my conscience was killing me.

Jackie and I had been sleeping with each other for almost a month. We got together only a day after we'd nearly been caught by Alison. I hadn't even gotten in the door from work that day when Jackie's car pulled into my driveway. Everyone in the congregation knew that Alison went straight to the hospital to see the first lady and didn't come home until visiting hours were over, so by the time Jackie entered my house and my front door was closed, it was on. Once we consummated our relationship, we couldn't stay away from each other. Jackie was like a drug, and I was an addict that had to have a fix at least once a day. We met in every cheap short-stay motel in Brooklyn and Queens, and it never seemed like enough. We both longed to spend more time together. So when this business trip to San Francisco came up, I insisted Jackie come along with me. I had the time of my life, being with Jackie without looking over my shoulder, fearing we might be seen by some church member. The trip was something I thought I'd never regret, but now that Alison had told me she was pregnant, I felt guilty. I think Jackie knew it, too.

"So, where does this leave *us*?" We'd just finished making love and Jackie was now playing with the hair on my chest. I was lying on my back, staring at the ceiling as I daydreamed about fatherhood. I began to contemplate packing my bags and heading home. There was no doubt I was in love with Jackie, but for the first time, I realized my place was with my wife, Alison, and our unborn child.

"I'm not quite sure what you mean." I was lying. I knew exactly what Jackie meant. What I didn't know was the politically correct way to say there was no *us* now that my wife was pregnant.

"Where does you and Alison having a baby leave *us*? You know, *us*, as in, you and me? I thought we were going to be together."

I took a long, deep breath. "I don't know, Jackie. Why don't we just take it one day at a time?"

"What? Oh, no you didn't!" Jackie rolled those beautiful green eyes at me with jealous anger, then threw the covers to the side and got out of the bed. "You've been screwing me every day for the past month and now you wanna take it one day at a time like I'm some whore you can discard at any time? I'm not a whore, Brent. You don't just pay me and I go away. I'm in love with you."

"I never said you were a whore, Jackie, and I love you too. But we're both married, and even if we weren't, the fact that you can't have kids stands in our way." Jackie sat up wide-eyed, bucking at the chance to lash at my remarks. I jumped to my own defense before a word was uttered. "Oh, c'mon, Jackie. It's not fair that you'd look at me that way. We've discussed this before. I want a family. I want to be able to go outside and throw a football with my son and go to gymnastics with my daughter. You can't give me that, and you know how bad I want a child."

"No, Brent. You're the one who's being unfair. I apologize that I can't have your baby, but it's also not under my control. If you love me so much, then what's wrong with the thought of adoption? We can do the same thing the white people do in Asia. We can go down to the Islands or even Africa and get us a baby—a little boy. We can even name him Brent Jr. How about that? I'd love him and care for him as if he was my own."

I let out a laugh, but by the look I received, I could tell I'd pissed Jackie off. "You can't be serious. You barely take care of the children you've got. Who's going to stay home with the baby? You or me?"

Jackie didn't have an answer for that right away, but I could see tears start to fall. I walked over and wrapped my arms around my lover's narrow waistline.

"I'll do whatever it takes to make you happy, Brent. I just need to know that you love me."

"Of course I love you. You know that. Now com'ere." I kissed Jackie's neck, figuring that some sex would be the key to calming the situation down. Then things would go back to the way they were.

Jackie pushed me away. "No, I don't know it. I'm starting to think you love her more than you love me. I guess the question is, do you?" Jackie posed, sistah-girl-style, waiting for an answer.

"No, Jackie, I don't love her as much as I love you. I've never loved anyone as much as I love you, but I do love her. I love her a lot. She's having my child."

"Well then, you're going to have to make a choice. I'm in love with you, Brent. I'm willing to give up everything for you. I just want you to do the same. I'm sick of living a lie."

Feeling torn inside, I paused before answering. Truth is, I'd never felt so alive as when I was with Jackie, but the bottom line was, Alison was my wife, and she was having my child.

"Answer me, Brent."

Finally, I cleared my throat and spoke in a firm voice. "Jackie, please don't force me to make a choice we both might regret."

"Answer the question. Should I stay or should I go?"

"What do you want me to do, Jackie? Leave my wife and unborn child and move out here to San Francisco with you?"

"That's exactly what I want you to do."

"What we have is good, Jackie, better than I could have ever imagined, and I don't want it to end . . . but I'm not leaving my wife for you or anybody else."

Jackie's eyes filled up with tears again. "So, there it is. I asked you to make a choice and you made it. I just hope you can live with it."

Jackie stomped over to the closet and pulled out a suitcase.

"Why are you doing this? You knew I was married when we started this whole thing. You're married. You said you just wanted to have fun."

"In every affair there comes a time when the mistress wants to become the Mrs. I just realized that I'm never going to be the Mrs."

27

James

I'd been waiting for almost a week before I finally got the call I'd been expecting from my mother. She left a vague message with Cathy that she had something she wanted me to pick up at her house. Of course, this drove Cathy crazy, but it wasn't the first time my mother had received deliveries for me and refused to share any information with my wife. She loved Cathy, but she was very good about protecting my interests. Besides, the things I had delivered to my mother's house were normally just gifts for Cathy that I didn't want her to open before her birthday, so my mother's secret-keeping was pretty innocent, at least until now.

I knew that this time the delivery would be the results of the DNA test, which were supposed to be sent in a plain envelope without the company logo on it. With the unmarked envelope, I was confident my mother had no idea what she was keeping for me at her home. I had decided to have the results sent to my mother's house instead of Sonny's because I couldn't be sure that he wouldn't open the letter before I had a chance to pick it up. I trusted him to keep the original DNA testing kit, but his curiosity would very likely get the best of him if he knew he held the results in his hand. I didn't want to risk that.

The call from my mother had come in the morning, and the wait to go over there and get it felt like torture. I wanted to go as soon as possible to get an answer about Marcus's paternity, but I couldn't leave until late in the afternoon, when my boys were off at Little League practice. They loved my mother, mostly because she was the type of grandma who spoiled her grandkids, so if they knew I was going to see her, they would have insisted on going with me.

All day, as I counted the minutes before their practice, Cathy bugged the shit out of me, trying to figure out what my mother could possibly have at her house. No doubt she assumed it was another gift for her, even though it was nowhere near her birthday or our anniversary. I made a mental note to stop at the mall and buy her something after I went to pick up the mail. When Cathy finally got the boys in the car to take them to practice, I had to stop myself from running to my car before they were out of the driveway, then I had to remind myself to drive somewhere near the speed limit.

When I pulled up in front of my mother's house, a wave of nostalgia washed over me. This was the home I grew up in, and memories flooded me as I sat, my engine idling. I looked up at the roof where I broke my left arm when Sonny dared me to leap off it in the fifth grade. My eyes traveled to the porch I used to jump from with my skateboard, then to the bump in the sidewalk where we used to pop wheelies on our dirt bikes. Those were the good old days, when life was simple . . . not the mess my life was now.

I felt like a little boy again, and although I didn't want to admit it, I wanted my mother. When my father died when I was seven, my mother stepped up to the plate, working midnights and taking care of me and my little brother and sister. She was always the one who could make everything all right, no matter what.

I still kept a key to my mother's house, so I let myself in. As soon as I walked into the house, the envelope seemed to jump out at me. It was sitting on the telephone stand where my mother always kept her mail.

"James, is that you?" my mother called out from the kitchen. I could smell her famous mustard greens and fried chicken. Usually, just the aroma of my mother's cooking could throw me into an incredible hunger, but today, I was too worried. I had no appetite.

"Yeah, Ma, it's me."

I picked up the envelope, but my fingers froze as I tried to open it. I heaved a deep sigh, walked around in a circle, then repeated the same steps counterclockwise. What was I going to do? This letter was like kryptonite to Superman. It could blow my newfound security with Cathy and my two sons straight out of the water. I kept saying to myself that I was going to tear it open any second now, but some invisible hand stopped me. I was too afraid. Finally, my mother came out of the kitchen, wiping her plump hands on her full-length apron, which covered her heavy girth. For a while, she watched me as I paced the room, holding the envelope clasped tightly in my hands.

"James, what is it?" My mother knew me like a book.

"Ma—" I couldn't finish the words because I didn't know where to start.

"What is it?" she repeated. I walked into the living room and my mother followed.

"You don't wanna know, Ma," I sputtered.

"Let me see that envelope." My mother took it out of my hand and I didn't protest, not even when she opened the envelope and read the enclosed letter. Her eyes searched my face for some explanation, but I still couldn't speak.

"James, what have you gotten yourself into? This letter says that there's a ninety-nine-point-nine percent chance that some child named Marcus could be your son. What is going on, James?"

I had to sit down before I collapsed. I took a few backward steps until I bumped into the nearest chair, then fell into it. So many times in recent weeks, I had tried to convince myself that a DNA test would solve all my problems. I guess because I wanted it to be true, I believed that the results would tell me what I wanted to hear: that I was not Marcus's father, and I would no longer have to deal with Michelle. Hearing my mother read the exact opposite of the news I wanted was a cold slap of reality, and I was struggling to process it. How could this really be happening?

My mother, on the other hand, had already processed the information in the letter and wanted some answers now. "James, is this true? Did you know about this child?"

I regained my senses enough to finally respond. "Ma, it was a mistake. Cathy and I were separated when I met Michelle. I just found out about Marcus."

"How old is this boy?"

"He's three."

"Have you seen the child?"

I nodded. "I've been babysitting more than you'd believe." She listened as I told her everything, from the first late-night phone call from Michelle to how she had been manipulating the situation. "But I still didn't want to believe he was mine, Ma. That's why I got the DNA test."

She looked down at the letter she was still holding. "Well, from the looks of this test, you'd better start believing it."

"What am I gonna do?" I asked. I felt bad about bringing this drama to my mother's doorstep, but part of me still wished she could just make it all better, like she could when I was a child. But I knew that wasn't possible, so the most I could hope for were some ideas about how to handle things now that I knew for sure I was Marcus's father.

"Well, since you had this delivered to my address, I'm assuming that Cathy doesn't know anything about it," she said.

"Not yet. She thinks the reason I'm out so often is that I took on a second job."

My mother raised her eyebrows as she recognized the web of lies I'd been weaving. "Well, I don't exactly condone you lying to your wife, James, but in this case, you might have been right. I don't know how she's going to take this news, considering you two have just started working out all your other issues."

"I know," I agreed. "That's why I don't know how I'll ever be able to tell her."

"Well, eventually you might have to, but not yet. At least wait a while. It looks like you and Cathy might make it, but things are still a little delicate. This would only tear apart all the work you've done to fix your marriage, and I would hate to see you lose your family over this mistake," she said. Though she referred to it as my "mistake," she knew it would undoubtedly be termed an ultimate betrayal by my wife, which was why she was advising me to keep Marcus a secret.

"I don't know how much longer I can keep the secret, Ma. If she thinks I have a second job, she obviously expects to see some money, and I can't keep borrowing from my friends forever."

"True. I have some ideas about how I can help you with that." She put her hand on my shoulder. "But first, I want to meet this child for myself."

I looked up at her, not sure how I felt about her request. Was it really a good idea to let her meet Michelle and Marcus? My mother had been known to go off a time or two when she thought someone was threatening one of her children. Michelle, with all her threats to tell Cathy, was clearly not someone my mother would like. I couldn't risk letting her get indignant with Michelle. It would only give Michelle one more reason to want to pick up the phone and call my wife.

"I don't know, Ma. You and Michelle might not—"

"Nonsense," she said, obviously trying to sound innocent. "I understand what you're trying to tell me, James, and I will not do anything to upset that woman. But that boy is my grandson, and I want to see him for myself."

I stood up reluctantly, still trying to protest. "But Ma, maybe—"

"Now, James. I want to go see him now, so call that girl and tell her we're coming." She spoke in that tone that I'd come to know so well as a child. When she spoke this way, Momma was giving an ultimatum. Although I was a grown man, I was still powerless to deny her orders once they were given this way.

She smiled at me, satisfied that I'd gotten her message. Placing the DNA results on the telephone table, she said, "I'll just go turn off the stove while you call and tell her we're on our way."

I pulled out my cell phone and waited for my mother to leave the room before I made the call. I dialed, and my stomach twisted and flipped as I waited for Michelle to answer. When she picked up the phone, I wasted no time with small talk.

"Michelle, my mother wants to meet you."

"Oh, hello to you too, James," she said sarcastically, "and hell, no, I don't want to meet your mother."

"Why do you have to be this way?" I asked.

"Because I can," she said with a quick laugh. "Besides, why would I want to meet your mother? It ain't like you and me are a couple or something."

Thank God, I thought. "No, we're not, but you are the mother of her grandson."

"Oh." This stopped Michelle's roll for a moment, like it just dawned on her that this wasn't all about her. There was a child involved.

Suddenly, an idea came to me. Ma could help me keep the secret from Cathy, and I wouldn't have to be out of the house as much as I had been lately. "She wants to babysit," I said, knowing my mother would most likely go along with this.

Michelle sucked her teeth, picking up the attitude right where she left off. "I don't know this woman."

"I know, which is exactly why I want to bring her by now to meet you. Trust me, you'll like her," I insisted, banking on my mother's promise that she would behave herself around Michelle.

"Now's not a good time. Besides, I don't think I want her babysitting Marcus. He's afraid of strangers," she said in all seriousness, forgetting that she had left me to babysit him the very first night he laid eyes on me. Now I saw what this was all about. Michelle knew she was threatening the stability of my marriage every time she called me out of my house at night to watch Marcus. Allowing my mother to take over some of the babysitting duty would take away that hammer she'd been holding over my head.

"Michelle, she wouldn't be a stranger to Marcus. She's his grandmother, for God's sake."

Ma had come back into the room at some point during my conversation. I don't know how much she heard, but she obviously knew that I was getting nowhere close to convincing Michelle to let us come over.

"Let me talk to her," Ma said, reaching for the phone. I handed it over quickly, glad for some relief from Michelle's constant arguing.

"Michelle, my name is Mrs. Robinson, and I'm James's mother." Her tone was gentle yet firm. She didn't pause long enough to give Michelle a chance to protest when she said, "If I have a grandson in this world, I'd like to see him. I may be of some help to you. I am a retired nurse, so I know how to care for children."

When she did finally give Michelle a chance to speak, Ma's expression told me that she wasn't getting any of that famous attitude I was so accustomed to hearing from Michelle. I was glad that as bad as she was, Michelle still had enough sense to show some respect to her elders. In fact, the conversation went on peacefully for several minutes, and Ma even laughed a few times during the call. By the time she hung up, Michelle had agreed to let us come over so Marcus could meet his grandmother.

After she handed my phone back, she got her coat and purse. "Let's go."

* * *

During the twenty-minute ride to Michelle's house, I felt like I was in the Twilight Zone. Here I was, sitting in the car with my mother, who was excited about the idea of meeting her three-year-old grandson, the one I'd fathered with someone other than my wife. At this moment, our emotional states could not have been more opposite. As eager as she was, I was nervous about seeing Marcus for the first time since getting DNA proof. I could no longer operate with that safety net in the back of my mind, the one that said, *Don't worry, he might not be yours.* Now I had to deal with him as my child, and I felt a sudden obligation to try to bond with him, something I wasn't sure I could do.

In my state of distress, my mind started playing tricks on me. I began to think maybe that 0.1 percent chance that he wasn't mine could still turn out to be the correct result. Maybe my mother would take one look at him and announce that he didn't look a thing like our family, that he couldn't possibly be my child. Now, I knew damn well that the likelihood of that happening was just about zero, but still, the thought crossed my mind several times before we pulled up in front of Michelle's place.

When we got there, my mother took the lead. I didn't know what to say.

"Hello, Michelle. I'm Mrs. Robinson, James's mother."

Michelle extended her hand in greeting, causing me to wonder who this woman was and what she had done with the real Michelle. "Hello, Mrs. Robinson. Pleased to meet you." She turned to Marcus's bedroom and called out, "Marcus, honey, come out here and meet your other grandmother."

Michelle was laying it on thick, and my mother was eating it up. Ma gave me a look that said, *I thought you told me this woman was not nice.* I just shrugged and kept my mouth shut.

Marcus came out of the room, holding his head down.

My mother always had a way with children. "Come here, sugar plumpkin," she said.

Marcus slowly ambled over to my mother and reached up and hugged her around her thick waist. Mama's eyes watered as she looked down at him. "James, this boy looks just like your dead Uncle Bob. He's like my oldest brother come back to life." There went my last ray of hope.

My mother picked him up and patted his back. "Oh, you're so precious." Over my mother's shoulder, Michelle gave me a smirk. I could've strangled her.

From there, the visit only became more bizarre, as far as I was concerned. We visited for about an hour. Michelle showed my mother baby pictures of Marcus—minus the ones with her and Trent, who she originally thought was the father. She was acting like she was pure as the driven snow as she showed Marcus's pictures when he was three months, six months, nine months, a year, two years, and now, three years. I was too dumbfounded to speak, but she and my mother chatted up a storm. It was as if Ma had completely forgotten that I was actually married to another woman who would probably want to murder us all if she witnessed this scene.

As we were leaving, my mother said to Michelle, "If you ever need anything, or need me to babysit, you can call me."

Michelle gave me a smug look. "Yes, ma'am," she said, closing the door behind us. I didn't know if this new, kinder, gentler Michelle was real or just an act for my mother, but if it helped me avoid facing the truth with Cathy for just a little longer, I was happy to accept it for now.

28

Sonny

"Hi, Uncle Sonny," Tiffany's daughter Nikki shouted as she opened her apartment door and jumped up into my arms.

"Hey there, pretty girl. I think you forgot something."

Nikki wrapped her arms around my neck and kissed me right on the cheek. "I didn't forget," Nikki insisted. "Rule number one: Always give Uncle Sonny a big kiss when he comes through the door."

"That's my girl. Now, go watch some TV. I'm gonna go get some Chinese food in a little while so your mom doesn't have to cook." I let Nikki down and walked over to her brother, Tony, who was playing with his Game Boy.

"What's up, partner? Can I get next?" I stuck out my hand and Tony slapped it without even looking up from the game.

"Sure, Uncle Sonny, but not right now. I just started on this game."

"That's cool. Hey, did you do your homework?" He pointed toward the kitchen table. Tony was a smart kid, but he needed someone to push him. Ever since Tiffany and I started dating, I had volunteered to be that someone. "Look, I'm going to a Yankees game next Friday with my friends. You wanna go?"

"Yeah!" He stopped playing his game and looked up at me for the first time.

"Okay, I'll set it up with your mom." I looked around. Tiffany was usually sitting in the living room when I came over. "Where is your mom, anyway?"

"She's in her room talking to my dad on the phone." Tony went back to his game.

"Oh, really?" My eyebrows shot up as I walked into the kitchen and eased the wall phone receiver off the base and hit the mute button. Now I could hear them, but they couldn't hear me.

"They're your kids, Kareem. Not his. Now, I need you to give me some money to help with your children."

"What part of 'I ain't giving you shit as long as you fuckin' that nigger Sonny Harrison' don't you understand? I don't give a fuck if they starve."

"You a triflin'-ass bastard, you know that, Kareem? Why I ever regarded you as a man at one time, I don't know. Only a sorry-ass bastard would be like this to his children. You'd rather see your kids hungry and out on the street than help me."

"Who you callin' a bastard, bitch? Don't make me come over there and whip your ass." I almost released the mute button and invited him over. One of these days, Kareem and I were going to tango, and when we did, he was going to wish he never met Tiffany.

Tiffany got quiet, then she said, "I'm not afraid of you anymore, Kareem."

"You should be. As many times as I put my foot in your ass. Now, stop calling my phone before seven. You running up my minutes."

Kareem hung up, and I heard Tiffany mumble, "Damn, now what am I gonna do?"

I smiled. Tiffany didn't have anything to worry about. Whether she knew it or not, I had her back. I hung up the phone, walking from the kitchen to her bedroom as if I hadn't heard a thing. She was sitting on the bed, trying to hide tears. I sat down beside her.

"Hey, babe, what's the matter?" I put my arm around her, patting her back, and she laid her head on my shoulder. "Are you all right?"

"No, I'm not all right. That bastard I married is tryin' to say he's not gonna give me child-support money anymore because I'm messin' with you. He promised me that money, Sonny. I was going to pay the kids' tuition with that money. God, I can't stand that bastard. He don't even care about his own kids." Tiffany balled her right fist and punched it into her open palm.

"Fuck him, Tiffany. I told you before I'd help you with your bills. Haven't I told you that I want to be here for you? Now, how much you need to pay?"

Tiffany lifted her head as if she was about to say something, but when I smiled at her, she lowered her head again as if she was ashamed. "Yes, I remember you said you'd like to help out, but I can't ask you for that kind of money, Sonny."

"Why not? I'm your man, aren't I? Don't make things harder than what they have to be, Tif. You've got me right here saying I'd like to help you. I'll take care of the kids' schooling bill. It's not a problem, okay?"

"Yes, but they're not your kids. He should be paying their tuition." I think Tiffany could tell I was a little hurt by the "not your kids" comment, because she grabbed my hand and spurted her second statement as quick as a reflex action. "The truth is, I may need you to help me with some other bills if I don't get a new job soon."

"New job? What's wrong with where you work? I thought you liked your job."

"I did, but they fired me today. They just let me go without warning."

"Oh, no. That sounds kind of fishy. Did you ask them what were their grounds for firing you?"

"Yes. I was told some crap about downsizing my position, but I think that shit was racist." She looked like she was about to cry again. I noticed her bottom lip trembled as she spoke.

"Don't cry, Tif. We're going to get through this. I've heard of workplaces being inconsiderate like this before, but we're not going to let this beat us."

"How am I going to pay my rent and keep my kids in private school? I don't got no job, Sonny." She looked so frustrated.

"I think I've got the answer to your problem."

"What's that?"

"You're worried about paying your rent and the kids going to good schools, right?"

"Yeah, and . . ."

"Well, why don't you move in with me? I've got this big old empty house that both you and the kids love. They can each have their own bedroom, which they don't have here. There's plenty of fresh air out there in Long Island, and the schools are good. They can play outside and not be stuck up in this apartment after school." I could see the wheels spinning around in Tiffany's head, and I was sure she'd come to the same conclusion I did, but I was wrong.

"No, Sonny." She shook her head. "It's a tempting offer, but I can't do it. Not yet, anyway. We just started dating, and I promised myself I wouldn't live with a man unless I was married to him."

"Is this a roundabout way to get me to ask for your hand in marriage?"

"No, this is me trying to convince myself I'm doing the right thing. 'Cause if one more thing happens to me, I might just take you up on your offer."

"So, Tiffany, if you don't come to stay with me, how are you going to pay your bills?"

"I've got a little money stashed away that my mother left me when she passed last year, and I can get unemployment. Oh, and I'm going to take my ex to court."

"Yeah, but Tif, are you sure everything will be taken care of on a measly little unemployment check? And who knows how long you'll be battling back and forth with your ex? Court could take a long while. You sure you don't need my help?"

"I'm not sure of anything right now, Sonny, and don't get me wrong, I'm going to need your help. I just can't move in with you right now, but I reserve the right to change my mind." Tiffany kissed me. "I love you, Sonny."

"I love you too."

"Uncle Sonny, are we going to get some Chinese food or what?" Nikki walked into the room and jumped on the bed.

"Yes, we're going." I stood up and smiled at Tiffany. "We're going to get through this together, me and you, all right?" Tiffany nodded and gave me a slight smile. "Look, let me run out and get this girl some Chinese food before she loses her mind. Come on, Nikki."

29

James

"Okay, James, have a nice time at the game." Cathy gave me a quick kiss and practically pushed me out the front door. I was headed to a baseball game with Sonny and Brent, and our boys were sleeping over at a friend's house for the weekend, so Cathy was looking forward to a full day alone in the house. As much as she loved her family and missed the boys whenever they were away from her for more than a few hours, I know she longed for those rare moments of peace that came when we were all gone. She had a few DVDs lined up on the coffee table, all chick flicks, of course, and water on the stove to make herself some herbal tea. After a movie, she would probably go upstairs and soak in a tub scented with some sort of feminine concoction she picked up at the Bath & Body Works.

"Thanks, honey. You enjoy your day at home," I told her.

"I will. Do you think you'll be going out to dinner or something after the game?" Her eyes looked hopeful when she asked the question, like she was trying to squeeze as many male-free hours as she could out of this day.

"Sure, babe. You don't have to worry about making anything for dinner. I'll pick something up before I come home."

"Sounds good," she said, already taking a few steps back into the living room, glancing impatiently toward the waiting DVD player.

I chuckled as I walked to my car. I was happy she was excited about her day. Cathy was a great mother, and she took good care of me too, so her time off was well deserved. Of course, my guilt over the situation with Michelle and Marcus probably made me even more anxious to see my wife this happy. I had this terrible feeling of dread that at some point soon I would have to confess to her about Marcus being my son, and then there might be very few moments of happiness in my household. If it was still my household.

As I drove down the street away from my home, my mind, as it had so many times since I received the paternity test results, raced through the many possible ways the scenario could play out. I still hadn't come up with a plan to reveal the truth to my wife without permanently damaging our relationship. One thing I was sure of, though, was that I had to be the one to tell her. The news could not come from anyone else.

That was why I was headed to Michelle's house before I met Brent and Sonny for the game. I had to keep the peace with her, so I promised to take Marcus from her for a few hours to give her a break. Funny how with Cathy I felt the break was well deserved, but with Michelle I still had this nagging feeling that she was taking advantage of the situation and would get rid of Marcus for a day any chance she got. But whatever the case, I was going to pick him up and take him to my mother's house.

Michelle seemed to be calling more and more frequently to demand that I babysit, and sooner or later it would be impossible for me to keep up with the lies. Cathy was satisfied with the lie that I had a second job, but at the rate things were progressing, I'd soon be "going to work" every damn night. Thank God my mother was willing to help out, though I knew Michelle still wished I would be the one watching Marcus all the time. She knew that all this babysitting would eventually cause a strain in my marriage, and I'm sure that's exactly what she wanted. Ever since we ended up wrestling over the phone that one night, and the kiss the night I'd been forced to give her when I got the DNA swab from her mouth, she'd been making suggestive comments about our once-active sexual relationship. *Didn't I miss it?* she wanted to know, making it obvious that she did. I guess she figured that if she could pull me out of my bed enough nights of the week, I would have no chance to have sex with my wife, and I'd be horny enough to take her up on her offer to rekindle our relationship.

Like everything else with Michelle, I played along. While I didn't act on any of her advances, I didn't come right out and refuse them, either. Because I let her keep that little bit of hope alive that we might get together again, I was reasonably sure she wouldn't try to contact Cathy.

This would be the first time that Marcus would spend a day with my mother, but I was confident things would be fine. They had actually hit it off well on the day she went to Michelle's house and met him. She always loved babies, and while this one was not conceived in the best of circumstances, he was still her grandchild, and she was looking forward to getting to know him. Michelle wasn't going to work that day, but she had called, claiming she just needed some time away from Marcus, and my mother had happily agreed to take him so I could still go to the game.

When I knocked on Michelle's door, she let me in, and I couldn't help but notice her appearance. I guess she wasn't planning to try to seduce me that day. Or, if she was, she was sure going about it the wrong way. Her outfit was nice enough, fitting her curves tightly the way she liked, but her face was totally without makeup, and her hair was wrapped in a dingy old scarf. I was actually relieved that it didn't look like we'd be playing any of her games. And the way she greeted me confirmed that she was all about business today.

"You know it's the end of the week, right?"

"Uh, yeah, Michelle, I looked at a calendar today. Thanks," I answered, reminding myself to try to control the sarcasm. I wanted to get Marcus and get out of there with as little hassle as possible.

"Shut up, James. You know damn well what I'm talking about."

Of course I did. This was Michelle's reminder that I owed her some money for child support. As long as I gave her something weekly, she agreed that she wouldn't go the legal route to get court-enforced payments. That was the last thing I needed—for the money to start disappearing from my paychecks. I reached into my pocket and pulled out two hundred-dollar bills, which I handed to her.

She looked down at the money and a smile came across her face. I seriously doubted that she was thinking about all the things she could buy for her son with that money.

"Marcus, your daddy is here," she called toward the bedroom. I still had to get used to being referred to as Daddy by another family. But regardless, I couldn't help but grin when I saw him come into the hallway. The kid really was cute, and he looked so eager to be going with me. He was innocent in this whole mess, and I didn't want to see him hurt, no matter how much I couldn't stand his mother.

"Hey, little man, you ready to go?" I asked as I reached my hand out to him.

"Yeah, Daddy." He gave me a big high-five and laughed.

"Okay, then. Why don't you go pick out a few of your toys to bring with you?" I suggested, knowing my mother didn't really have anything in the house he could play with. Marcus ran to his bedroom to gather his toys, and I stood waiting in the living room.

"You can sit down if you want," Michelle said, sounding like she couldn't care less what I did, before she headed for the kitchen.

I took a seat on the couch and checked my watch. There was plenty of time for me to get Marcus to my mother's house and meet Sonny and Brent in time to see the first pitch.

"Yeah, girl, it's me." I heard Michelle's voice coming from the kitchen. She was obviously on the phone talking to one of her friends, who was probably someone else's baby mama headache.

"What? Yeah, he's here. Uh-huh. I got two hundred." I rolled my eyes when I heard that. I wondered how often she and her friends compared notes on how much money they were able to extort from their babies' fathers.

Michelle laughed, then I heard her say, "Hell, yeah, we're still going. Call up and find out how crowded it is in there today. I don't want to be waiting all day to get my hair done. What? No, I don't want to skip it. Janay is gonna watch Marcus for me tonight when James brings him back, and you know my hair gotta look good for the club tonight."

It took every bit of self-control that I had not to jump off the couch and go into the kitchen. Now, I know there are probably plenty of men out there who have their suspicions about where their child-support money actually goes, but I was a brother with living proof that not a penny of that money was going to benefit my son. That two hundred dollars was going to end up in the hands of some weave-wearing, gum-popping chick down at the hair salon, who probably had a few baby daddies of her own on the hook for loot every month. That shit burned me up.

I was on the couch doing some deep breathing to calm myself down when Michelle strolled back into the living room. "Marcus," she yelled, "hurry up. You don't want to keep your daddy waiting."

"What's the matter?" I asked. "You in a hurry to get to your hair appointment?"

She rolled her eyes at me but didn't bother to answer my question as she picked up her purse and pulled out her wallet.

"I can't believe you, Michelle."

"What is your problem?" she asked calmly, like she didn't have a care in the world. Shoot, she didn't, now that she had my cash safely tucked away in her bag.

"You know what my problem is. I gave you that money to take care of Marcus, and you don't even have the decency to *pretend* you're gonna spend it on him."

"Oh, I know you're not gonna go there," she started, turning to me with an ice-cold stare. "Shoot, as much money as I spend on that child every day, I'm broke by the end of the week. As long as your son is provided for, you shouldn't care where your share of his support money goes. Trust me, Marcus gets everything he needs."

"Somehow I doubt that, Michelle." I stood up and stepped closer to her. "You're so damn concerned about going to get your party on at the club tonight, you're gonna leave him with my mother all day and then leave him with another babysitter tonight. As a matter of fact, whoever this Janay person is, why couldn't you have called her all those times you called me to come babysit?"

"Oh, no, you didn't just say that. I'm a good mother to my son, James, and just because I want to go out once in a while don't mean I don't take care of my baby. And as far as calling you to watch him, shit, he's your son. Be glad I don't make you take him for a whole weekend."

So much for getting out of there without a hassle. . . . Her attitude, like she was doing me some kind of favor with our current arrangement, had me at the boiling point. My anger was out of control now, and I didn't stop to think about what I said next.

"You know what? Forget you. Maybe your girl Janay can

watch him all day, 'cause I damn sure ain't gonna let you take advantage of my mother as your new babysitter. It's bad enough you keep calling me to watch him and bring you money all the damn time. I can see it now," I said, mocking the sistah-girl tone she'd used on the phone a few minutes before, " 'Yeah, girl, I got his mother wrapped around my finger. She'll watch Marcus any time I want.' Well, guess what, Michelle? It ain't happening. You can watch him your damn self!" As I shouted, I spotted Marcus out of the corner of my eye. He had come into the room while we were fighting, and he stood there now, his arms full of action figures he had been planning to take to my mother's house, his face full of confusion and pain.

I felt like shit, but there was nothing I could do now. The stress of everything Michelle had been putting me through for weeks now had pushed me to this point. There was no turning back. I headed for the door.

"You'll be sorry if you walk out that door, James," Michelle threatened. I didn't care what she had to say. My legs carried me forward until I was in my car, driving away from her house.

It wasn't until I was almost a mile away before I realized the seriousness of what I had just done. The image of Marcus's sad face was still stabbing at my conscience. I had done exactly what I had hoped would never happen; I had hurt him. And even worse, I had enraged Michelle, and I knew what she was capable of when it came to revenge.

I gathered the courage to dial my home phone. As I listened to it ring, I said a silent prayer that Michelle hadn't already called Cathy. If she had, I didn't know what I was going to say, but there seemed to be no choice but to make this call. Depending on what Cathy had to say, I could either go to the game with my boys, all the while worrying that Michelle still might call, or I'd head home to try to pick up the pieces of my marriage.

As it turned out, neither one of those things happened. The answering machine picked up at my house. Cathy must have turned off the ringer when she sat down to watch her movies. If I was lucky, she had also turned down the volume on the answering machine. Maybe the worst that would happen was Michelle's number showing up on the caller ID. I would just have to get home early enough to check the messages on the machine before Cathy got to them. My breathing returned to a more normal rate as I realized I just might be able to handle this mess.

I went to the game with Brent and Sonny, though I don't remember much of what happened there. My mind was still on overdrive, thinking through my dilemma. When should I tell Cathy? And would she ever be able to forgive me? Or was it already too late? Had Michelle left a message that Cathy had already listened to? My boys noticed how preoccupied I was, and it was easy for them to guess who was the cause of my bad mood, but they didn't push for details. I told them I didn't want their day to be ruined the way mine had been, and they left it alone after that.

By the end of the game, I was more than ready to go home. I know I had promised Cathy I'd stay out later so she could have more time alone, but I needed to see her now. As much as I tried to find a way around it, the time had come for me to admit everything to her. Things with Michelle were not going to get better. At this point, it seemed like it was just a matter of time before she got pissed off enough and contacted Cathy, if she hadn't already, and I could not let it happen that way. My wife had to hear it from me if there was any hope of saving our marriage.

On the drive home, I came up with the words I would say to my wife to tell her about my son. I couldn't think past those first few sentences, because I had no idea how she would react. It wasn't possible to plan my defense if I couldn't be sure she'd even want to listen to me once I broke the news. I would just have to let things flow whichever way they did once the conversation was started. I was just grateful that my boys would not be home that night to hear any of this.

As I headed up the walkway to my home, I tried to prolong my confession just a little longer by taking slow, tiny steps. By the time I reached the door, my hands were shaking and I had to fight not to lose the contents of my stomach all over the steps. I put my hand on the doorknob, but before I could turn it, the door flew open.

There was Cathy, fury on her face. I looked down and had to grab the railing to steady myself when my knees gave out. In one hand she held a suitcase, and standing beside her, action figures still in his hand, was Marcus.

30

Sonny

I drove down South Road, headed toward the projects, and tried my best not to show any fear. The last thing you can do in the hood is act like you're afraid. Fortunately, I'd grown up in South Jamaica so I knew a little about how to handle myself, but things were different back then. People just got drunk on the weekends, and when dudes fought, they battled with their fists or maybe a knife. Nowadays, everyone was packing hardware, so you never knew when you might get caught up in some shit.

Wearily, my eyes scanned the street. I'd never seen more drug dealers, ten-year-old lookouts, and crackheads in one area in my life, all going about their business like five-oh didn't exist. I guess I must've looked like new money pulling into the neighborhood, because all eyes were on me as I headed to my destination.

My cousin Leroy, better known as Lowjack, was a master thief in his own right, and still lived in my old building. I was headed to his place because I knew Lowjack was just the man to help me carry out my little scheme. The only problem was that showing up unannounced could be detrimental to my health. Lowjack was always up to some unlawful shit. I usually stayed away from him for that reason, but this day, I could care less about what he was up to. I only hoped he'd agree to what I was about to ask him to do.

After I parked my car, I reached into my glove compartment and took out an empty mayonnaise jar with holes nailed into the tin top. As I headed to Lowjack's apartment, I looked down at the empty jar and thought of how I was only moments away from having the crucial elements to making my plan a success. I rushed into the building, stepping over a couple of winos and baseheads passed out in the hallway. Before reaching the fourth floor, I endured the smell of piss, body odors, and soiled Pampers, strong enough reasons to make me want to turn back before losing everything I'd eaten. But I remained focus on what I came for.

Once I made it to Lowjack's door, I paused before knocking. It had been a while since we saw each other, and there was still the possibility that he'd tell me he wouldn't be able to help me. I also knew that I'd never know unless I tried, so I knocked on the door.

"Who is it?" a gruff voice called out.

"Sonny."

"Sonny who?"

"Your cousin Sonny, fool. Open the door."

"Sonny! Oh, shit, what up, nigga?" Suddenly the door opened.

It must have been my work clothes, because Lowjack looked me up and down like I was the police. Then he stepped outside the door to look down the hallway. He finally let me in after he was satisfied no one else was with me. I'd always known him to be a paranoid brother, but when he started to frisk me, I started to get worried that maybe I shouldn't even be in that apartment. My suspicion was that my cousin was back to boosting again, something that was confirmed when I entered his apartment to see, amongst the filth, more stereos, TVs, DVD players, and computers lined up along the walls than in a Circuit City warehouse. My eyes popped out of my head when I saw the new IBM laptop computer that all the computer geeks were talking about online. I didn't even think they were out yet.

"Hey, cuz, long time no see. Sorry about all this frisking and shit, but a brother can't be too safe in my line of work." I was still staring at the laptop, wondering how much he was selling it for, when Lowjack snapped me out of my trance by grabbing me up in a bear hug. For a moment, I could hardly breathe, and then he let me go.

"I heard you moved back to New York. What you been up to? And where's that fine-ass wife of yours, anyway?"

"Man, I had to kick that bitch to the curb," I lied as we pounded fists. "I'm back with my old girl, Tiffany. I been meaning to come by and holler at you before now, but you know how things can be with work and all."

Lowjack cut his eyes. "Man, you know I ain't never worked no real job."

I looked around nervously. My skin was crawling, his place was so dirty, but just standing there, I knew I'd come to the right place for what I was looking for.

"So, what brings you back to the hood? Can I interest you in a TV or a DVD player? I saw you looking at that laptop. I got a special on computers. Don't you work with computers?" I followed him over to the couch, but I couldn't bring myself to sit down next to him.

"Well, cuz, I'm tempted, but what I really need is a favor."

Lowjack scratched on his day-old shadow. "A favor, huh? Damn, how come only time family comes to visit me is when they need a favor?"

I wanted to say, "Have you ever taken a good look at your place?" but I didn't speak at all. I think he got the hint anyway.

"So, what kind of favor you need?"

I fumbled around in my head for a minute for the right words. Lowjack sat patiently, awaiting my reply. I soon realized there was no other way to put it than to just ask, so I let the words roll off my tongue.

"What I need is some roaches." I was serious, but I don't think he took it that way.

"You need some what?" He looked at me with a wrinkled nose and twisted lips. "What the fuck you mean, you need some roaches?"

"Like I said, I need some roaches. And from the looks of this place, you got plenty of roaches."

Lowjack glared. "Yo, man, you ain't got to insult my crib. I know I got roaches. Everybody in these projects got roaches."

"No, man, you don't understand. I really need some roaches." I handed him my empty jar.

Lowjack held up the jar, staring into the pricked top. "You're serious, aren't you?"

"Yep, I sure am."

"Well, aw'ight then." He gave me the jar. "If you're serious, I guess you came to the right place." He pointed at a door in the rear of the room. "The biggest ones are in the kitchen under the sink. Go knock yourself out."

"Hold on there, cuz. This isn't exactly what I was thinking. I ain't going in there by myself." I handed him the jar again. "I want you to collect them for me."

"What! Man, are you serious? You want me to get you some roaches?"

"Yep, I sure do." I nodded.

Lowjack stared at the jar, then smiled. "Aw'ight, I got this. But it's gonna cost you."

I reached into my pocket and pulled out a twenty-dollar bill. Lowjack snatched the money out of my hands. "I guess you don't want too many roaches, 'cause a jar full of roaches costs more than twenty dollars around here. I'd say a jar full of roaches gonna run you at least fifty bucks."

I shook my head, reaching into my pocket to pull out another twenty and a ten. This was starting to cost more than I expected, but if things went the way I planned, it would be well worth the money.

Lowjack took the cash from me with a smile. "Now you gonna get a lot of roaches. Follow me."

I walked behind him into his small kitchen. He put the lights on, and I swear to God, you would've thought the walls were moving, so many roaches scattered from the light. Lowjack knew how to catch some bugs, too. He went over to this spot under the sink and within ten minutes, he had my jar three-fourths filled, and not soon enough for me. I was scratching and itching so much, I was starting to feel like I had hives. All I wanted to do was get the hell out of there and take a shower.

"That all you want?" he asked quizzically. "'Cause we got some real good rats in the basement. I could let you have a couple of them real cheap."

I wasn't sure if I should laugh or not, but I actually contemplated his offer. No, I decided, a few rats would probably be over the top. "Naw, man, this is fine."

"Okay, cuz, don't use them all in one place. There's plenty more where these came from, and if you call ahead next time, I can deliver."

"I'll remember that."

Lowjack kissed his fifty dollars as he let me out the door. "You know what, cuz? You one crazy muthafucka."

I left his apartment with a big smile plastered on my face.

Even the winos and junkies didn't bother me as I sauntered down the hallway with my roaches.

Twenty minutes later, I was walking through Tiffany's front door. She didn't know it, but I'd made my own set of keys when I took her car to the car wash last week. By the time she got back from picking up the kids at school, I'd be long gone. I placed the jar of roaches on the kitchen table, then reached into my jacket and pulled out a cigar. I lit it up and walked around the house, letting the smoke waft throughout the rooms.

I made my way back to the kitchen, staring at the jar of roaches. In one swift move, I opened the lid and let half of them out in the kitchen. They scrambled out of the jar like, "Free at last! Free at last!" I released the other half in the living room, making sure to leave about an inch of them in the jar, which I spread across Tiffany's bed. You'd think after driving around with them for twenty minutes I'd be used to them, but they still gave me the willies.

If this didn't get Tiffany to move in with me, nothing would. I hated to do it, but after spending all that time making those calls to get her fired, I had to do something. Tiffany, like most women, just didn't know what was good for her. And as her man, it was up to me to help her to make those decisions. The key was not to get caught.

I crushed the cigar's burning end out between my thumb and forefinger, then put the butt in a candy dish in the living room. I looked around before I left and was satisfied with the job I'd done. The roaches were crawling everywhere.

I'd just walked in the door when my phone rang. I didn't expect Tiffany to call this soon, but when I looked at the caller ID, I saw her number. I took a deep breath, trying to keep myself from laughing when I answered the phone.

"Hello," I said nonchalantly.

"Sonny, Sonny, you gotta help me!" Tiffany screamed hysterically into the phone.

I held the phone away from my head and chuckled quietly. "What's the matter, Tif?" I asked calmly. I was proud of myself for the acting job I was doing.

"Roaches!"

"What's that?"

"I said, roaches. We've got roaches. They're all over the place. Even in my bed."

"C'mon, Tif, stop exaggerating. Just step on it."

"I'm not exaggerating. There's millions of these things in here."

"Calm down, Tiffany."

"I can't calm down. These things are crawling on me," she whimpered.

I could imagine her brushing one off her arm as we spoke. "Tiff, don't panic," I said soothingly.

"Don't tell me not to panic, Sonny. Goddammit! I can't stand roaches. I've never had them before."

"I know. Maybe they bombed the apartments next door."

"They ain't bombed shit. It was Kareem. I can still smell his stinky-ass cigar. I know it was Kareem."

My face broke into a satisfied grin. God, do I love it when a plan comes together. I'd found a pack of Kareem's cigars a few weeks ago in a box of his personal shit that Tiffany had planned on giving back to him. She'd mentioned that one of the things she couldn't stand about him was his nasty-ass cigars, because of how the smell lingered in her furniture. That's why I brought a few of his brand of cigars to leave as evidence. What better scapegoat for the roaches than her pain-in-the-ass ex-husband?

"How do you know it was him?"

"He left a cigar. And he always said no nigga gon' be walking on his carpet in his house and over his kids. He will do anything to bring me down. As if I'm not going through enough."

"Calm down, baby."

"I can't calm down, Sonny. Is that offer to move in still open?"

I had her just where I wanted. The plan had worked to perfection. "Sure, you can move in anytime you want."

"Thank you, Sonny."

"No problem, baby." I got straight to the point now. "But we just have to come up with some household rules if we're all going to be together under one roof."

"Sonny, I'm not worried about no rules. Just get a truck and come move my stuff."

"All right, I'm on my way. I just have to see if I can get a hold of James and Brent to help me move you. You know we're gonna have to leave everything outside and spray it before we move it into my house," I told her, still feeling queasy at the thought of all those damn bugs crawling everywhere.

"Whatever, Sonny, just hurry up."

I hung up happily. Things had finally fallen into place the way I wanted them to. I stepped outside to the U-Haul truck, which was waiting in my driveway. I called James and Brent to let them know I needed help moving Tiffany and her kids because they had an unexplained roach infestation at their apartment. I hated to use my friends in my schemes like this, but you know what they say. . . . What they don't know won't hurt them.

31

James

The look on Cathy's face as she stood in the doorway holding Marcus's hand was enough to make me want to turn and run away as fast as I could. Only problem was that my legs wouldn't move. My heart felt like it was already running in a hundred-yard dash, but my feet stayed firmly planted on the top step, so I was forced to look into my wife's eyes and see the accusation within.

"Hi, Daddy," Marcus said happily, oblivious to the anger shooting out of Cathy's pores.

"Hey, Marcus," I said weakly, wishing he could just disappear into thin air. "Uh, hi, Cathy."

"Oh, so you know him, huh?" She spat the words at me like each one was a poisonous dart aimed at my head.

With a quick glance toward Marcus, I braced myself for what I knew would be the longest night of my life. "Yeah, I know him. His mother Michelle's a friend of mine from my old route. Did she bring him by?" I asked in a lame attempt to string together some sort of lie that Cathy might believe. I don't think I was doing such a good job, though.

"Yeah, she brought him by, all right, but she didn't say anything about being your friend. In fact, she called herself your baby's mama." Her lips were twisted into a horrible grimace as she recounted the details of how she came to have my son here with her. Aside from the anger and attitude she was giving me, it was clear that Cathy was in emotional pain right now. I felt sick knowing that I was the sole cause of her heartbreak.

"Cathy. . . ." I started to speak, but didn't really know what I could say to make this better. She wasn't about to help me out, either. She stood with her arms crossed over her chest, her eyebrows raised, as if challenging me to try to lie my way out of this one. I finally found the courage to ask, "Can I come in so we can talk?"

"What could we possibly have to say that I would want to hear, James? Some bitch just dropped off your kid on my doorstep. I think that says it all."

"But I just found out about him myself," I said desperately. I looked down to Marcus, who had wandered away from Cathy's grasp and was sitting on the floor near the front door, playing quietly with his superheroes. I hoped he was engrossed enough in his game that he wouldn't be listening to this conversation.

"Oh, that makes sense. You just found out about him, huh? Well, he sure seems familiar with you, *Daddy*." Her sarcastic tone almost made "Daddy" sound like a dirty word. I guess in her mind, the fact that I'd fathered a child outside of our marriage was actually a pretty obscene idea. "Just answer this for me, James. Is he your son?"

"Well . . ." My eyes wandered everywhere except to Cathy's face. I couldn't bear to look at her as I admitted, "Yes, he is my son. But—"

"There is no but, James!" she shouted at me, her voice trembling like she was on the verge of tears. "You have another child! You're my husband, but another bitch had your baby! How do you think that makes me feel?" Her tears were now flowing freely.

I reached for her hand, but she snatched it away. I stood helplessly and watched her sob for a few seconds. Finally, she let me touch her arm and I guided her to the step so we could sit down. I didn't try to put my arm around her as she cried, knowing she probably wouldn't allow me. But as I sat next to my wife and watched her in agony, I kept murmuring quietly, "I am so sorry. I can't tell you how sorry I am."

At one point, Marcus tried to come out to the steps with us, but I quickly told him to go back into the boys' bedroom, where he would find lots more toys. He ran away happily. I was glad he was young enough to ignore what was going on between me and my wife.

When Cathy's tears slowed a little, she turned to me with glistening eyes and asked, "How old is he?"

"He's three."

She looked across the yard, and I could tell she was trying to do the math in her head.

"Yes," I assured her, "he was conceived during the time you and I were having so many problems."

She cut her eyes in my direction. "Is that supposed to make it all right? No matter how many problems we were having, we were still married, James. Did you really think going out to fuck another woman was going to *help* our marriage?"

I cringed at the truth of her words. In hindsight, I knew that having an affair with Michelle was not the smartest choice. Obviously it couldn't improve my marriage, but at the time, I was feeling terrible, and having another woman desire me when my own wife was so disgusted with me seemed like just the thing I needed. I didn't begin the affair thinking about what might happen in the future. I wasn't thinking about the fact that I might be able to fix my struggling marriage, and I certainly wasn't thinking about the fact that Michelle might have a child. I was only thinking about what I needed at the time, which was a boost for my wounded ego. Once I got what I needed, I had no more use for Michelle and the affair ended. But now I would be suffering the consequences for the rest of my life. And Cathy was here to remind me that I wasn't the only one who would be affected by my mistake.

"What exactly am I supposed to tell our boys?" she asked.

As I looked at her and thought about how I'd damaged my family, my own tears started to flow. "Oh, baby, I am so sorry."

My attempt at tenderness just made her roll her eyes. "Please do not try to be kind to me right now, James, after you just ripped my heart out. Just tell me what you plan to do with this boy."

"Well," I started, not really sure what I could do. The only thing I was certain about right now was that I wished I could murder Michelle with my bare hands. "When his mother comes back to get him, we can sit down and decide how to tell the boys."

"You must be joking," she said, her tears now dried up, her anger back in full force. "First of all, I don't know why you think that boy's mother is coming back to get him. Only thing she said when she left him was, 'James will know what to do with him.' She didn't say anything about being back anytime soon. And that bitch was dressed like she was going out to the club. . . . Either that or to walk the streets, I'm really not sure. But you can bet she ain't coming back here at least until tomorrow."

I squeezed my eyes shut tightly, still wishing this was just a bad dream that would be over soon. But with my eyes closed, an image flashed across my mind of Cathy standing in the doorway when I got home. She was holding Marcus's hand, but it was her other hand that concerned me now.

"She left him with a suitcase, didn't she?" I asked in a defeated tone.

Cathy looked like she wanted to hit me for being so slow. "You damn right she did. Now, do you still wanna talk about 'when his mother comes back to get him'?" she asked, mimicking me in a voice that probably sounded as stupid as I had.

"She's just doing this to fuck with me," I said, trying to convince myself as much as to convince my wife. I stood up and went to the living room, each step feeling like a walk down death row. Part of me knew I was going to find a hell of a lot more in that suitcase than clothes and diapers for one overnight visit. But in no way was I prepared for what was really in there.

As I held my breath and unzipped the small suitcase, I cursed myself a thousand times for every day I'd slept with Michelle. The breath escaped from my lungs and I had to suppress a scream when I saw what Michelle had packed for Marcus. On top of several outfits were two things that made it more than clear what Michelle planned. She had packed his birth certificate and his Medicaid card. She had no intentions of coming back to get Marcus anytime soon, if ever.

My hands were flat on the floor beside the suitcase, and I stayed on my knees, trying to control my breathing before I started hyperventilating. I couldn't get myself together enough to form a coherent thought. Could this shit possibly get any worse?

Cathy was standing over me now, looking at the contents of the suitcase, and in a low, vicious tone, she said, "You are such a stupid asshole. The least you could have done if you were going to fuck around was stay out of the ghetto, James. But no, you had to pick a woman so low, she would dump her own baby just to get your attention."

I turned my head to look up at her, and again, all I could manage to say was, "I am so sorry, Cathy."

"Yeah, you damn sure are sorry. You are one sorry-ass man. Now get *your child*, and get the hell outta my house."

I looked at her, knowing there was no argument I could make at this point to change her mind. I closed Marcus's suitcase and pulled myself up off the floor. Without another word, I went to the bedroom to get him.

"Where are we going?" he asked as I led him toward the living room.

"Well, Marcus, I think we'll go stay with my mother tonight," I explained, trying to sound like this was just a little change of plans, and not, quite possibly, the last time I would set foot in this house I shared with my wife and sons.

"Oh, good," Marcus answered. "I like your mother."

Cathy spun around, looking like she could spit fire. "Did he just say he likes your mother? Your mother knows about him?"

I sighed, too drained to even try to explain. "Yes, Cathy, my mother knows."

"You son of a bitch. Get the fuck out my house," she said ominously. "Take your goddamn child and go to your fucking momma's house. She's probably already got a room fixed up for him."

"Cathy, please. . . . She—"

Her palm was in front of my face in an instant. "I do not wanna hear a word you have to say, James. Just be a fuckin' man and get out now." She turned her back on me, and there was nothing I could do but take Marcus's hand and lead him outside to my car.

Marcus was sound asleep by the time we reached my mother's house. I carried him in my arms up the steps to the front door. Just like Cathy had done earlier, my mother pulled it open before I even had a chance to knock.

"Hi, Ma. How did you—"

"I just got off the phone with your wife," she told me, the annoyance clear in her tone. "I don't appreciate her cursing me out like that, James."

My shoulders slumped, and I had to hold on to Marcus tighter so I wouldn't drop him. "I'm sorry, Ma." It seemed like I was going to spend the rest of the night, and perhaps the rest of my life, apologizing for the mess I'd created. "I didn't know she was gonna call you. I guess she told you what happened, huh?"

"Yes, she told me." Her eyes traveled down to my arms, and she looked at Marcus, who was still sleeping. "You might as well bring him in and put him down in my bed."

I followed her inside and carried Marcus into my mother's bedroom. Once he was tucked under the covers, I headed back out to the living room to receive the lecture I knew was coming. I sat on the couch and looked at my mother expectantly.

"What are you looking at?" she asked. "Don't you have anything to say for yourself?"

"What can I say, Ma? I fu—I mean, I messed up, and now I'm gonna be paying for it for the rest of my life. Cathy looked like she doesn't ever wanna talk to me again. What did she say to you, anyway?"

"You mean, after she got through cursing me out for being a part of your 'elaborate deception,' as she called it? Well, she told me that since I seemed to support you and all your lies, I could keep you and your illegitimate child here."

The way she said it, I knew my mother had no intention of letting me stay with her for too long. I know she loved me, and she had offered to help with Marcus once in a while, but my mother enjoyed her privacy, and she sure wasn't looking to give it up just because of my stupidity.

"Ma, I know we can't stay here forever, but I have nowhere to go right now. Can we at least stay here tonight? Tomorrow I'm gonna find Michelle and make her take Marcus back anyway."

She frowned, but I knew there was no way she would refuse me. "You can have the couch. And I don't have any food for a child, so in the morning you'll have to go get him some cereal or something."

I nodded. "I really appreciate this."

"Mm-hmm. I bet you do. Now, what are you gonna do about your wife? You can't lose your family over this mess, James."

"I don't know what I'm gonna do." I stood up and headed to the door. I opened it, then turned to finish the conversation. "I have to give Cathy some time, I think, but I'm gonna do whatever it takes to get my family back together."

"And what about this boy's mother? What was she thinking about, leaving her child like that?"

"I wish I knew. I knew she was low class, but I didn't think she would stoop to this level."

She shook her head. "We talked about this, James. I thought you understood that you had to keep Michelle happy so she wouldn't do something like this. What happened?"

"I think she was just mad at me 'cause we had a fight and I told her I wouldn't watch Marcus for her tonight. I know I shouldn't have fought with her, but you just don't know, Ma. She knows how to push my buttons, and I just lost control." I looked at my mother, hoping she'd understand, but she still had a disapproving look on her face. "I'll find her tomorrow and talk some sense into her. She'll take him back." As I went to the car to get Marcus's suitcase, I could only hope that I was right—that it was possible to convince Michelle that this was not the way to go.

32

Brent

The doorbell rang, and I let go of the mattress I was carrying to the basement in order to run up the stairs and answer the door. I'd been cleaning out what used to be our guestroom so that it could be transformed into the baby's nursery. Alison and I had big plans for this room, including adding crown moldings and hardwood floors. I loved working with my hands, and planned on doing most of the work myself. It would be a welcome distraction from the depression I'd been going through after Jackie had broken up with me three weeks ago. I guess that old cliché was true, you don't know what you have until it's gone, because I felt like a piece of me had been missing ever since Jackie walked out that door in San Francisco. I loved Jackie more than I wanted to admit. Don't get me wrong, I made the right choice by coming home to my wife and unborn child, but if I had to do it all over again, I wouldn't even think twice about having another affair with Jackie.

"Who?" I yelled as I approached the door. Like every other time I answered the door, I was praying it would be Jackie, but of course, it wasn't.

"It's Jason, Mr. Williams." I opened the door, and there was the high school kid from two doors down who cut my lawn. I'd heard him out back mowing the grass, so he was obviously looking to get paid. Jason was as good as any of the local lawn service guys, and much cheaper at twenty-five dollars.

"Hey, Jason, how many weeks do I owe you for?"

"Just one. Your wife paid me last week."

"Good, let me go get my wallet."

I walked into my bedroom and took thirty dollars out of my wallet, hoping Jason had five dollars change. When I walked back to the front door, I froze right where I was standing, and Jason's money dropped to the floor. I could not believe my eyes. Standing next to Jason was Jackie.

"How you doing, Brent?"

I didn't answer, although Jackie's words seemed to float into my ears. Jackie walked over and picked up the money I'd dropped, handing it to Jason. "I think this belongs to you."

Jason took the money and counted it. "It's too much money, Mr. Williams. I don't have any change."

I snapped out of my trance, although I was still staring at Jackie. It took everything I had not to run across that room and tongue my baby down right in front of my neighbor's son. "Don't worry about it, Jason. You can keep the change."

Jason grinned. "Thanks, Mr. Williams." He walked out of the house and Jackie closed the door behind him, taking a few tentative steps toward me.

"You never answered my question."

"Huh? What question?" I still hadn't moved out of my spot.

"I asked you how you were doing."

"Better now that I know you're all right. When did you get back in town?"

"About two weeks ago."

"Two weeks ago?" I snapped. "Where've you been? I called your job and you weren't there. And you haven't been in church for the past three Sundays."

"I was at home getting my life together."

A twinge of jealousy hit me, but I played it off. "So you and Trustee Moss are working things out."

"No, I told you in San Francisco that I was no longer going to live a lie. Me and Trustee Moss are getting divorced." There was no remorse or regret in Jackie's voice, almost to the point that it scared me. "Oh, there was a lot of cursing, then crying and more cursing. And believe me, there's going to be a lot of talking about me in church this Sunday. But in the long run, I think what I did was for the best."

"Did you say anything about us?" I held my breath as I waited for the answer.

"No, I didn't give out any names, but I did say I was in love."

I swallowed hard, thankful that my name would be left out of the impending church gossip. "So, what are you going to do now?"

"Something I've wanted to do for the past three weeks." Jackie closed the three-foot gap between us, then reached up and placed a hand gently behind my neck, pulling my head down until our lips met. I parted Jackie's lips with my tongue as my hands began to roam.

"I missed you so much, Brent," Jackie whispered between kisses.

"I missed you too, baby." I was now kissing Jackie's neck and earlobes, while at the same time, Jackie's hands were exploring my chest and lightly pinching my nipples.

"Take this off," Jackie moaned, gesturing for me to pull my shirt off. I glanced at the grandfather clock on the far side of the living room. It was six o'clock. Visiting hours at the hospital wouldn't be over for at least another two hours. We had plenty of time.

As my shirt came off, I eased my way toward the sofa. Without missing a beat, my lover began to kiss and nibble on my chest until both my tiny nipples were hard as b.b.'s. I felt wet kisses across my abdomen, and spider-like fingers massaging my manhood through my baggy jeans.

"I don't wanna lose you, Brent. If you wanna play house with Alison, then fine, but I don't wanna lose you."

"I just want things to be the way they were, sweetheart. I just want us both to be happy." My pants fell to the ground and my penis poked at my boxers.

"Oh, God, I just wanna taste it," Jackie moaned.

In what seemed like no time, my boxers were down on the floor with my pants, and I was stepping out of both. I stepped back and fell onto the sofa. Jackie, who was still standing, slid down to one knee. I watched in lustful anticipation as my lover's head came closer and closer to my groin. When it finally reached its destination, I was moaning loud enough to wake the dead.

Jackie was putting it on me like I'd never had it done before, and I defied even Super Head, the Video Vixen, to match my lover's skill. I closed my eyes, trying my best to catalog the pleasure I was receiving in my mind. With any luck, on one of those bad days sexually with Alison, I'd be able to pull up this memory. But enough about her. It was time to concentrate on the business at hand, because Jackie's head was bobbing and twisting around my penis like a waterspout. When the moment arrived for my ejaculation, my body went into uncontrollable convulsions and I screamed at the top of my lungs as I sat straight up. I opened my eyes to both the most pleasurable and the most terrifying moment of my life, because standing behind Jackie was my stunned wife.

33

James

"James, will you stop pacing before you wear a hole in my damn floor!" my mother shouted from her seat at the kitchen table.

She was right. I was probably doing some damage to her living room carpet as I walked back and forth, holding the phone against my ear, listening to Michelle's home phone ring endlessly. Marcus had been with me for three weeks now, so I had practically worn a path on the floor I walked across each time I called Michelle and waited in vain for her to answer.

I hadn't been able to reach Michelle at her house or on her cell phone. I knew she had been back to her house at least once, though. For the first few days, I had been able to leave messages at her house. Now the answering machine wasn't picking up, so she'd obviously shut it off. It pissed me off to know that she'd ignored my calls, and even worse, she'd ignored the one where I let Marcus speak into the phone. He was doing all right at my mother's house, and I'd gone to buy a few toys to keep him occupied, but he really missed his mother. I couldn't understand how Michelle could be so cold when she undoubtedly heard his sad little voice on her answering machine.

I clicked the phone off angrily and headed into the kitchen to sit with my mother. She slid a cup of coffee across the table to me but didn't say a word. I know she was probably getting sick of seeing my face every morning when this was only supposed to be a one-night stay.

"She's still not answering," I said, stating the obvious.

"Why don't you just go by there? She has to come home sooner or later, doesn't she?"

"I've been by there a few times, Ma, but she's never home. I don't know what the hell is going on, but she's hiding from me. I just can't believe she doesn't want her son back."

"I know. It's hard to imagine a woman who could abandon her child, but at this point, I don't think you should be surprised by anything she does. You've gotten yourself into one hell of a mess, haven't you?" She couldn't hide her annoyance as she frowned at me.

"Ma," I asked cautiously, "do you think you could watch Marcus for a while today?"

"Why? What are you going to do?" She did not sound pleased. Although she had initially offered to help me with Marcus so I could keep the secret from Cathy, now that the truth was out, Ma seemed a little less eager to be involved.

"I've gotta find Michelle. If I have to, I'm gonna sit outside her house all day until she comes home. She can't keep ignoring me like this."

"Go ahead," she said abruptly, clearly still upset with me.

"Thanks, Ma," I said as I stood up. "And if Cathy calls—"

"James, don't. You know she's not going to call you. You're going to have to be the one to start that conversation with your wife."

"I know," I said sadly. "That's why I have to find Michelle. I can't talk to her until Michelle takes Marcus back. If Cathy has to see him again, it would be a constant reminder of the affair."

"It sure is, but you better get over there to see her soon. There's no telling what she said to your boys. They probably think you've abandoned them at this point."

I don't know if she said it to hurt my feelings, but my mother's words were like a slap in the face. I missed my boys so much, it caused me physical pain. I left my mother's house determined to find Michelle and settle this whole thing.

I sat outside her house for hours, waiting for Michelle and thinking about everything that had happened. I still couldn't understand how she would just leave her son like that, but it was starting to sink in that this was much deeper than I thought. She hadn't left him just to make a statement after our fight. There was more to this, but I wouldn't know what it was unless I could get her to talk to me.

In the meantime, I had to face the possibility that she might not ever want to take Marcus back. What would I do if that happened? As much as I didn't want it to be true, he was my flesh and blood. If his mother didn't want him, could I reject him too? Would I put him into foster care if it were the only way my wife would let me come home? I didn't really want to consider these possibilities, so I just kept telling myself that sooner or later, Michelle would come home and I'd get her to realize what a mistake she was making.

My patience finally paid off six hours after I parked across the street from her house. A cab pulled up in front and Michelle stepped out, carrying a shopping bag from Macy's. I shook my head. I guess since she didn't have to buy diapers and food anymore, she had a little extra to spend on herself.

I jumped out of my car and ran across the street as Michelle stood in front of her door, searching for keys in her bag. I shouted her name as I approached. She turned around and cursed.

"Stay away from me, James. I ain't got nothing to say to you." She continued searching frantically for the keys. It didn't matter. I was not about to let her go into that house without me.

"You have nothing to say to me?" I asked incredulously. "How about, 'How's my son?' Don't you even care how Marcus is doing since you dropped him off with my wife?"

She smirked wickedly. "Oh, yeah, I bet she liked that, didn't she? I saw on my caller ID that you're not calling from home anymore. She kicked your ass out, didn't she?" She placed her key in the lock and turned it, laughing at the domestic turmoil she'd set into motion.

My fingers clenched into tight fists, and I crossed my arms over my chest to stop myself from punching her like I wanted to. "This is not a fuckin' joke, Michelle. You might think it's funny to be fucking with my marriage, but how could you use your son to do it? What kind of woman are you?"

She whipped her head around and glared at me through dark eyes. "Don't go there, James. You ain't been around the last three years. You have not earned the right to judge me, 'cause you have no fuckin' idea what it's been like for me."

I followed her into the house when she opened the door. She paused for a moment like she was thinking about telling me to get out, but then she just dropped her Macy's bag on the table and slumped onto the couch. I followed her, standing beside the couch to look down at her.

"What the hell are you talking about? Do you know how many women are out there raising children by themselves? And they don't dump their kids just because they want a little time to themselves. Shit, I don't know what you're complaining about. I might not have been there from the start, but I sure as hell have been watching him for you plenty of nights ever since I found out I was his father." I sat on the arm of the couch and waited for her reply.

"It ain't even about that," she finally said quietly. I was surprised by how defeated she sounded. She'd lost her fire so quickly this time. Maybe she did miss Marcus. Maybe this was an opening for me to get her to change her mind and take him back.

"What is it, then?" I asked, trying to keep my tone gentle. "Why did you leave him, Michelle? Your son misses you."

She remained tight-lipped, so I kept prodding.

"Is it the money? I know it's been hard for you to raise him by yourself. Look, if it will help, I'll increase the amount of child support I give you each week so you can cut back on your hours at work. Marcus needs his mother. He needs to be with you. I can't give him the nurturing that you can." As I said the words, I hoped it didn't sound like the bullshit I knew it was. Obviously Michelle wasn't giving him much nurturing if she could just dump him like some orphan.

"It ain't the money," she said with a sigh. "You just don't get it, do you?"

"No, Michelle, I don't get it. You need to explain it to me."

She dropped her head into her hands, and I waited patiently for her to speak. I felt like I was getting close to an answer, so I didn't want to set her off now. I desperately needed her to open up to me so I could help her with her problem and send Marcus home. Finally, she looked up at me.

"How am I supposed to give love to my child if I ain't got no one giving love to me?" she asked.

Was she kidding? Was she really that selfish? If she was trying to imply that she would take the boy back as long as I showed her some love, then she was out of her damn mind.

"Michelle," I started carefully, "you know I love my wife. I know you're lonely, but I can't possibly—"

"Oh, please." She rolled her eyes. "I do not want you."

Now I was lost. "Then what are you talking about?"

"It's Trent," she answered.

"Trent? You mean, your ex-boyfriend?"

She nodded.

"What about him? I thought he dropped you as soon as he found out the results of the paternity test." Michelle had told me that story not long after I started going to her place to babysit Marcus. Trent had been her boyfriend before I hooked up with her, and when she had Marcus, she wasn't really sure who his father was. She hoped it was Trent, though, because he was supposedly the love of her life. They got back together for a while when Marcus was an infant, and she convinced Trent that he was the baby's father. The relationship wasn't all roses, though. Trent had a shady side of his own, and he had another woman he was stringing along for her money. To make a long story short, Trent and Michelle ended up taking a paternity test—on the daytime talk show *Two Sides to Every Story*, no less—and Trent found out in front of millions of viewers that he was not Marcus's father. Michelle said that the day they taped the show was the last time he talked to her, so I had no idea what he had to do with the mess I was in right now.

"Trent came to see me at work a few weeks ago. We've been talking," Michelle admitted. Something about the way she said his name made it obvious she still loved this guy. From everything I'd heard about his personality, these two deserved each other.

"If that's what you want, I'm happy for you, Michelle. But what does that have to do with your son?" I had to keep her focused on Marcus if I had any hope of sending him back home to her.

"Trent wants to get back with me."

"Like I said, that's great. Now, what about Marcus?"

She looked into my face and said calmly, "He says he can't stand the thought of raising another man's child," as if this was a perfectly acceptable thing for a man to demand of his woman.

"Are you saying what I think you're saying?" I asked, unable to believe she was. Could she really be willing to abandon her child just to be with her ex? The irony of it was making me sick to my stomach. She could understand Trent not wanting to raise another man's child, yet she was expecting Cathy to raise another woman's son. Then again, I realized, she probably hadn't given a thought to Cathy's feelings. Yes, she was that selfish.

"What else am I supposed to do, James? I am so sick of being lonely. Every time you came over to babysit, I tried to open the door for us to have a relationship again, but you made it more than clear you didn't want me. And now that Trent has come back, I know he's the only man I want in my life. I love him, and I'll do anything to keep him this time."

My head was starting to hurt from trying to understand how a mother could think this way. "Are you listening to yourself, Michelle? Don't you love Marcus at all?"

"Yes," she said, "but I love myself too. If I lose Trent again, I'll just end up being lonely and miserable, and you wouldn't want me to take that out on Marcus, would you? It's better off that I send him to live with you now, before I do any damage to him."

"You've already damaged him!" I was through trying to understand her. "That boy cries every night, asking when his mommy is coming to get him. Are you really going to be able to live with yourself, knowing you abandoned your child?" This was my final effort to get her to change her mind, but it was no use.

"Don't worry about whether I'll be able to live with myself. Plenty of women have abortions, and they get over it and get on with their lives." My mouth hung open in disbelief as I listened to her warped logic. "Shoot, at least I gave the boy life. I coulda had an abortion like all these other girls out here, and then he never woulda been born. He's young. He'll forget all about me. You'll take good care of him, James." She got up from the couch and went to the mirror to fix her hair.

"Now, if you don't mind," she said casually, as if we hadn't just been discussing the fate of her child, "Trent is coming over in a little while, so I need you to get outta here. He's the jealous type, you know."

I sat speechless for a moment, my mind reeling with confusion. This conversation had not gone anything like I had expected. I truly believed I would be able to talk some sense into Michelle and things would go back to the way they were; I would convince Cathy to take me back, and Michelle would be satisfied with child support and an occasional night of baby-sitting. This new reality was not something I was ready to comprehend.

Michelle stood humming, admiring herself in the mirror and applying lipstick like she didn't have a care in the world. Her son's life was about to be forever altered, and all she seemed to care about was her boyfriend's upcoming visit.

As I let myself out, I prayed for some direction. Things would never be the same for Marcus, but these events would also affect my other sons and my wife in ways I could only imagine. In time my shock would wear off, and I would have to decide on the next step of my plan, the one that would inflict the least amount of pain on everyone involved.

34

Sonny

I walked into my house and smiled. I could smell the Pine Sol from the cleaning Tiffany had given the house. Now, this is what family life was supposed to be about—my house was clean, Tony was at the kitchen table doing his homework, Nikki was next to him, trying her best to sound out the words in a Dora book, and Tiffany was in the kitchen cooking our family dinner. B. Smith, Martha Stewart, and Betty Crocker herself couldn't have put together a better home than my woman.

Both kids jumped up from the kitchen table when they saw me. "Hey, Uncle Sonny," they said in unison. I kissed each of them on their foreheads and they went back to their homework.

"You got one of those for me?" Tiffany asked.

"I got something better." I walked over and wrapped my arms around my woman, kissing her tenderly. "I missed you, Tif. How was your day?"

"I missed you too. My day was interesting. I've got something important to talk to you about after the kids go to bed, but it can wait."

"Are you sure? Because we can talk about it now if you like."

"It can wait." She dipped a spoon in a pot and brought it to my mouth for me to taste.

"Mmm, now that's good. When are we gonna eat?"

Tiffany smiled. "In about ten minutes."

"Sounds good. I'm going downstairs to my office to mess around with my computers for a few minutes. Call me when dinner is ready."

I went to the basement and turned on the laptop, which I'd gone back to buy from my cousin Lowjack, then entered my password and clicked on my video webcam recorder, also courtesy of my cousin's "business." Tiffany didn't know it, but I had installed hidden cameras throughout the house right before she moved in. I know it's a little extreme, but when you got a woman as good looking as mine, you can't take any chances with the mailman or UPS drivers like James. Working at UPS these past few months, I'd heard too many stories about the affairs between the drivers and the housewives they deliver packages to. Besides, if I'd done this when I was with Jessica, I'd probably still have my other family.

I pushed PLAY and watched Tiffany going through her daily routine. I watched in fast-forward as she cleaned the house for the better part of the morning, then talked on the phone for a while. I was going to have to listen to the phone tapes later, but it was probably just the usual bragging she did with her girl-friends about what a good man she got and how she loved staying home. Everything I saw on the tape looked completely normal until around one o'clock, when she had a visitor.

"What the fuck?" I shut down my computer and ran up the stairs. As I passed through the living room, I shouted, "Tiffany, get the fuck upstairs, now!" then ran up another flight of stairs into our bedroom.

Tiffany rushed in, and I commanded, "Close the goddamn door."

She did as she was told, looking bewildered. "What's the matter?"

I closed the gap between us, and when she was close enough, I reared my hand back and smacked the shit out of her. She fell on the bed, holding her face. Tears immediately welled up in her eyes.

"What the fuck is wrong with you? Why'd you hit me?"

I raised my hand again, this time swinging even harder. She screamed in pain. "You had that motherfucker in my house?"

"What are you talking about?" she asked, holding her cheek, where a bruise was forming.

"You think I'm stupid? You think I don't know what you've been doing? This is my house. The neighbors tell me everything that goes on around here." I gestured like I was going to slap her again, and she scampered across the bed.

"Sonny, what are you talking about?" I slapped her again, just for thinking I was so damn stupid.

"Kareem! You had Kareem in my house, our house."

It was clear from the panic in her eyes that she knew what I was talking about now. "Oh, my God, Sonny, I was gonna tell you about that."

"When? When were you going to tell me?" I had my arm in the air, ready to slap her ass again.

"After the kids went to bed. Remember, we were supposed to talk?" She was now on the other side of the bed, curled up on the floor.

"I talked to you eight times today, and you didn't tell me a damn thing about Kareem coming over here. Why didn't you tell me before I got home? And how the hell did he even know where we live?" She was shaking now, cowering in fear, but I didn't care. I jumped on the bed, then onto the floor in front of her. "I asked you a question."

"I . . . I told him."

"You did what?" I swung at her again, catching part of her arm and face. "Did you fuck him? Did you fuck his ass?"

"No! No, I didn't do anything like that," Tiffany insisted. "He told me he was going to bring me some money for the kids."

"Well, where's the money?" I demanded.

"He didn't give me any. He was lying, just like he lied and told me he didn't plant those roaches in my apartment. I'm sorry, Sonny. I should have listened to you."

I shoved her. "Sorry ain't good enough. That's why we have rules around here, remember?" I walked toward the door, then looked back. "Don't come out this fucking room until we're finished eating." I slammed the door behind me. Something told me she was telling the truth, she hadn't slept with Kareem, but I had to go back and look at the entire recording to be sure. I was also going to have to get that software installed at my job so I could watch her ass all day while I was at work.

The kids and I were sitting in front of the TV playing video games later when Tiffany left the bedroom and came downstairs. They had heard us thumping around upstairs, but during dinner I managed to convince them that Tiffany had just tripped over something. Tony looked a little uneasy with my explanation, but when he said he was going to check on her, I told him she was sleeping and he shouldn't disturb her. As soon as I challenged him to a battle on his favorite video game, he seemed to forget all about her anyway.

When Tiffany came into the room, I handed the remote control to Tony, then stood up and approached her. "I left a plate in the microwave. You hungry?" I tried to guide her toward the kitchen, but she flinched when I reached for her. She had a few red marks on her face, but it didn't look like anything serious.

"I'm sorry about your face, but I'm not gonna apologize for anything I said or did. You were wrong." She looked at me, but obviously she wasn't seeing my point of view about this situation. I took a deep breath and explained, "Now, you've got three choices. Number one, you can go in there and call the police to have me locked up. I won't stop you, but I'll probably lose my job and this house, and you and the kids won't have anywhere to stay."

She didn't move toward the kitchen or the phone, so I guess she wanted to hear her other choices. "Number two, you can pack your shit and leave. I don't know where you're gonna go without a job and with two kids, but again, I won't stop you."

She didn't move toward the bedroom, so I continued, giving her the final option. "Number three, you can accept that what I did earlier wasn't meant to hurt you, but rather done out of love and a sense of family. You broke the rules, Tiffany, and no family can exist without rules, so you have to accept the consequences. Now, what you wanna do?"

I waited with arms folded for her answer. She stood quietly for a few seconds, her eyes glistening with tears. Finally, without speaking, she went over to the couch and sat next to her kids, pulling them both close against her. That was the answer I was hoping for.

35

Brent

Ten minutes earlier, I had been the happiest man on earth. My friend and secret lover had shown up at my door after being MIA for almost a month. We'd started back right where we left off, and our passion brought us to my living room sofa, where Jackie proceeded to give me the best oral sex of my life. Unfortunately, when it was over, I opened my eyes to my worst possible nightmare. My pregnant wife Alison was standing behind Jackie, staring at us in bewilderment, and then she went into a holy dance as streams of tears rolled down her face.

"Oh, Jesus, Lord," she screamed, grabbing her chest as if she was about to have a heart attack. I immediately tried to get up to attempt an explanation, but my legs were still feeling the effects of Jackie's oral pleasure, and I couldn't get off the sofa. "Lord, please just take me right now! Please, Lord, take me! I wanna be with my mama because I done married the devil."

When my legs no longer felt like jelly, I pushed Jackie to one side and stood, calling Alison's name. The response was almost demonic. Alison's once-cute face was now twisted evilly in anger and grief. Cautiously, I took two steps toward her, but stopped when she jerked her arms repeatedly to keep me at bay.

"Don't touch me, you heathenous bastard. Dear Lord, how could you let me be pregnant by him?" She broke down in long, horrifying sobs, then started to slam her hands violently against her stomach.

I screamed. "Alison, please! You're going to hurt the baby. It's not what you think! It's not what you think."

Alison froze, glaring at Jackie, then stared wide-eyed at me like I had two heads. "I don't have to think anything, Brent. I have two eyes and I can see! And what I saw was a man sucking my husband's *dick*!"

I'd been sleeping with Jackie off and on for the better part of two months, but I'd never once thought of it as being as repulsive as I did when I heard Alison say those words. Yes, it's true, Jackie was a man, named after the famous baseball player. Jackie Robinson Moss was a church organist, father, husband to a popular church trustee, and yes, he was my lover. I bet you actually thought Jackie was a woman, but not once did I ever refer to him as anything more than my lover.

"And I was sucking it well too, wasn't I, Brent?"

Both Alison and I turned toward Jackie, shooting him evil darts with our eyes. I couldn't believe he'd just said that, and I was afraid he might say more and make things worse.

"Jackie, please . . ."

He cut me off. "No, Brent. The cat's out the bag now. It's time to come clean, baby. Come on, tell her how you really feel."

"Jackie," I said, "shut up."

"I'm just trying to help."

"Goddammit, Jackie, will you shut the hell up?" I cursed through clenched teeth.

"You know, I've heard about men like you," Alison said tearfully "What do they call it? 'On the down-low.' But I never thought I'd marry one. And you, Jackie . . ." She eyed him with distaste. "You are so nasty. Wipe your mouth." Jackie rubbed his chin as Alison continued. "I don't even wanna think about what Trustee Moss is going to do to you."

Jackie got defensive. "I've left my wife. And Brent's going to leave you too, aren't you, baby?"

What did Jackie say that for? The spell was broken. The next thing I knew, Alison raised her fists, let out a war whoop, and charged at Jackie. She would have beat him to death if I hadn't jumped in between the two of them.

As I held her back, Alison swung and clawed like a deranged animal. "I'll kill you. I'll kill you, nasty dick-sucking fucker! You did this to him," she bellowed. I swear, her voice sounded like the demon in *The Exorcist*. My once soft-spoken, proper wife looked possessed, her eyes were so wild. I'd never known this side of Alison. Then again, she'd never known this side of me either.

"Alison, calm down before you hurt the baby."

"This baby would be better off dead than with you as a father. How could you, Brent?" She was still struggling to release herself from my grasp. "I can't believe this. The entire time I'm trying to run off all those women eyeing you in the church, you sleeping with a man."

Suddenly, Alison stopped pacing and began to bite, claw, and kick at me. I tried to pin her flailing arms to her side, but it was as if she had the strength of two men. The truth be known, I was afraid of her myself. I managed to hold her, though, until finally, some of the fight went out of her. At last, she stopped swinging. She was out of breath and her hair was standing up on her head. My face was stinging from her scratches.

"Alison, please. We can work this out."

"Work it out, my ass. I'm not working anything out with you." She pulled away from me. "You two heathens deserve each other. I'm outta here." With dignity, she threw her head back and stomped out of the house, slamming the door with a resounding thud.

Dealing with my new status as a homosexual had me spinning. Was I gay or was this just a gay episode? How could I tell my boys, Sonny and James? Should I come out of the closet to the world or did I want my wife back? And, if Alison would take me back, could I stay straight? I didn't know if I was upset because I'd gotten busted or if I was truly upset that Alison was gone. She was the first woman who I'd ever felt comfortable with in all my adult life. Ever since I could remember, I'd sublimated the feelings I had for men, yet those feelings had been there. Waiting . . . insidious as a detonator, waiting to explode . . . and Jackie had seen in me what he knew was in him. Is that what had made him come after me?

But even before Jackie, those feelings for men had been there, keeping me the oldest virgin in our group, and they had been there, keeping me from having a serious relationship with a woman—until Alison. I'd tried to escape those feelings through the church, through celibacy, and then, look what happened! When I'd acted on those urges, they had destroyed my life.

36

Sonny

For two hours, I'd been waiting outside for this bitch he had in his apartment to leave. I was starting to think she was a little more than a booty call and was going to spend the night. Usually she left around eleven so he could get ready for work. It was quarter-past now, so either they were just finishing up the second round or he had called in sick. I picked up my cell phone and dialed his job.

"Home for the Aging," a female voice answered.

"Hi, is Kareem there? This is his brother, Jihad."

"Kareem won't be in until midnight."

"Okay, thanks."

Just as I hung up the phone, a cab pulled up and the bitch walked out the door. How Kareem could choose to mess with her instead of Tiffany, I didn't understand. She looked like a hooker. Then again, she did work in a strip club, so she was probably doing tricks.

I waited about five minutes, until the street was clear, then got out of the car and headed for the door, wearing all black and carrying a baseball bat. I'd broken all the streetlights with rocks three days earlier, so aside from small lights on some of the houses, the block was dark. I put on my ski mask and knelt behind a bush beside the front door, waiting for the door to open. Twenty minutes later, Kareem walked out. I stepped out from behind the bush.

"Who the fuck are you?" he said boldly.

"I'm your worst fucking nightmare." I swung the bat and heard his arm break with a loud crack. He lost his footing, and I pushed him back into the house. I hit him again along his back and ribs, and he fell to the floor. He must've thought I was trying to rob him because he kept telling me he didn't have any money.

"I don't want your money, muthafucka." The bat landed against his legs.

"Aaahhh! Then what do you want?" He grimaced in pain and I wanted to laugh.

"You really don't know what this is about, do you? It's about your wife. Or should I say, my fiancée?" I pulled the mask off my face, and shock registered in his eyes.

"What the fuck do you want, Sonny?"

"I got everything I want, Kareem. I've got your family." I swung the bat again. This time I could hear his ribs crack. I wondered if I should go over to the stereo and turn the music up to avoid alerting the neighbors. "The question is, what do I need?" I kicked him in the ribs. "C'mon! Ask me what I need."

"Ooohhh . . . what . . . do you . . . need?"

"I need you dead. I need you out of the way. Tiffany thinks she needs you giving her money to help out, but she don't know what's good for her. I know what's good for her. So, with you being dead, she'll come to realize that I'm the only family she and the kids have. Her mama's dead, her daddy's dead, she doesn't have siblings, and soon her ex-husband will be dead."

"Man, you crazy!"

I tilted my head, giving his statement some thought. "You really think I'm crazy? Now, that's interesting. Here I am thinking I was just highly devoted to my woman."

"Man, don't kill me," he said, gasping for air. "You can . . . have her. I never really . . . liked that bitch anyway. Come on, man. There ain't . . . no reason . . . to kill me . . . not over no woman."

I had to chuckle. "That's where you're wrong. The only time a man *should* kill is over a woman. Then again, I guess you've never been in love before."

"Man, you're crazy!"

"I thought we already established that. I'm not crazy. Maybe a little obsessive, but not crazy." I hit him again. "One last question before you go, Kareem. I always wanted to ask somebody who was about to die: Where do you think you're going? Heaven or hell?" He looked at me silently, though his eyes were still pleading for mercy. "You look like you need a little more time to think about this. Too bad your time is up." I lifted the bat and swung it at his head. When I was through, there was no doubt in my mind that he was dead.

I had no remorse. I did it for love.

A few minutes later, I picked up the phone at the house, still wearing my gloves, and called Kareem's job.

"Home for the Aging," a female voice answered.

"Hey, this is Kareem." I lowered my voice a few tones, trying to imitate his voice as closely as possible. It wasn't close enough, though, I soon learned.

"Hey, Kareem," the woman said, flirting. "You don't sound quite like yourself."

"Yeah, I'm a little down and out," I said quickly. "My grandmama down South just passed away."

"Oh, I'm sorry to hear that."

"Me too. Look, can you tell them I'm not gonna be able to come in for a couple of weeks? I gotta go down there to get everything straight. She left me everything, ya know."

"For real?" Her voice perked up at the mention of an inheritance. "Maybe I need to go down there with you."

"Yeah, maybe you should," I said. I didn't know if she was serious, but I had to play along just in case Kareem had been sleeping with this girl or something. I couldn't risk saying the wrong thing and raising her suspicions. "After I get my business straight, I'll give you a call."

"Aw'ight, Kareem. Don't forget me, now."

37

Brent

I'd tried my best to throw myself into my work to take my mind off everything, but it didn't help. I kept thinking about Alison and Jackie and how I loved both of them in such different ways. And yes, despite everything you might think, I did love Alison, only my love for her was more like the love you have for a sister than for a lover. I know that sounds kind of creepy, considering we were having a child together, but the truth is, that's how I felt since the first day we were introduced by the first lady. I just wasn't man enough to admit it to her or myself because of my own insecurities. I did wish I could work things out with Alison, though, for the baby's sake.

The love I had for Jackie, on the other hand, was that deep, passionate love that you dream about all your life. Whenever I was around him, I felt like a boy again, when I had a crush on the captain of the basketball team. The problem with loving a man, though, was that it came along with taboo and ridicule. Even if I chose to remain in the closet, it would still bother me that so many people consider it wrong, especially when it comes to being a Christian. First Corinthians 6:9 specifically says: *Do not be misled: Neither fornicators, nor adulterers, nor men kept for unnatural purposes, nor men who lie with men . . . will inherit God's kingdom.* I interpreted that to mean that a lifetime of love and happiness with Jackie would only bring me an eternity of hell in the afterlife.

I thought about going back to the bishop to talk to him about my dilemma, but he'd just given a sermon on the sins of homosexuality, so I was pretty certain I knew what his opinion would be. Still, I needed to talk to someone so desperately that I even picked up the phone one afternoon and called James. I was going to tell him everything, about Jackie and me getting caught and the whole nine yards, but after he told me about his problems with Cathy finding out about Marcus, I didn't even want to bother him. And Sonny . . . well, Sonny had been a homophobe for years.

So, as I drove home from work, I still had quite a bit on my mind. When I pulled in front of my house, I was actually surprised to see Alison's car parked in the driveway. Usually around this time she was at the hospital with the first lady. Plus, we hadn't spoken since the incident with Jackie earlier that week, and considering how badly that turned out, I was almost afraid to enter the house. Was she alone? Was she there to pick up clothes? Was she there to talk? Or was she there to kill me? I really couldn't blame her for it if she was. Whatever she was there for, it was time to face my wife as a man.

When I entered the house, I was even more confused. I expected to find Alison waiting there, ready for another fight. Instead, I saw that the lights were turned down and white vanilla-scented candles were everywhere. Teddy Pendergrass's song "Close the Door" was playing in the background on the stereo.

"Alison," I called out.

"I'm in here, Brent," she answered from the dining room in a surprisingly sweet voice.

When I entered the dining room, I had to stop and take it all in. The room was bathed in candlelight, and the dining table was covered with our most expensive tablecloth and set for two with our wedding china and crystal stemware. But what caught my breath was the sight of Alison. There she was, sitting at the head of the dining room table. Her hair was pulled to the side, and she was dressed in a slinky black, off-the-shoulder dress. She was looking good and smelling good. Even her makeup looked different. She actually looked stunning. Then it hit me. My wife had gotten a makeover!

I approached her tentatively, not quite sure what was going on. This whole scene was so surreal, considering how she was acting the last time I saw her. Alison stood up from her chair in a slinky motion like I'd never seen before, and eased off my tie. Then she unclipped my cell phone from my waist.

"Baby, sit down. I've got your favorite dinner, and then we're going to make love all weekend. I've cut the ringer off, and it's just going to be me and you. We're going to shut off the world."

As wonderful and attentive as she sounded, this was a side of Alison I'd never seen, and I knew this sex-kitten act wasn't her true self. In my heart of hearts, I knew it was about Jackie. She was trying to compete with him. But could she compete? Can a woman ever outdo a man in bed once that line has been crossed? I didn't know, but I wanted to see if I could forget Jackie. I did want this thing with my wife to work, for the sake of God and my unborn child.

I still found myself hedging around the issue, uncertain if I could go through with the sexual act. I didn't necessarily want to go to bed with her now that I'd admitted to myself that I really didn't have strong sexual feelings for women, but I didn't want to hurt her fragile feelings either. I searched for an out.

"Aren't you worried about hurting the baby? Maybe we shouldn't be doing it in the first trimester."

"You know the doctor said I'm doing fine. We can make love safely up until I'm eight months, as long as there are no complications."

So I sat down and ate, all the while going through the motions of pretending to enjoy my favorite dinner of steak, baked potato, and asparagus. Every attempt Alison made at seduction fell flat, though I forced myself to smile each time. When she placed her finger in her mouth to lick off some melted butter, I knew what she was trying to do, but it had the opposite effect on me. It only served to remind me of the night I watched Jackie sucking on ribs from The Rib Shack. I forced the memory out of my mind and tried to remain focused on my wife. My mind was cooperating, but my heart wasn't with the program yet.

Finally, after dinner, Alison got down to the business at hand. She started out by massaging my shoulders and my back. As Teddy crooned, "Baby, I've got so much love to give and I want to give it all to you," Alison began to kiss me on my body in ways she'd never done before. It felt uncomfortable, and in a crazy way, it felt dirty.

Alison eased out of her dress, and underneath she was wearing a revealing black negligee, which accented her plump curves. Her nipples were standing up at attention, but they didn't arouse me.

"Just take me here, baby," she whispered, pointing to the champagne-colored carpeting as she gyrated to the music. I knew she was getting worked up.

I couldn't do that. Jackie and I had been together on this same floor, and I knew I would have felt too much guilt to take my wife here now. But as I remembered my encounter on this carpet, thoughts of Jackie ran through my head once again. How come it was so different with Jackie? I had no problem getting or maintaining an erection with him. In fact, just the thought of Jackie generally made me hard. I'd used those thoughts on many occasions to enable me to perform my husbandly duties with Alison, but tonight I didn't want to fantasize about Jackie in order to make love to my wife.

"No, let's go to the bedroom," I said. Thankfully, I had never allowed Jackie to come into that room, so I hoped that his memory would stay out of my marital bedroom now.

Alison was obviously so set on pleasing me, she didn't protest even slightly. Holding hands, we climbed the stairs and went into the bedroom, where she had placed more candles. She lit them and turned on the music as soon as we entered. On the bed I saw she had placed new red satin sheets and covered them in red and white rose petals. Jackie loved roses, I thought, then shoved his memory out of my mind once again. It was such a struggle to keep myself present with Alison, but I was going to keep trying.

Once we slid under the covers, Alison tried to kiss and fondle me again. No matter how much I wanted to, I still couldn't get hard. I was limp.

"What's the matter, baby?" she said. "I'm willing to do whatever you want. We can even have anal sex if that's what you like."

It was painful to hear her say that. I knew that she would never have offered that to me if it weren't for the situation we were in. It was not something she believed a good Christian woman should be doing, yet she was offering it to me now. I heaved a deep sigh. "I don't know, Alison. Maybe it's because we really haven't even talked yet about what happened the other day. I'm feeling really guilty, and—"

"Shh," she said soothingly. "I don't want to talk about that right now. All I want is for us to be together. Make love to me—then you'll know I've forgiven you."

Forgiveness. That sounded so good to me at that moment. I hadn't yet been able to forgive myself, I wasn't sure if God could ever forgive me, and here was my wife, the woman I'd hurt deeply, offering up forgiveness so freely. Part of me wanted to make love to her just to feel forgiven. If I allowed myself to think freely about Jackie, I could get hard enough to make love to Alison. But I knew that was wrong. Even if I could complete the act now, it would only be a temporary fix. After it was over, I would still feel passion for Jackie, not for Alison. This would never work between us, and I now understood that I'd been fooling myself when I thought that it would. When Alison discovered me with Jackie that night, she had cracked open the door of the closet I'd been hiding in. Just cracking that door had shed some light on the truth that I was now coming to terms with: As much as I didn't want to be, I was a gay man. And as desperately as I wanted to be part of a family that society would accept, it was not who I was, and I would never be able to do it.

Before I could even turn to Alison to tell her how I felt, she already knew. She lay beside me, crying quietly.

"I'm sorry, Alison. I truly wish things could be different, but this is who I am."

She turned to look at me and asked, "Why, Brent? I love you so much. Why can't you feel that way about me?"

"I do love you, Alison, but not in the way a man should love his wife."

"I don't understand," she said as she sat up in the bed and wrapped her arms around her knees. Her body language said she felt a need to protect herself, and she was right. Anything I had to say to her right now could only hurt her.

"I don't know how to explain it, Alison. I love you like a best friend, but physically, no matter how much I want to, I just can't make my body desire you."

Tears streamed over her cheeks. "Is it because of my weight?" she asked. "What if I lose some weight?"

"No, it has nothing to do with your weight." I reached out to hold her hand. "Please don't think this has anything to do with your appearance. You are a beautiful woman, Alison."

She shook her head like she didn't want to believe me.

"It has nothing to do with you, Alison. You have to believe that. There's no other way to say this except that when I think about men, I get aroused, and when I think about women, I don't."

"That can't be true, Brent," she said. "If you don't desire women, then how were you able to make love to me as many times as you did? How did you get me pregnant?"

It was a legitimate question, but I was sure she had asked it thinking that the fact that we had conceived a child together was proof that I wasn't really gay. Unfortunately, that wasn't the truth.

"Well," I said, wishing I didn't have to, "those times that we were making love, it wasn't you I was thinking about."

The hurt flashed in her eyes as she realized what I was saying. "You were thinking about Jackie every time? Even on our honeymoon?"

I nodded. "I'm so sorry, Alison."

"Why did you do it, Brent? Why marry me in the first place if you knew you weren't attracted to women?"

"I wanted to believe I could be straight. I wanted a family so bad, and I loved you more than I ever loved any other woman. I thought if I married you and we started a family, I could just make these urges go away."

"Maybe you still can," she said hopefully. She released her knees and I saw her body relax as she turned to me, sounding almost eager. "We're going to have this baby together, and if you tell Jackie you can't see him anymore, we can still be a family. Maybe once he's out of your system, you'll be able to kick this. We don't have to make love yet, but over time, God will help you find your way down the right path. He wants us to be together, Brent. I just know it."

"No!" I said with enough volume that it startled her. "I can't do this anymore. I told you, I *thought* I could make these urges go away. I know now that they never will." Alison's eyes started watering again as I continued. "I will be there to provide whatever our child needs, but I can't be here as your husband. I've made my decision, and I'm going to live my life as a gay man."

"But what about the church?" she asked. "You know the bishop preaches that homosexuality is a sin."

I stopped for a moment to calm myself before answering her. That issue had been one of the hardest for me to come to terms with, but I knew I only had one choice now. "I know what the church teaches, Alison, but I also know that I can't change who I am. If the church can't accept that, then I'll leave the congregation."

"Bishop Wilson will never forgive you, you know."

"It's not for the bishop to forgive me. The only thing I need to worry about is God's forgiveness, and if He's a merciful God like I believe He is, then all I can do is live my life and pray that in the afterlife He will forgive me for being who He made me."

She looked dumbstruck. I'm sure she thought that I loved the church too much to ever consider straying from its teachings. After much soul-searching, though, I understood that I could leave the church if I was forced to, and I would still be all right.

"This is the only way I can do things, Alison. I refuse to live a lie anymore. I'm leaving for San Francisco tomorrow, and when I come back next weekend, I plan on announcing my truth at Sunday services."

She jumped off the bed and gestured wildly as she yelled at me. "You can't do that! You're making a huge mistake! Please don't make that announcement, Brent."

"I'm going to do it, Alison. There's no turning back now." I stood up and headed for the door. "I'm going to sleep in the guestroom, and I'll be gone in the morning."

Alison called after me before I left. "So you call yourself a man?"

I didn't reply, but I wasn't really sure if I could.

38

James

"Daddy, Daddy, throw it to me!" my oldest son, James Jr., was yelling as I jogged with the football. His younger brother, Michael, was chasing behind me, grabbing at my knees to try to knock me over onto the grass and capture the ball. Marcus sat on a blanket near the edge of the yard, laughing and clapping as he watched us play.

This, to me, was pure heaven. All three of my boys were there with me, and everyone was happy . . . until Cathy stormed into the yard and grabbed the two oldest boys.

"What the hell do you think you're doing?" she screamed, holding them tight against her body. "I didn't tell you that you could come over here and see the boys."

Both boys looked at her in bewilderment. They were too young to understand what was wrong. Before she came, this had been a great day for all of us, a reunion after being separated for way too long. Now their mother was yelling like we'd been caught doing something criminal. My heart ached for them and the confusion I knew they must be experiencing.

"Cathy, we were just playing football," I said. "I just wanted to see my boys."

She took a few steps backward, pulling my sons farther away from me. "That's too damn bad, James. You should have thought of your boys before you went and had another son with some other b—" She stopped herself before she cursed in front of the boys.

As she pulled them across the yard, James Jr. looked at me, then at Marcus, then back at me. Michael was still too young to understand what was happening, but I could see the wheels turning in my oldest son's head. He was starting to understand what his mother had accused me of, and he didn't look too happy now. I cursed myself under my breath. I should have had the guts to tell them myself that Marcus was their little brother. I should have been a man about it. Now, James Jr. had heard the news during his mother's outburst, so Marcus, even if they grew to accept him as a brother, would always be a reminder of Cathy's pain at this moment.

I wanted to chase after Cathy and pull the boys out of her grasp. I wanted to sit down with them and find a way to explain this whole thing. It was important that they knew that I never meant to hurt their mother, and that I still wanted us to be a family. But my legs wouldn't let me move. It was as if the grass had grown in a tangle around my ankles and was holding me in place as I watched my sons disappear.

I felt Marcus poking me now. "Daddy?" he said quietly. I was still frozen, and I couldn't even open my mouth to answer him. He just kept poking my ribs and calling my name until finally, my eyes popped open and I realized where I was.

I was in the guest bedroom in my mother's house, where I'd been for over a month now. She'd finally let me move off the couch when she came to terms with the idea that it would be an extended stay. Of course, she was still dropping hints and making suggestions every day about how I should go about getting my family back, but it was nothing I hadn't been thinking about myself.

Every night I would have dreams about going to see Cathy to work out a solution, but this was the first time my sons were there too. The image of their faces was still fresh in my mind, and I had to wipe away a single tear before I turned to look at Marcus, who'd been sleeping next to me.

"Hey, Marcus," I said, trying to sound much more cheerful than I felt. "How are you, little man?"

He asked the same question I heard every morning as soon as we woke up: "Daddy, can I go see my Mommy today?"

And every morning, I had to give him the same answer. I had concocted a story about how his mother just went on a little vacation. She would call us whenever she came back, I promised, and then we could go see her together.

"And then I can stay with her?" he would ask, and I could only give him a halfhearted smile as I answered, "We'll see, okay?" The conversation was the same every morning, and each time, I would find a way to distract him as quickly as possible so that I could stop lying to him.

This time, I asked, "Hey, you wanna go in the kitchen and see what kind of cereal we have?"

"Okay," he said, still sounding sleepy.

I took his hand and helped him climb out of bed, then guided him to the kitchen cabinets, where we examined the choices. There were plenty of boxes to choose from, courtesy of my mother. Once she heard about Michelle's decision to abandon Marcus for Trent, she resigned herself to the fact that we were going to be with her for a while. Although she acted like it was a great inconvenience for her, the shelves were overstuffed with treats for a child, which told me that she wouldn't have had it any other way. She knew Marcus was suffering from his mother's absence, and she wasn't about to add to that pain by rejecting him too.

I felt the same way, which was why I was still here with him. The possibility of contacting social services and finding a placement for him had crossed my mind a few times, but it always left me feeling ashamed to have even considered it. I would keep Marcus as long as I had to, even if I still hoped that someday his mother would want him back.

As I watched him eat the bowl of sugary cereal he had chosen, I thought about my other sons. I wondered if they felt abandoned by me. Did they miss me the way Marcus missed Michelle? I had no idea what Cathy had told them about my sudden absence. They were a little too old to believe the story of the "little vacation" I'd used on Marcus, but I hoped she'd come up with another believable story. The only other alternative was to tell them the truth, that she'd kicked me out when she found out I had a baby with another woman. Just like in my dream, I had a sudden urge to speak to them, to explain my side of the story before they heard their mother's version and decided I was a monster.

After I got Marcus settled in the living room with his toys, I went to the phone hanging on the wall in the kitchen. I picked up the receiver and stared at it, wondering if I could really gather the courage to make the call. I'd only tried to call once before, but hung up before anyone answered at my house. I wasn't ready then to face the conversation where I had to tell Cathy that Marcus was still with me, and he would be indefinitely. If he was gone, I would have begged her to let me come home. Now I knew going home was out of the question. I missed my sons terribly, though, so this time I was going to stay on the line until Cathy answered. What I would say to her remained to be seen, but I had to get her to let me see the boys.

When I heard Cathy's voice, I couldn't speak. My heart raced and my palms were sweating, but I couldn't make my mouth form a word.

"I know it's you, James." Somehow, she managed to say my name in a way that made it sound like some sort of infectious disease. "Your mother's number comes up on the caller ID, you know." She waited for an answer, and when I remained silent, she said, "Oh well, guess you're too much of a coward to speak, so I'm gonna hang up the phone now. Have a nice li—"

"No!" I shouted, finally finding my voice. "Please don't hang up. I . . . I really want to talk to you."

"Hmmm . . . let's see. Are you calling to talk about when you're going to send me some child support? 'Cause if you're not, then I don't think there's anything we have to talk about."

"Cathy, please don't be like that."

"Like what? Like a woman who's pissed off because she found out that her husband is a fuckin' cheat and a liar? Like a woman who just found out her husband has another family?"

I tried to protest. "We're not a family."

"Oh, really? Well, what do you call it when you have a mommy, a daddy, and a baby?" I could just picture the way her face was twisted up, her eyebrows raised as she demanded answers from me.

"We are not a family," I repeated. "I probably won't ever speak to Michelle again."

"Don't fool yourself. She's your baby mama now. You have to deal with that woman for the next eighteen years. I, on the other hand, will be happy to never speak to you again. You can just mail me my checks."

"No," I said quietly, "I might never speak to her again because she left Marcus with me. She doesn't want him back."

Cathy was quiet for a minute. I expected her to yell, but when she finally spoke, it was slowly and practically in a whisper. "Did you just tell me she left her child?"

"Yes," was all I managed to say.

"What kind of ghetto trash were you messing with? What kind of mother abandons her child?"

We were both quiet, and when I could no longer stand the silence, I said, "I want to see the boys."

"Why?" she asked in an icy voice. "You have one son with you, so why would you need to see *my* boys?"

"Come on, Cathy. You know that's not right. I need to speak to them. I want them to understand why I haven't been around. That I love them." I waited a few seconds before asking the question that I was afraid to hear answered. "Do they hate me?"

"No, James," she said with a sigh, "they miss you."

I couldn't suppress the smile that came across my face. It was such a relief to hear there might still be some hope for my relationship with my boys, though I had serious doubts about any possible future for me and Cathy.

"They don't hate you," she continued, "because they don't know like I do who you really are."

This took me by surprise. "You haven't told them anything?"

"No. I'll leave that up to you. You're the one who fucked up and had a child outside our marriage, so you should be the one who has to look into their eyes and watch their hearts break when you tell them what you did."

As scary as it was to imagine admitting my failings to my boys, I was relieved that Cathy hadn't poisoned them against me. "When can I see them?" I asked with a mixture of excitement and dread.

"You can see them this afternoon, if you want. But I have two conditions."

"What are they?"

She laid down her rules. "One, you can't stay here with them. You'll have to take them out somewhere, because I don't think I can stand the sight of you right now. And two, you can't bring your *other* child with you. Maybe in the future, but this time is for them."

Poor Marcus, he was so young and innocent, yet it was clear that Cathy hated even the thought of his existence. Still, I could understand her point. I would have to talk my mother into watching him while I went to see my two oldest boys.

"No problem, Cathy. I just really need to see them. I can't tell you how much I miss them," I said.

"Mm-hmm," she said with skepticism. "Like I said before, it's too bad you didn't think of that before you got that bitch pregnant."

"Okay," I said, feeling defenseless. "I'll be by this afternoon, but I'm going to tell them about Marcus."

"Uh-huh," she said with as little interest as possible. "Oh, and James . . ."

"Yeah?" I asked, hoping she might say something to give me even a glimmer of hope for our marriage.

"Bring me a check when you come. I've got some overdue bills to pay."

39

Brent

The next day, when I caught my plane to San Francisco, my mind was made up. I couldn't live without Jackie. At the same time, I was still shamed that Alison had caught us together in our house, and that I couldn't make our marriage work, but in a way, I was relieved. The question was, how would we be received? What would people think? Neither one of us fit the profile of a flaming gay guy. For one, we were both very masculine and clean cut. We were both prominent members of the church. Would this change how people viewed us? I definitely think it would.

Why couldn't life be simple? Why couldn't Jackie be Alison, where I would get all the backing from the church? And, come to think of it, what would people say about me leaving my pregnant wife? I knew they were going to say there was something depraved about what Jackie and I had, but I'd never felt so clean. It all felt so right for me now. I couldn't help it. I loved Jackie. He made me feel complete.

After I attended my business meetings, I went to my hotel. I needed time to do some soul searching. My whole life was getting ready to change. I still hadn't talked to Sonny or James to let them know what was going down, although I did leave voice-mail messages that it was important that they come to church on Sunday. As soon as I unpacked, my hotel room phone rang. It was Jackie. "Hey, baby." His voice wavered and he sounded uncertain.

"Hey, Jackie. I guess you got my message."

I heard Jackie draw a sigh of relief on the other end of the phone. "Yeah, I got it, and I just wanted to make sure you made it safely."

"I'm fine. When I get back we need to talk."

"I guess it's over with Alison." Jackie sounded hopeful.

"Yeah, it is. I can't pretend anymore. I'm going to announce that I'm gay at church on Sunday."

"Do you want me to be there with you? So we can go as a couple?"

"I sure do."

"Well, I'll be there waiting for you. Sunday's as good a day as ever to come out of the closet."

I was lying on the bed in my hotel room, replaying my last conversation with Jackie over and over in my mind. I had reached the point where I was ready to leave Alison and be in a relationship with Jackie, but would I be able to go through with announcing our homosexual love to our church congregation as I promised? So much had happened in my life so quickly, I was actually glad for the chance to be in San Francisco, away from everyone, while I tried to put it all in perspective. I grew tired as I lay in the room, my emotions running the entire spectrum, from elation over a budding relationship with the man I loved to grief over the loss of my friendship with Alison, and the relationship I might never be allowed to develop with my unborn child. When I could no longer stand the thoughts swirling around in my head, I decided to go get something to eat. I hoped that sitting outside at a café and taking in the sights of this beautiful city would be enough of a distraction to make me forget everything for a while.

I headed across the street to the Harbor Café, where I ordered a sandwich and a coffee, then carried my tray to the outdoor dining section. When I sat down and unwrapped my sandwich, I looked around at the other diners, some of whom were obviously gay, wondering if any of them had problems as serious as mine were. That's when I spotted a familiar face. She resembled Alicia Keys, and although we were never really that close, I'd recognize that face anywhere. I thought that perhaps talking to her might divert my thoughts for a while. I got up, gathered my meal onto the tray again, and approached her table.

"Jessica?" I looked down at Sonny's wife, or ex-wife, or whatever she was now. He hadn't mentioned getting any divorce papers, but the last time I talked to him, he told me things with

Tiffany were great and he was planning on asking her to marry him soon. I assumed this meant he had moved on with his life. I wondered if Jessica had too.

"How are you?" I asked casually, though in my mind I was conjuring up a million more questions about what she'd done to my boy Sonny.

Apparently she wasn't in the mood to engage in small talk, though, and got right to the point. "Brent . . ." she said quietly, looking at me through glasses so dark I couldn't see her eyes. "Please don't tell Sonny you saw me here."

I wondered why she sounded so nervous and her hands were trembling. Now she had my curiosity aroused. I wanted to ask some questions, but obviously she wasn't going to talk to me unless I assured her I wouldn't tell anyone.

"Sonny doesn't even know I'm here, but I'm sure he'd love to know where you're at, considering you kidnapped his kids. Besides, he's been a little preoccupied lately, so I don't get much chance to talk to him."

"I did not kidnap his kids—I saved them from him. And what do you mean, preoccupied? He hasn't been trying to find me, has he?" she asked, obviously jealous.

"No," I answered, unable to resist a jab at this woman who had broken my friend's heart. "He's moved on with his life, Jessica. He met a really great woman, and they're living together now."

"He's got another woman? Oh, thank God." I was surprised by her interest in Sonny's dating habits. I would have guessed it was jealousy, except that she actually looked happy when I told her Sonny had another woman in his life.

"Yeah. So, can I sit down?"

"Oh, yeah, sorry." She gestured to the chair next to her. I sat down and unwrapped my sandwich again.

"So, who's this woman Sonny is with now?" Yeah, she could pretend to be relieved, but she was jealous.

"Her name is Tiffany. It's someone he went to high school with."

"Didn't he used to date someone named Tiffany?"

"Yeah. It's the same woman," I said, even more surprised by her constant questions. "Jessica, can I ask you something?"

She looked uncomfortable. "I suppose, but I can't promise I'll answer you."

"Well, why are you so interested in Sonny now that he has another woman? Could you possibly be feeling guilty for leaving him the way you did?" I asked, hoping I hadn't overstepped my bounds. I wanted to get as much information as possible because I knew that Sonny would want to know as much as possible. To my surprise, she answered it, but in a strange way.

"If I know that Sonny is with someone else, then I can be a little less scared that he might be trying to hunt me down."

I was taken aback by her choice of words. "Hunt you down? Sure, you broke his heart, but I wouldn't say it was as serious as all that. As a matter of fact, he seemed to get with Tiffany pretty soon after he came back from Seattle." Now that I thought about it, Sonny did bounce back quicker than I would think any man would be able to. Either he was an incredibly strong person, or he was still dealing with some unresolved issues. The only thing that was strange, now that I considered it, was that I'd never heard Sonny mention missing his kids. It was like Jessica and the kids disappeared, so he just plugged another family into the empty slots.

"Let me ask you a question, Brent. What did Sonny tell you was my reason for leaving him?"

"Well, he hasn't really talked about it much, but he said he thought you had another man."

"And he hasn't been talking about coming to find me?"

"Not that I've heard. Like I said, he hooked up with Tiffany pretty quick."

She rested her elbows on the table and said sadly, "Whoever this woman is, I want you to get a message to her. Tell her to get away from him as soon as she possibly can and don't stop running until she's in another state."

That was wrong of her, as far as I was concerned. She left the guy, and now she wanted to make sure he stayed lonely forever, I guess. I had to speak my mind. "You know, Jessica, that's pretty messed up. I don't know what your reason was for abandoning him and taking away his kids, but it's just not right for you to try to get in between him and his new woman now. Can't you just let the guy have some happiness?"

"Why, he never let me have any happiness. You don't know

why I left him. . . ." she said, her voice fading away. Her hands started to shake again as she raised them toward the dark sunglasses she'd been wearing. "This is why I left Sonny." She removed her glasses, revealing a recently healed wound that traveled from the corner of one eye, across her brow, and ended over the bridge of her nose. It appeared to have needed stitches, and would definitely leave a scar above her eyelid, which drooped lazily over what were once striking hazel eyes. Now they looked frightened and sad.

"He did this to you?" I asked, already knowing what her answer would be.

She nodded. "It's taken almost five months to heal. I've got plenty of other scars from places he's hit me, kicked me, bit me. One time, he broke three of my ribs with a bat."

I was stunned. Could we really be talking about the same guy? Sonny was always talking about his family; he seemed so devoted to them. It was hard to imagine him hurting someone he seemed to love so much. I wondered if maybe she was just making this up. After all, she'd only shown me a scar on her face, and all I had to go on was her version of events. For all I knew, the cut over her eye was caused by some accident unrelated to Sonny. I didn't want to believe he was capable of this. Maybe if I kept asking questions I'd catch her in some sort of lie.

"How long has this been going on?"

"It started almost as soon as we got married," she said, putting her sunglasses on again. That's when I noticed a few small, circular scars on the back of one hand. *Could they be cigarette burns?* I wondered. "In the beginning, it wasn't so bad. Once we moved out to Seattle, though, things just kept escalating. He had this set of rules that I had to live by, and if I broke one of the rules I had to be punished." Now that I thought about it, Sonny always said you had to have rules if a marriage was going to work. I just never thought he meant that so literally.

"Why didn't you leave him sooner?" This seemed to be an obvious question. If things were really as bad as she was saying, why wouldn't she have gotten out?

"That's not as easy as it sounds. Once we moved to the West Coast, I was basically a prisoner. He wouldn't let me work. He wouldn't give me any money unless I went to the store with him. He'd go through my purse. At first he made me account for my every minute out of his sight in a journal, and then he just stopped letting me out of his sight altogether. Why do you think he lost his job? It got so bad that he started locking me in the closet whenever he was going out. Even if I wanted to run, where was I supposed to go? I didn't know anyone in Seattle. I didn't have a car that I could just hop into and get away. If he hadn't left for New York for your wedding, I might have been dead by now."

"But if he wasn't letting you out of his sight, why would he travel all the way to New York without you?" I asked.

She pointed to her sunglasses. "The week before the wedding is when he gave me this scar. We were supposed to go with him, but he couldn't exactly bring me to your wedding with stitches all over my face."

This story was so contrary to the picture Sonny had painted of his perfect family life in Seattle. "Jessica, Sonny told me things were great with his family, and now you're telling me all this. How could your two versions be so different?" I asked, still grasping at the hope that her story was false.

"I don't expect you to believe me. I know you never liked me, Brent. Sonny made it perfectly clear that you and James always thought I was bad for him. I know he never defended me when you guys would talk bad about me, because that was exactly how he wanted it to be."

I didn't respond, mostly because I was embarrassed by how right she was. James, Sonny, and I had spent plenty of nights discussing Jessica, and he really hadn't put much effort into changing our opinions of her. In fact, we'd never really had much contact with Jessica, so our opinions of her were based on things he would tell us about her.

"Yeah, it was perfect that you two didn't like me enough to want to come visit us in Seattle. In fact, I bet he never invited you, did he?"

"No, but I just assumed—"

"You assumed that it was because I didn't like you," she said, and she was correct. "But the truth is, he couldn't let you guys come to Seattle to see what was really happening in our home. No one was ever allowed in our house. The kids weren't even allowed to have friends over."

"Okay," I said, trying not to sound confrontational, though I was still looking to poke holes in her story. "If he wanted to keep you away from us, then why was he planning to move you back to New York?"

"I don't really know," she answered. "I suppose he just really missed you guys. His abuse had gotten so out of control, maybe he just lost touch with reality. He might have really convinced himself that he could hide me away even if you and James lived close by. Who knows? Maybe he planned on killing me once he got us there. All I know is that I was sure it was my only chance at freedom, so I told him the move was a great idea. As soon as he left for your wedding, I started packing everything."

"How are the kids? Are they here with you?"

"I don't wanna talk about them," she said firmly. "I know Sonny's your boy, and I can't risk letting you give him any information. I can't even be sure that you won't tell him about this."

She sounded so scared. I wanted to be able to assure her that I wouldn't give her up to Sonny, but I couldn't. After everything she had told me, I had a lot to process. Her story was so far from the image I had of my friend and his marriage that it was hard to believe it could be true. Still, she didn't seem to be faking the fearful state she was in. And now that I'd mentioned her kids, she began fidgeting in her chair, until she finally stood up.

"I know he's your friend, and I don't expect you to make me any promises. All I can do is ask you not to mention to Sonny that you saw me here. And now that you have, I'll probably be moving again anyway." She turned to leave. "But if you give some thought to everything I've told you, I bet you'll realize that your friend is capable of this."

I had very little to say at that point. Either I was talking to a pathological liar or I was talking to a woman who had been tortured by my good friend for years. I still didn't know which version of their marriage was real. "Take care, Jessica," I said.

"If you do decide to talk to someone about this, Brent, consider talking to that woman Tiffany. You might be saving her life," Jessica said, then disappeared into the crowd of window-shoppers on the sidewalk.

I had been right to think that talking to Jessica would take my mind off my problems for a while, but I had no idea that she would be handing me a whole new set of issues to deal with. Whatever the truth was, I knew that now I had to talk to Sonny as soon as I finished my business in San Francisco.

* * *

I thought I would be able to wait until I got back to New York to talk to Sonny, but the conversation with Jessica had been weighing so heavily on my mind that I called him from the plane before we even landed at LaGuardia.

"Sonny, it's me, Brent. You got a minute?"

"For you, I got as many minutes as you need. What's up? Does this have anything to do with you insisting we all go to church tomorrow?" His question caused my stomach to lurch.

"No, that's an entirely different issue. What I wanna talk to you about directly involves you."

"I'm all ears. What's going on?"

"You're not going to believe this, but I saw Jessica." There was silence on the line. "Sonny, you there?"

"Where'd you see her? Did you see my kids? Are they all right?" Sonny didn't know that I had been in San Francisco, and he didn't know I was calling from the plane, and until I figured out what the truth was, I didn't necessarily want to tell him where I'd seen Jessica.

"I didn't see the kids, but Jessica seemed all right . . . although she seemed scared."

"Where is she? Do you know where I can find them?" He was insistent. I suppose any man would be anxious to find out where his kids were after they'd been taken from him so suddenly. Then again, maybe he had another reason to be eager to find Jessica. Either way, I couldn't tell him in good conscience.

"That's not important right now. What is important is what she had to say."

Sonny's breathing was heavy and agitated. "I don't give a damn what she had to say. I know you didn't believe anything that lying heifer had to say, did you?"

I contemplated my response, wishing I could tell my friend I had no doubt Jessica was lying. "I'm not sure what to believe, Sonny. But I'm pretty sure she didn't give herself those scars on her eye and her hands."

"I didn't give her those scars. Brent, you don't know what she's capable of. That woman's crazy. You saw how she sold all my shit." He sounded desperate for me to believe him, like a guilty person often is. I was starting to feel uneasy, but still wanted to give my friend the benefit of the doubt.

"How did she get those burns, Sonny?"

"Look, Brent," he said suddenly, "Tiffany just walked into the room. Can we talk about this later? Why don't we just meet somewhere?"

"I'll be home in a couple hours. Why don't you just meet me at my house?"

"Sure, man, but don't be jumping to no conclusions until I have a chance to talk to you. Oh, and let's just keep this between us. Trust me. There's a logical explanation."

"I would hope so, man. I would hate to think that you're capable of something like this."

"I'm not, man," he insisted.

Two hours later, I pulled my car into the driveway and saw that all the lights were out, letting me know that Alison was most likely staying at the hospital with the first lady. I'm sure she was still upset that I was going to announce to the entire congregation that I was gay, and she had probably stayed away on purpose, knowing I was due to arrive home. The first thing that came to my mind was to call Jackie. Then I realized that I had asked Sonny to stop by, so I would have to put my own issues on the back burner long enough to clear up this stuff with him. If it turned out that he had indeed been hitting Jessica, I would do what I could to get him some help as soon as possible.

I stepped out of the car, then opened the rear driver's-side door to retrieve my bag. That's when he stepped out from around the side of the house carrying a baseball bat. He was dressed in all black and wearing a ski mask. Before I had a chance to think, he swung the bat at me, hitting me directly in the arm. His next swing hit my knee, and I fell helplessly to the ground. I covered my head as the bat continuously struck my back and lower spine. I knew I was in trouble when I heard my back crack. The pain was incredible, and I could only pray that my life would somehow be spared.

40

James

Cathy's call woke me up about two in the morning. She told me to get over to the house right away because it was an emergency. I tried to find out what the hell was going on, but the only answer she gave me was, "Just hurry," and then she hung up the phone. Well, you know I got up right away and told my mother to watch Marcus because I had to go see about my family.

Cathy met me at the door in her housecoat.

"What's wrong? What's going on?"

"Come on," she demanded, grabbing my arm and gesturing for me to follow her up the stairs. Why the hell was she being so damn mysterious? If she was taking me upstairs, there was obviously something wrong with one of the boys. As I realized this, my heart began pounding. I was relieved when we passed James Jr.'s room, but I almost burst into tears when she stopped in front of Michael's room.

"What's wrong with Michael?" I pleaded.

I reached for the door handle, but she stopped me. "Shh, you'll wake up the boys." She pushed me across the hall into what used to be our bedroom, where she closed the door, then took off her robe. She was naked underneath. I didn't have to be told what to do next. I kissed her like I'd never done before. Whatever brought on this complete change in her behavior toward me, I wasn't going to complain now. Getting Cathy to take me back had been the only thought consuming me for weeks, and now here we were, in our bedroom, about to make love. I couldn't have asked for more.

"I missed you so much, baby," I confessed as I picked her up and carried her to our bed. She didn't say a word, but her body's reaction was all I needed as I kissed and caressed every inch of her. When I finally went down on her, I wasn't just trying to make her have an orgasm, I was trying to make a statement—no man, no matter who he was, could do what I could do to her.

When I'd given her enough oral pleasure, I slid up over her body, positioning myself to enter her.

"Wait." She reached over to her night table, then handed me a condom. "I want you to wear this."

"For what? You've got your diaphragm in. I could feel it when I put my finger in you." I hated condoms, and I only carried them for times Cathy and I wanted to be spontaneous.

"So what? I don't know who you've been with." Her expression was set, and she obviously wasn't budging from this position, so before the mood was gone entirely, I ripped open the condom wrapper and put it on.

It wasn't the most ideal situation for me, but I made the best of it. Cathy seemed to be happy, and actually pleaded with me for a second round. When we finished, she got up to go to the bathroom, and I got under the covers to get some sleep. I don't know how long it took me to doze off, but I did hear the shower running. Don't ask me what time she woke me up, but I'm sure I wasn't asleep long.

"James, get your ass up." She shook me.

"Huh? What time is it?" I hadn't even opened my eyes yet.

"Time for you to get your ass up."

I looked at the clock radio. "Come on, Cathy. I don't have to get up for another two hours."

"I'll be damned. Your ass is getting up now." Her voice was dead serious.

"Why?" I sat up and stretched, staring at her. She was standing in front of me with her robe on and a towel around her head. In her hands were clean sheets.

"Because I don't want the boys to see you."

I raised an eyebrow. "Why not? We just made love. We're on the road to getting back together."

"Getting back together? Making love? Are you seeing the same picture I'm seeing? Because all I saw was a booty call."

"A booty call!" I couldn't believe what I was hearing. "Is that really what it was to you?"

"Uh-huh, that's it. Why do you think I made you wear that condom? Now, can you get out of my bed?"

I got up in a huff. "Why the fuck would you call me for a booty call?" I was hurt when I realized that my dreams for a reconciliation had been hopeless. But even more than being hurt, I was insulted. This was my wife, and she had just used me like a gigolo. I had been so damn foolish.

"Why do you think I called you? I was horny." She started to strip the bed as I got dressed. "I thought about going to a bar or something like that, but the boys were here. Besides, new dick is like playing Lotto. Sometimes you come so close, but you never know if you're gonna hit. I knew what I was getting with you. Shit, I even got a little extra, by the way. Thank you. But now you got to go."

"This was fucked up, Cathy."

"So was you having a baby with another woman, James. So I guess we're both fucked up."

"Whatever." I started to walk to the door.

"Hey, James." I turned to see her smirking at me. With a hand on her hip and head cocked to the side, she said, "Just so you know, there was one other person I could have called."

"What are you talking about?"

"You're not the only one who had a little something on the side when we were talking about divorce," she said devilishly, clearly getting pleasure out of sharing this news.

"You—" I started, but she cut me off.

"Yeah, I did, but at least I wasn't stupid enough to go have a baby by someone else."

My stomach went into knots. As stupid as it might be, considering I had an affair myself, I felt jealousy coursing through my veins at the thought of my wife with another man. I wanted to know who the hell she had been with. And who was watching my children while she was out screwing some other guy? Yeah, I knew I was being totally unreasonable, but it's what I was thinking, and there was no way I could stop it as I dropped my head into my hands and wondered how my life had gotten to this point.

When I walked out of the bedroom door, my son Michael was walking out of the bathroom.

"Daddy!" he yelled, running into my arms and calling out to wake his brother. "Jay-Jay, come quick! Daddy's home, and he's coming out of Mommy's room." He turned to me and asked, "Daddy, did you bring our other brother with you?"

Before I could even think about how to answer him, James Jr. appeared at his door and ran toward me, arms out for a hug. "Dad!" he shouted. I held both of my boys tight. "Dad, are you staying? Are you coming back home now?" He sounded so sad.

I turned to Cathy, who was standing in the doorway. "Son, that's up to your mom. But that's a conversation for another day."

She rolled her eyes at me, but then looked at our sons. There was no denying the joy on their faces, and she knew it as well as I did. "No, boys," she said, "Daddy's not coming home . . . but he can come by and see you anytime he wants now." She turned around and went back into the bedroom, shutting the door. I carried my boys into their bedroom to tuck them into bed with a promise to be back to see them very soon.

41

Sonny

I'd been watching Tiffany clean the house, then work out to her Pilates tape, via webcam at work for the past half-hour. It's absolutely amazing what you can do with technology these days, and having a cousin like Lowjack brought the price of going high-tech right into my range. For the past four weeks, Tiffany couldn't fart without me knowing it. I had the poor woman so paranoid that I think she thought I had mind-reading abilities after the last couple of ass-whippings I'd given her for breaking the rules. She kept asking me how I'd found out what she did, but of course I came up with some excuse that made it look like my neighbors told me or that she'd been stupid enough to leave some type of incriminating evidence. I've got to give her credit, though. She'd been pretty good the last two weeks. I hadn't even had to raise my voice even once, which supported my theory that women are like children; they need discipline, structure, and a firm hand.

As I watched Tiffany exercise, I actually thought about going home for lunch. She looked so sexy in that Lycra doing those stretches, I was getting horny as hell. A little lunch time pu-pu would have been nice. Unfortunately, my show was ended abruptly when she stopped doing her exercises and stood up. I watched her go from the family room to the front door and made a mental note to put my foot in her ass for opening the door wearing that skimpy-ass workout gear. I wanted to scream when she invited two men in suits into our house and they sat down on the sofa.

I pushed a few buttons on my computer, activating the listening device in the living room, then turned up the volume. I almost hadn't taken the sound equipment, but my cousin talked me into it. Now I realized how invaluable it was to me. Next time I saw Lowjack, I was going to have to give him a little extra for hooking me up with everything I needed to keep Tiffany in line.

"Fuck," I mumbled under my breath. It was the cops, and they were asking Tiffany about Kareem. I should have expected this. I mean, it had been over a month since his death, and she was his ex-wife. It's a good thing I didn't leave his body behind in his house.

The cops spent almost forty minutes talking to Tiffany, and if you ask me, they were doing a little bit too much staring at her legs and breasts. I actually saw one of them bend his whole body to the side to get a good look at her ass when they were following her to the door to leave. I was going to have to teach her a real lesson when I got home. Maybe it was time to break out the cigarettes.

I picked up my phone and dialed the department secretary when the cops left. "Stacy, I think I'm going home for lunch. Can you have my calls forwarded to my cell?"

"Sure, Sonny. Just remember, you've got a two o'clock meeting with shipping."

"Don't worry. I'll be back way before then."

By the time I pulled in the driveway, Tiffany had called three times, probably to tell me about the cops. I didn't answer the calls, but I was happy to see she made them. I was still gonna whip her ass for sitting in front of those cops with that tight-ass Lycra, but because she'd called me before I got home, I'd forgo the cigarette punishment for now.

When I opened the door, Tiffany was sitting on the couch, still in her workout clothes. "Sonny, what are you doing home?"

"I came home for lunch. Why, did I miss something?"

"Well, sort of. The police were here." She looked at me, probably wondering if I'd already known, considering how many times I'd demonstrated my "mind-reading" ability over the last few weeks.

"Yeah, I know. Mrs. Pollock from down the street told me when I pulled up."

Tiffany shook her head. "Doggone it, Sonny. Why do you have the whole damn block spying on me?"

I smiled. "Don't get mad at me because I've made friends on the block and you haven't."

"It's kind of hard to make friends when everyone in the neighborhood thinks they're on your payroll. I'm surrounded by spies. And how did she know those guys were cops, anyway? Did you have her listening at the door or something?"

She didn't know how close she was to the truth. "C'mon, Tif. People in this neighborhood can spot an unmarked cop car from a mile away. Anyway, you wouldn't be calling our neighbors spies if you didn't have something to hide."

"That's bull and you know it."

I waved my hand at her. "Whatever. So, why were the police in my house? And were you wearing that when they came in?" I gestured in the direction of her tight short shorts.

Tiffany wasn't stupid. She knew what I was implying, and she did not want to be punished for breaking another rule, the one that said that no other man should be allowed to see her in anything shorter than knee-length. She avoided the second question, looking frightened as she said, "They came to ask me some questions about Kareem. He's missing, and he hasn't been seen in over a month."

"Well, good riddance. He's probably somewhere doing some shit he's not supposed to do," I said nonchalantly. Tiffany didn't respond to that. "Hey, can a brother get a sandwich? I'm starved." I figured I better eat before I put my foot in her ass.

"Sure, baby." She got right back to the subject of Kareem as we walked into the kitchen. "This sure isn't like him to disappear like this. They said he didn't even cash his income-tax check, and I know that's not like him."

"Well, you never know. If we're lucky, they'll find him floating in a river somewhere and you can collect that life-insurance policy you took out on him."

"Sonny, I don't want him dead," she said with mild disapproval in her voice. "That's my kids' father."

I slammed my hand down on the kitchen table and spun around to face her. "No, they're my kids! That motherfucker didn't do shit for them or you. That's why I killed his ass." Tiffany froze, and I realized that my temper had possibly gotten me in trouble. I tried to clean it up. "I didn't mean that. I was just joking."

"You killed him?" This sounded like some kind of cross between a question and a statement.

"No, I didn't. I just said that in anger," I answered, opening the refrigerator casually and assuming the conversation was finished.

She wasn't ready to let it go yet. "Sonny, tell me you didn't have anything to do with this."

I took the orange juice out of the refrigerator and placed it on the counter. "I already told you, I didn't have anything to do with it. Now, can I get my sandwich?"

I expected to hear, "Sure, honey," but when I turned to look at her, she was staring at me like she was still waiting for me to say something about the subject.

"What the fuck are you looking at, damn it? I told you, I didn't have anything to do with it."

"You fuckin' killed him!" She knew I hated it when she talked to me this way, especially when she got up in my face.

"Lady, you better slow your fucking roll, 'cause you are fuckin' cruisin'," I warned.

"Cruisin' for what? You gonna kill me like you killed Kareem?" She put her finger in my face, and that was the last straw.

I grabbed her by the neck and dragged her to the basement door. "You wanna know if I killed him? I'll show you if I killed him!"

"Sonny, nooooooo!"

I opened the door and threw her down the stairs. "I told you to get outta my face, didn't I?"

At the bottom of the steps, she was still moving around pretty good, but she wasn't so damn talkative now. I walked down the stairs and over to a wine barrel in a corner of the basement. I pried off the cover, and the strong scent of vinegar filled the room. "You wanna know if I killed that motherfucker? You damn right I killed him. I beat his head in with a bat, then I put him in a barrel of vinegar so he wouldn't smell." I reached into the wine barrel. Tiffany screamed as I pulled out Kareem's head.

"I love you, Tiffany, and as you can see, I'll kill anyone who tries to get between us." I walked over and pulled her to her feet. She was shaking as if it were fifty degrees below zero. "I think we have a little dilemma right now. I may love you, but I don't trust you. I never did. That's why I built this room before I asked you to move in." I pointed to a cinder-block room with one door. "From now on, when I'm not home, you're going to stay in there. I can't have you talking to those cops again now that you know the truth about what I did for you."

"No, I'm not. I'm not," she protested, struggling to free herself from my grasp.

I smacked her. "Oh, you're going in there, all right. And when I let you out, you're going to be the perfect wife. 'Cause if you aren't, I'm going to use Tony and Nikki for batting practice, then put them in barrels right next to their daddy." She covered her mouth, her eyes wide open in horror. "Do we understand each other?"

She nodded as the first few tears escaped from her eyes.

"Good. Now get in there. The phone's ringing, and I gotta go back to work. I'll call the school and tell them that I'll be picking the kids up from the after-school program on my way home this evening."

42

James

I'd just stopped off at the Jamaican joint over by Rochdale Village for a beef patty and some coco bread when my cell started to ring. I got back in my UPS truck and checked the caller ID. It was my house, which didn't make any sense because Cathy should have been at work.

"Hello."

"Can you talk?" It was Cathy, all right, and she didn't sound happy.

"Yeah, Cathy, what's up?" I was still pissed off at her about the booty call last month, but she had been good about letting me come to see the boys whenever I wanted. She'd even let me bring them to my mother's house to meet Marcus once. So, even if there wasn't much warmth between us right now, we were on speaking terms, and I was grateful for at least that much. I still loved her after everything we'd gone through, and until she was ready to try again, I would always be there for her and the boys.

"I just got back from the school," she said. "It seems we have a problem with Jay-Jay."

"What type of problem? I know he ain't fighting again."

"Yes, he was fighting, but that's not just it. I had a meeting with the school psychologist today. Jay-Jay's grades are down, and he's been acting up in class."

"I'm gonna whip that boy's ass."

"No, James, it's not his fault." I was surprised by Cathy's tone. Normally, when our sons misbehaved, she was right there with me, ready to discipline firmly.

"Not his fault? Whose fault is it?" I asked.

"Yours and mine. The psychologist seems to think that our

separation is directly related to James's behavior. . . ." She was quiet for a few seconds. "And I think she's right."

Now I understood why she sounded so defeated, so tired. Our problems had been taking their toll on everyone, and now that it was following the boys to school, it felt like the final straw.

"Well, what are we supposed to do?" There was no sound on the other end, and for a moment, I thought maybe my cell phone had dropped the call. "Cathy? You still there?"

She answered quietly. "Maybe you should move back in." My mouth dropped open in shock, but before I could respond, she added, "Not in my bedroom, but in the basement. What do you think?"

Now it was my turn for silence. This was exactly what I'd been waiting for, a chance to move back home, but did I really want to do it this way? I wanted my wife to ask me back home because she wanted me there, not only because it was the right thing to do for the kids. And, of course, there was still one major obstacle—Marcus.

"I'm sorry, Cathy, but I can't do it. . . ." I didn't even finish my sentence before she jumped in.

"What?" If it was possible, she sounded more upset than she'd been in a while, and lately her emotions had been running pretty high. "How could you not do this for your son?"

I didn't let her anger get me riled up. "Cathy," I said gently, "you know I love them and I'd do anything for my sons. I love you too. There's nothing I want more than for us to be together as a family again."

"Then what the hell is your problem, James?"

"It's Marcus. Don't forget, Cathy, he's with me now, and he's my son too. Are you ready to handle having him move in with you?"

After a long pause, her voice was less agitated when she answered. "That's a lot to ask of me, James."

"I know that, but his mother already deserted him, and I won't do it too. He's a good kid, and I'm going to do right by him. If you want me to come home, then he's coming with me. But I'm giving you the choice. If you can't handle it, tell me you don't want me to come home, and I'll understand. We'll find another way to help Jay-Jay get through this."

"Can't you just ask your mother to keep him?" she asked, but her tone told me she already understood that solution would be impossible.

"That wouldn't work, and you know it. My mother needs her life and her house back, and Marcus needs at least one of his parents with him."

Cathy didn't speak for a long time. I waited patiently, knowing this was not an easy decision for her to be making.

"You're a good father, James," she finally said. "Jay-Jay and Michael need you home."

"I love my boys, Cathy. But do you think you can handle this? I don't want you to say yes now and then take it out on Marcus once we're living in the house."

I heard her release a long sigh. "You know, we both made mistakes when we were having problems back then. The only difference is that she got pregnant and I didn't." The reminder of Cathy's affair stabbed at me a little, but I knew this was a huge step toward reconciliation, so I remained silent. "He's innocent in this whole thing, just like our boys are. We have to do what's best for the boys . . . all three of them. Come home, James."

"We'll be there tonight," I said, unable to suppress my excitement.

"You know, you're going to have to do a lot more around the house and with the kids," she pointed out.

"That would only make sense," I responded, still unable to suppress the huge grin on my face.

"Don't be asking me for no sex, either."

"I won't even go near your room unless you invite me in."

She sighed heavily again. "All right, we can try it. But I reserve the right to kick both of your asses out at any time."

"Done. We'll see you after I get off work." I closed my phone and started the truck, confident that my family would soon be whole, and my marriage could once again become strong.

43

Brent

I woke up to a blinding bright light. Was I dead? I knew I'd been attacked by a man with a baseball bat, I did remember that, but I felt no pain. It was almost as if I were floating. The light seemed to get more intense and closer to my eyes. Was it the light I'd heard people talk about on those documentaries about crossing over? In the church, people always talked about wanting to go home. Was that light the road home? Was I about to meet my maker, the Lord Himself? And if so, did this mean He'd forgiven me for my homosexuality and my adultery and was allowing me into Heaven? I waited for a voice. It didn't take long before I heard one.

"Brent. Brent, can you hear me?" Was that it? Was it the voice of God calling me? It seemed so normal. I guess I was just conditioned to think that God's voice would sound as deep as James Earl Jones's or be followed by an echo or something spectacular. Then again, the Bible says that man was created in God's image, so why couldn't God's voice sound normal?

"Brent, can you hear me?" the voice called again.

"Yes, I can hear you. Is that you? Is that you, God?"

After a momentary pause, I heard laughter. The light seemed to be moving farther away, and I started to panic. "God, is that you?" There was more laughter, and for the first time it hit me. Maybe I wasn't in Heaven; maybe I was in Hell. Maybe that voice wasn't God's, but the voice of the devil. I closed my eyes in fear and called out for God one last time. "God, is that you?"

I finally got a reply.

"No, Brent, I'm not God." When I opened my eyes, the light had been removed, and leaning over me, although my vision was still blurred, I saw a bearded white man. "I'm your doctor. My name is Dr. Rosenthal, and you're in Long Island Jewish Hospital."

A voice came from behind him. "Do you remember what happened?" The figure came closer, and as he came into focus, I realized he was a black man in a police uniform.

"All I remember is getting out of my car and some guy attacking me with a baseball bat," I said in a voice that was still weak.

"Did you get a good look at his face?"

"He was wearing a mask."

"Did he say anything before he hit you? Was there anything familiar about the person?"

"Hey, leave him alone. He just woke up. You can ask him all the questions you want once he gets himself together." There was no mistaking Sonny's distinguishable voice as he approached. "You okay, buddy? You don't have to answer this guy's questions right now."

"Where's James?" I asked groggily.

"I'm right here, Brent. We're all here." James came up on the right side of the bed, across from Sonny. "Alison's here, too. So are Cathy and the kids. They're outside in the waiting room."

As my memory came into focus, I recalled the most recent events in my life. I remembered the conversation with Jessica in San Francisco. I had called Sonny from the plane to ask him about it, and not long after, I was waking up in a hospital bed. Now I had some serious suspicions about my attack and the possibility that the two incidents were related.

"Sonny, where's Tiffany?" I asked.

"She's . . . with the kids at the house."

"Tell her I wanna see her. It's important."

"Sure, Brent. I'll tell her . . . but I can't promise you anything. Tiffany hates hospitals."

I tried to turn my body to Sonny to get a good read on his body language, but for some reason, I couldn't move. I tried to sit up, but my limbs wouldn't react to my commands. Panic overtook me. "Oh, Lord, I can't move. I can't move!"

The doctor pushed Sonny out of the way. I think he rested a hand on my shoulder, but I couldn't feel a thing. "Calm down, Brent. During your altercation, your back was broken, and you have some severe spinal injuries."

"Oh, Lord! How bad is it?" Again I tried to get up. "Will somebody tell me something?" I screamed.

The next voice I heard was Alison's. She'd taken James's place and was holding onto the bed railing. "Brent, honey. You're going to be all right, baby. I'm going to take you home and take care of you, and we're going to raise our baby together just like we planned."

"What are you talking about? You know what I had planned." I was about to out myself right then and there, but Alison stopped me.

"Brent, I think God has changed your plans. Baby, I don't know how to tell you this. . . . the doctors think you can regain the use of your upper body, but you'll never walk again."

"Nooo!" I screamed, closing my eyes. "No, this can't be happening to me. Where's Jackie?" I continued to try to move something, any part of me, but the only things that were mobile were my head and my neck. I glared at Alison. "Where's Jackie? Did you tell Jackie?"

"You mean the organist dude from your church?" James chimed in. "He came by earlier. Dude was crying too. Said he couldn't take seeing you this way, that it was a sign from God, and that he knew what he had to do. He was going home with his wife and kids to pray."

"Amen to that," Alison hollered.

I closed my eyes again and wondered if death would have been preferable to this.

44

James

I knocked on the front door and got no answer, so I made my way around to the back door, peeking in the sliding glass door. Why the hell I was snooping around Sonny's house was beyond me. Believe me, if Brent hadn't been in the hospital and hadn't insisted I do this, I'd be sitting up with Cathy, happy that we were finally putting the pieces of our lives back together. I hated the idea that she had me sleeping in the basement, but our complete reconciliation was not going to happen overnight, and I was just happy to be sleeping in my own house again, with all three of my boys under one roof.

I went to the side of the house, and before I used the key that Sonny had given me when he first moved in, I pulled out my cell phone and called Long Island Jewish Hospital.

"Can I have room 653, Brent Williams's room, please?"

"Please hold."

The phone rang twice before Brent picked it up. "Hello."

Every time I heard his voice on the phone, it damn near brought tears to my eyes, because it was a miracle he could even pick up the phone in the first place. Two weeks ago, he was paralyzed from the neck down, and now, it was only by the grace of God that he could sit up and use his arms.

I was still concerned, though, that the attack had done something to his psyche. When he told me he believed Sonny had something to do with it, and that Sonny might actually have been the masked attacker, I didn't know what to do. I planned to talk to the doctors about his mental state, but in the meantime, I knew they wanted to focus on him regaining some physical strength. It was important for him to concentrate on that, and he wouldn't be able to do it if he was agitated over this imagined evil side of Sonny. To pacify him, I agreed to go check out the house after he'd been trying to convince me for over two weeks. I figured that once I could tell him Tiffany and her kids were fine, he would give up on this theory that Sonny was out to get him.

"Brent, it's James."

"Are you in? What did you find? Is she there?" I barely understood what he said because he was talking so fast.

"Nah, I'm outside the door, but it doesn't look like anyone is here."

"Well, what are you waiting for? Go inside. That girl's in trouble, James. I just know it." Brent had so much concern in his voice, and I knew he believed what he was saying about our friend. "I just hope she ain't dead."

"Look, Brent, stop exaggerating. You know she's not dead. I spoke to her on the phone last night. She said she was fine."

"He could have been sitting right next to her."

I held my breath and counted to three to calm myself before I lost it. I still couldn't believe all of this had started because he ran into Jessica while he was in California. I didn't have any doubt she told him that crap about Sonny being dangerous, but I also knew she was a liar. Sonny had been telling us that for years, long before she packed up the kids and the house and ripped apart his family. I had no idea why Brent believed her story, but I assumed the beating had scrambled his brains a little.

"Look, man," I said when I felt like I could speak without yelling at Brent. "Maybe we should just talk to Sonny. Why don't I come back tonight after he's off work? I'll see what's up, then we'll come talk to you at the hospital."

"No! You've been over there three times, and every time you get there, Tiffany's mysteriously been away. I want you to go in that house."

"Look, Brent, that's easier said than done. What if someone comes home? God, what if Tiffany's in there asleep? I don't want to scare the girl."

"I just talked to Sonny at work. And if Tiffany shows up, make up a lie. Matter of fact, you can blame it on me. Tell her I wanted a picture of her kids to put in my room with my other godkids. She'll believe that. Everybody believes paraplegics as long as we're not asking for money."

"All right, man. I hope you're right . . . wrong about this."

"I hope so too, but I doubt it. And make sure you check all the closets. Jessica said he used to lock her in them." Why Brent was pushing me to betray my boy Sonny's trust for something that bitch Jessica said was beyond me. I took out my key and opened the door.

It didn't take but about five minutes to check the downstairs rooms and closets. The upstairs took a little longer because I had to check under the beds. There were no dead bodies or abused girlfriends like Brent feared, but I did find something interesting under Sonny's bed. I never knew it, but he actually had a gun. Once the upstairs and downstairs were checked, I called Brent and gave him my report.

"Did you check the basement?" he asked.

I wasn't happy about it, but I knew I had to check down there. If I didn't, Brent would still be insisting Sonny was guilty. I had to check every nook and cranny to satisfy his paranoia. I'd be relieved when this was done.

The only thing I found in the basement other than Sonny's computer equipment was an old wine barrel. I cracked open the top, but immediately turned my face away and shoved the cover back down when my nostrils were overcome with the strong scent of vinegar. Damn, that shit was nasty.

I was about to go upstairs and leave when I noticed a gray door that just seemed out of place. I became even more intrigued when I noticed it had not one, but two combination locks on it. Could it be . . . ? I banged on the door, and to my surprise, I heard movement.

"Is anyone in there?" I shouted.

As faint as it may have been, I heard a panicked voice. "Yes."

"Tiffany, is that you?"

"Yes," she replied, this time a little louder. Jesus Christ, Brent was right! Sonny's ass was crazy. "Hold on, Tiffany. I'm gonna get you outta there!"

My eyes searched the room for something to break the locks, but it was empty except for the computer equipment. Then it hit me: the gun upstairs in Sonny's room. I could shoot the locks off.

"Tiffany, don't worry. I'll be right back."

"No, please don't leave me," she pleaded, but I had no

choice. I didn't even answer her before I ran to retrieve the gun. It might have seemed like a lifetime to Tiffany, but it didn't take me long at all to get back downstairs.

"Tiffany, back away from the door, sweetheart. I'm going to shoot off the locks." It took five shots, but I finally got both of them off. When I finally opened the door, Tiffany came out crying. She fell into my arms.

"Everything's okay," I assured her. "You're safe now."

"You don't understand," she said, close to hysterics. "We have to get out of here. He told me he has cameras all over the house and he watches them while he's at work. He's probably on his way back here right now."

"Don't worry. He can't hurt you now."

"You don't know what he's capable of!" she cried. "He's already murdered my ex-husband." She pointed at the wine barrel. I felt my stomach lurch. Was there really a body in there? For the first time, I was actually scared.

"Come on, my car's outside. We'll go to the school and get your kids. We can call the cops on the way."

She ran up the stairs. Was this really happening to me? I took one last look at the wine barrel before following after her. I tripped on the bottom step, and by the time I regained my footing, she was already in the kitchen. I heard her scream.

"Bitch! How could you?" Sonny was there with her, and he sounded ready to commit another murder. Fuck that, I wasn't taking any chances. I went back to get the gun. Sonny might have been my best friend, but he was definitely not stable.

I crept up the stairs, but Sonny was there, waiting for me with a gun to Tiffany's head. I pointed my weapon at him.

"Why the fuck are you interfering, James?"

"I'm here to get you outta trouble, buddy." I tried to remain calm. I didn't want to set him off. Tiffany's life, and maybe my own, was at stake.

"It's too late for that. Now, back off, James. I don't wanna hurt you, man."

"Believe me, bro. I don't want you to hurt me either, so why don't we put these guns down?" My hand was starting to shake, I was so damn scared.

"I can't do that, bro. You know I love you, but I can't do

that." Sweat poured down Sonny's face, but his hand remained steady and his expression was locked in determination.

"Come on, Sonny, why can't you just put it down? We can work this out."

"Because this bitch here fucked everything up." He pressed the gun against her head. "Things were going to be different this time, James. I had the rules set and everything. I even gave her a written copy when she moved in. She signed them." Finally his demeanor cracked a little. I could hear a slight change in his voice.

"So what do you want me to do?"

"I want you to walk out that door so I can finish this. I'm not going to jail. I'll kill her and I'll kill myself before I go to jail."

"If you're going to kill yourself, man, I understand it. I don't agree with it, but I understand it. But don't kill her. Let her go, Sonny."

"I'm sorry, James, but if I can't have her, nobody will." I took a few cautious steps toward him and he pulled her in tight. "You're going to have to shoot me, James."

"No, Sonny, I'm not going to shoot you."

"Yes, you are. Because if you don't shoot me, I'm going to shoot her. I can't live without her, James."

"Yes, you can. You lived without Jessica."

"Jessica wasn't my soul mate, James. I know that now. Tiffany is."

I knew something about having a soul mate you didn't want to let go of, so I believed he really did feel that way. Granted, the level he had taken his obsession to was dangerous and extreme, but some small part of me understood.

"I'm going to count to ten, James, and if you don't shoot me by then, I'm going to shoot her and then I'm going to shoot myself. Are you willing to watch both of us die?"

He moved Tiffany to the side, giving me a clear shot at his chest and head. Then he started to count.

When he got to five, I screamed, "Sonny, don't do this!"

"Six . . . . Pull the trigger, James," he said, without the slightest fear in his voice. "Seven, eight . . ."

I closed my eyes and squeezed the trigger. Tiffany's screams filled the room. When I heard a thud, I opened my eyes. Sonny was on the ground, bleeding from his chest.

I dropped to my knees, screaming, "I'm sorry, man. I didn't wanna do it. You made me do it." Tiffany ran from the house immediately, but I couldn't budge. I sat beside my friend and cried openly as I watched the life drain from his body.

I don't know how much time passed before I heard my cell phone ringing. Barely conscious of my actions, I pulled it from my pocket and opened the phone.

"James!" It was Brent. "You didn't call me back. Are you still in the house? What happened in the basement? Did you find her?"

"Yeah," I answered, barely able to speak through my tears, and unable to believe that what I was saying was reality. "Sonny's gone, Brent. Sonny's dead." I dropped the phone in a pool of my friend's blood and buried my face in my hands.

Epilogue

One year later—Brent

The phone rang just as I was changing my son B.J.'s diaper. Being in a wheelchair, I knew I couldn't get his Pamper on and still answer the phone in time. I let it ring and continued to tend to my son's needs. The answering machine would get it, and I'd return the call later. Besides it was probably just Alison, checking up on us for the fourth time today.

Alison gave birth to our beautiful baby boy about three months ago. We named him Brent Jr., B.J. for short, and he was the true love of my life. B.J. made waking up each morning worthwhile, even if it was only to lift my useless legs and struggle into a wheelchair. Though I had regained the use of my upper body, nothing below my waist would ever be the same. The doctors predicted I would never walk again, and I could take Viagra all day long and it wouldn't cure my permanent impotence. My life as I had known it was over. So now I lived my life for my son.

I was still married to Alison, but she had become my caretaker in many ways. True to her word, she stuck by me through three surgeries and countless hours of rehabilitation. She was the rock of our family, working two jobs to support me and B.J. I hoped someday to be able to go back to work and provide for my family, but for the time being I was still too emotionally distraught about everything that had happened. Alison never complained about anything. She told me countless times that the only thing that was important to her was that we were still together as a family. Now that B.J. was born I totally understood what she was trying to say.

Jackie was no longer a threat to the stability of our marriage and our family. Once he figured out that the sexual part of our relationship would never again be possible, he returned home to his wife and children, and remained in the closet. His vow to re-veal his sexuality to the church never came to pass, and Trustee Moss was more than happy to help him keep that secret.

On Sundays, when I saw Jackie in church, though, I knew he was still up to his old tricks. It burned me up every time I saw him at services flirting with a new young man, especially since he wouldn't say more than five words to me at any given time. I thought our love was more than that. Hell, I was still the same man inside, even if I couldn't get it up anymore. His latest "friend" was Deacon Ferguson's son, Todd. They didn't think anyone knew, but it was obvious to me every time Jackie changed lovers. I guess it's just something another gay man can spot.

Yes, I am still a gay man. Just because my equipment is mal-functioning doesn't mean the desires aren't still there. I still loved Jackie more than anything in the world. I missed the times we spent together, and sometimes while I watched him play the organ, my mind got filled with images of the day he wore noth-ing under his choir robe. Once, Alison caught me staring so hard during service that she turned my wheelchair around so my back was to the choir. I tried to turn the chair around again, and she whispered that if I even thought about it, she'd leave me home alone the following Sunday. Like I said before, my life was no longer under my control.

That was why I was grateful for the fact that I was at least able to care for my son's basic needs. I finished changing his dia-per and placed him in his crib, then wheeled myself to the tele-phone to check the answering machine. I pressed PLAY and smiled when I heard James's voice.

James and Cathy had just come home from a much-needed vacation with the boys. They had a long way to go to repairing their marriage, but whenever I talked to him, James seemed hopeful. He and Cathy were seeing a therapist to work out their issues. Each of them was coming to terms with the other's affair, and Cathy had been able to accept Marcus as a new addition to their family.

James was also spending time one-on-one with a therapist to help him deal with the horrible fact that he had killed his best friend. Rationally, he knew that his actions saved Tiffany's life and spared her children from growing up without their mother. Even Jessica had called when she heard the news, thanking

James for his bravery. But while others praised him as a hero, he was torn up inside, still wondering if maybe he could have talked Sonny into dropping his gun that day. He was making strides in his therapy, but I don't think even I could fully understand what it must have been like having to make the decision he did that day. James was a strong man, and all three of his sons would grow up to be better people because they had him as a role model.

Marcus was getting along well with the other boys, and James had him in counseling as well to help him work through any feelings he had about his mother's abandonment. Michelle still had not contacted them to check on her son, but for the time being, it was probably better that James and Cathy could work on their marriage without Michelle complicating things. Maybe some time in the future she would try to make amends with her son, but for now, James was just happy to be headed back toward a normal, drama-free family life.

I was looking forward to hearing all about their trip and was sorry I had missed his call. As I listened to his greeting on the answering machine, I became even more disappointed. All I got was "Hey, Brent, it's James. Hope you're doing well. Cathy and the kids and I just—" before I heard a squeaking noise and the message stopped.

I cursed under my breath as I lifted the cover to retrieve the small cassette tape, which was now a tangled mess inside the machine. Before I married her, Alison had been thrifty, but it had allowed her to build up a decent savings. Now that I was unable to work, our accounts had dwindled, and she had to become even more of a penny-pincher. That was why we were still using this ancient answering machine with the tiny cassette tapes to record messages. I think we were probably the only people under the age of seventy who had not yet switched to a digital answering machine. Now this broken tape was just one more reminder of how my injuries had changed every aspect of my life, including finances.

I tossed the tape into a wastebasket, wheeled my chair to the desk in the corner and opened the top drawer, where Alison usually kept a few cassettes. I grabbed the first one I saw and went back to the machine. After I placed it in the answering machine, I rewound the tape then pressed PLAY. Sometimes Alison threw used tapes into that drawer, and I wanted to listen to be sure I

wasn't recording over something she might have wanted to save. What I heard caused my blood to run cold.

"Yo, it's Bubba. I took care of that thing you wanted me to do. I don't think you gotta worry about that dude going anywhere real soon. That bat did the trick. I wouldn't be surprised if old boy was paralyzed for life. I don't know what he did to make you want to hurt him like that, but . . . oh well, whatever. When you gonna call me back so we can talk about you paying me the other half of my money? You still owe me twenty-five hun'ed."

My hands shook as I reached out and stopped the tape. Confused thoughts raced through my head. Whoever this Bubba was, he obviously came from the streets, and I couldn't imagine how Alison would know someone like that. My mind was struggling to make the connection between my devoted, caring wife and everything I had just heard this man say. Could it be possible that Sonny hadn't been the one to attack me? Had Alison paid someone to beat and maybe even kill me? I felt bile rising in my throat as I realized that this might actually be true.

I retrieved the cassette from the machine, not quite sure what I was going to do with it. I knew I had to confront Alison with what I'd heard, and demand an explanation. In the meantime, I would search for any more clues in the house.

I put the tape on my lap and moved back over to the desk to find the file folder containing Alison's bank statements from the past year. Rifling through the papers, I found the statement from the month after the attack and examined the column that listed all the previous month's withdrawals. Tears collected in the corners of my eyes when I saw it—a cash withdrawal in the amount of twenty-five hundred dollars, made just days after I ended up in the hospital. Scanning backwards over the list, I found the other one, another withdrawal in the same amount, made while I was on my last trip to San Francisco.

The papers fluttered to the floor around my wheelchair as I sobbed uncontrollably at the horror of my situation. While I was on the West Coast, planning to come home and reveal my sexuality to the church, my wife was on the East Coast, preparing to have me assaulted. And now I was in a wheelchair, almost entirely at her mercy.

When I had no more tears left, I sat silently and considered my options. Alison had committed an unthinkable act, a crime,

and I knew I had to call the police to report it. But as I imagined the events that would follow her arrest, I wasn't so sure it would be my best move. I was able to take care of B.J.'s basic needs— changing his diapers, warming his bottles, putting him down for his naps—but beyond that, how much could I really do for him if Alison was in jail? How would I handle it once he learned to walk? I couldn't even get to the phone in time to answer it, so it was pretty unlikely I could chase behind an energetic toddler to keep him out of danger all day long. The closest thing I had to a family was James, and he was too busy with his own life right now to ask him for any help. I could hire a babysitter, but that cost money, and until my doctors said I was fit to return to work, I would never be able to afford it. The truth was, Alison was the one supporting our family, and without her, I would be virtually helpless, unable to give my son the life he deserved.

As I thought about the frightening truth, B.J. began to cry. I went into his room, stopped beside the crib to take him out, and once he was in my arms, his cries subsided. I rocked him gently until his eyelids drooped and he drifted off to sleep. A single tear fell onto his shirt as I watched him sleep and tried not to cry again. My first concern, I knew, had to be the safety and happiness of my child. I wondered, though, if running away with B.J. would be a wise choice. Just like if Alison went to jail, who would help me raise B.J. if I took him right now and ran away? I realized that taking away his mother would not be in his best interests.

Of course, I still had to question whether we would be safe here in the house with Alison. After all, she had done something so unimaginably horrible. She had robbed me of my ability to function as a man . . . but the act was so out of character for her. The Alison I had known was mild-mannered and kind, so willing to give of herself, to care for me in my time of greatest need. What had driven her to such an act, I wondered. Had Alison gone crazy?

Then it hit me. With great sadness, I realized that it wasn't really Alison who had done this to me; I had done it to myself. It wasn't her fault that she married a flawed man. Alison was, in fact, the sweet woman I had first known her to be. She wasn't a deranged criminal with violent tendencies. No, I was the one who turned out to be something other than what I said I was in the beginning. If I had been honest with myself about my sexuality from the start, I probably never would have married her. All she really wanted was someone to love her, someone to start a family with. I let her believe she could have those things with me, and even gave her the child she wanted. So, how did I expect her to react when I threatened to take all of that away from her in the blink of an eye? Yes, she went further than she should have to keep her family together, but I knew that as long as I wasn't planning on leaving her, I would never have to worry about Alison harming me again. In fact, I knew that all she really wanted to do was care for me better than anyone else ever could. And when I was truthful with myself, I had to admit that I needed her to do that now. I needed Alison's care, and so did B.J., the only person who really mattered now.

I looked down at my wheelchair and sighed. I would be staying in this chair for the rest of my life, and my family would be staying together, in spite of it all.

SO YOU CALL YOURSELF A MAN

CARL WEBER

ABOUT THIS GUIDE

The suggested questions are intended to enhance your
group's reading of this book.

DISCUSSION QUESTIONS

1. Do you think James should have told Cathy about Marcus right away? If not, why? And when would have been the right time?

2. Did you think that Sonny was going to kill the couple in his apartment?

3. If you were James, would you have let Michelle continue to blackmail you into babysitting after the first few times?

4. In what previous Carl Weber book was Michelle also a character?

5. Were you surprised when Jackie's true identity was revealed? Did you look back to see if you had missed clues, and if so, did you find any?

6. If you were Tiffany, would you have moved in with Sonny after you came home and found roaches all over your apartment?

7. Would you be able to leave your child behind as easily as Michelle did?

8. Do you believe Brent was ever physically attracted to Alison?

9. When did you realize that Sonny was crazy?

10. Do you think you have people like Jackie and Brent in your church?

11. Would you have let James back in the house if you were Cathy?

12. What was your opinion of Sonny's wife, Jessica, before Brent met her in San Francisco?

13. What did you think of Alison? Did you feel sorry for her? Did she go too far to protect her reputation in the church?

14. Could you kill your best friend to save someone else's life?

The following is a sample chapter from Carl Weber's
eagerly anticipated upcoming novel
THE FIRST LADY.
It will be available in January 2007
wherever hardcover books are sold.
Enjoy!

Prologue

"Hey, Charlene, you ready to get started?"

My good friend and confidante, Alison Williams, smiled as she walked into my hospital room. I tried to smile back when she kissed my forehead, but the abdominal pains I was experiencing wouldn't allow it. So, I lay there in my bed, grappling through the pain as I watched her sit in the chair next to my bed and pull out a notebook and pen. I pressed the button that controlled the morphine drip in my arm, and Alison waited patiently for my pain reliever to kick in. Six months ago, I refused to use any type of pain medication, but now I understood why the Lord invented addictive drugs like morphine and Demerol. Without them, I probably would have died from the pain of my cancer weeks ago. As it was now, I was pushing the damn drip button every fifteen minutes and I was on the highest dose there was, which meant I only had a few weeks left to live.

I wasn't afraid of dying, though. I'd lived a good life, married a wonderful man, Bishop T.K. Wilson, raised two fantastic children, and had the honor of being the first lady of absolutely the best church in Queens, New York. If the Lord was ready to call me home, although I considered myself still pretty young, I was ready to go. The only thing I was afraid of was what would happen to my family—more importantly, my husband, T.K., after I was gone. So, I was making preparations to make sure my man was taken care of from the grave.

You see, as good and honorable a man of God as T.K. was, he was still just a man with desires and needs; and men, no matter how bright they may appear to be, are very naive when it comes to women, *especially* slick-ass church women. I could see it now. Fifteen minutes after they put my body in the ground, those church heifers would be in my house trying to figure out the best way to redecorate my shit out. Say what you might about my choice of words, but I'd seen these so-called church women in action too many times in the past.

Last year when Sister Betty Jean White passed away, within six months her worst enemy, Jeannette Wilcox, had weaseled her way into that woman's house and was sleeping with her husband. A few months after that they were married, and if you walk into that house today, there's not one memory that Sister Betty even lived there. So, I could envision T.K. in his moment of grief and loneliness letting somebody manipulate him into doing just about anything she wanted, and I was not about to allow that. That's why, with the help of Alison and possibly my daughter Donna, I was making plans to stop her and any other threats to my family.

I hope you don't get me wrong. I wasn't trying to stop my husband from moving on with his life after I was gone. On the contrary, I wanted him to find someone to spend the rest of his days with and be happy. I just wanted to make sure that whoever the woman was, she had his best interests at heart and wasn't just some ambitious, gold-digging floozy disguised in a church hat and a flowered dress.

I felt the pain medication finally kick in, and Alison helped me as I struggled to sit up. She placed a pillow behind my head then sat back in her seat to take notes as I began to dictate the fourth of seven letters to be given out after my death. The first one was to T.K.; the next two were to my son, Dante, and daughter, Donna. The final four letters, which we would write this day, were to the four women I thought were possible candidates to one day replace me as T.K.'s wife and become the first lady of First Jamaica Ministries.

I started my dictation with a letter for T.K.'s first love, Marlene, the mother of his illegitimate daughter, Tanisha. I never really told anyone this, but I liked Marlene. She had spunk, and from what I heard, a loyalty to T.K. that almost rivaled mine. I must admit, though, that I liked her more when she was living in D.C. with her daughter and my son, who, believe it or not, were married. But that was before I was diagnosed with cancer, when I made it a point to keep any women that might interest T.K. as

far away as possible. Now I was happy to hear that she had recently moved back to Queens and had even shown up at a few church services. She, unlike any of the other candidates, had a connection to my family, which made her a very favorable competitor in the race for T.K.'s heart. Her only flaw was that she was a recovering drug abuser . . . but then again, so was my husband.

The next letter was to be written to Ms. Monique Johnson, the first lady of plastic surgery and implants. I'm sorry, but there was no way a forty-year-old woman with two kids could have a body like hers without something going south. Not only was her body fake, but so was her personality. I'd never met a phonier woman in my entire life. She was always smiling in my face and grinning at my man. She knew she wanted him. Rumor has it that she'd had relationships with at least two high-profile members of the church, both of them married. In fact, when Monique was around with her flirtatious self, every wife in the congregation had her man on lockdown. Like I explained earlier, there was no doubt in my mind that Monique had her sights set on T.K. Some of my girlfriends from the church confirmed that her overtures toward him had become even bolder since I'd become hospitalized. I was sure T.K. hadn't even given the woman a second thought with me being sick and all, but a question still remained: Would he be strong willed enough to stay away from her after my death?

After we wrote Monique's letter, the pain was starting to come back, but I fought through it as we started on Savannah Dickens's letter. Savannah was the church's new choir soloist. She was a quiet, attractive woman in her midthirties who kept to herself. I didn't know much about her because she was new to the church and the community, but I will admit I wasn't much for quiet folks because they were usually hiding something. She was, however, the niece of Trustee Joe Dickens, one of the more prominent older members of our church. Joe was looking to become the chairman of the Board of Trustees. I was sure that after my death he would be trying his best to push T.K. and Savannah together in an effort to consolidate power. It was a move I wasn't against, because it would probably benefit T.K. in the long run. What I didn't like was the fact that she was only thirty-five years

old. I wasn't objecting to her age so much; she was only ten years younger than T.K. What I was worried about was the fact that she was thirty-five and didn't have any children. A woman under forty who hadn't had a child probably wanted kids of her own, and that was out. The last thing T.K. needed after raising Dante and Donna and putting them through college was another baby to support.

Right before we finished the sixth letter, the pain hit me hard and I had to push the drip. I lay back down and Alison insisted that we'd done enough for the day. God willing, we'd finish the seventh and final letter the next day. It was to my good friend, Sister Wilma Mae Jenkins, one of the church's Holy Rollers. Although I'm not going to reveal its content, I can assure you that it would shake up a whole lot of people. Six months from now, I'd be dead, but I could guarantee my presence would still be felt.

Can you dictate the lives of your family, friends and enemies from the grave? Those were the thoughts I contemplated as I waited for the new dose of pain medication to take effect. I could picture the scenario now: The first lady of First Jamaica Ministries is dead. Who will win the bishop's heart and become the next first lady? Time would only tell.